KATHERINE STONE is the bestselling author of fifteen novels, including *Thief of Hearts*, *Bed of Roses*, *Home at Last*, and *Twins*. A physician who now writes full time, Katherine Stone lives with her husband, novelist Jack Chase, in the Pacific Northwest.

## ALSO BY KATHERINE STONE

# KATHERINE STONE

# A MIDNIGHT CLEAR

**WARNER BOOKS**

A Time Warner Company

WARNER BOOKS EDITION

Cover art by Franco Accornero
Hand lettering by Andrew Newman

Warner Books, Inc.
1271 Avenue of the Americas
New York, NY 10020

Visit our Web site at
www.twbookmark.com

A Time Warner Company

Printed in the United States of America

First Paperback Printing: December 1999

10 9 8 7 6 5 4 3 2 1

# A MIDNIGHT CLEAR

# PROLOGUE

*Christmas Eve*
*Loganville, Colorado*
*Twenty-two years ago*

It was 11:00 P.M. Time to leave. For Jace had made a promise to a five-year-old.

The actual promise had been that at precisely eleven he would go to bed. But Jace's plan, to leave the house at the designated time, would accomplish the spirit of the pledge—to be far from the white-brick fireplace through which Santa Claus would appear, and from the lopsided but beloved Christmas tree beneath which even more brightly wrapped packages would be placed, and most of all from the platter of cookies Grace had baked for the jolly Yuletide visitor and the bundle of carrots, freshly washed by her, for Santa's flying reindeer.

Grace Quinn's instructions regarding Jace Colton's whereabouts, where he *must not* be, had been specific. Emphatic. But she hadn't sounded in the least worried about whether Jace would comply. Grace trusted him completely. It was an astonishing trust, one that Jace had spent every second of the past eleven months trying to deserve.

There *had* been worry, however, when Grace had wondered aloud how he could be so unfamiliar with the Christmas Eve rituals of the merry St. Nick. Jace was fourteen, and she was only five. The nine-year age difference should have made him an expert.

Jace could not tell her, would never tell her, that he had never believed in Santa Claus, had had no reason to believe. So he reminded the five-year-old innocent of the truth. This was his first Colorado Christmas. She needed to acquaint him with Santa's Rocky Mountain routine.

"He tries to come exactly at midnight," Grace explained. "But he *could* come a little early, a half an hour or so, and sometimes, he can't help it, he might be a little late."

And there was, Grace realized, something one needed to be mindful of in snowy Loganville, not balmy Savannah. Fire. It was *okay*, she reassured, that flames had blazed within the white-brick fireplace throughout this Christmas Eve day. And even the care they had taken to add no new logs after 7:00 P.M. had been unnecessary. Santa's boots were fireproof, as were his clothes, and he had magical ways of dousing even the most raging of flames.

But if the ashes were cold, as they would be in Grace Quinn's home long before midnight, Santa wouldn't have to spend time brushing glowing embers off his boots. It would be rude, Grace asserted, to do anything that might disrupt his schedule. And it would be very mean for all the other children who were counting on him. Not, she added, that Santa would disappoint anyone. *Ever*.

Santa was as reliable, as trustworthy, as Jace.

Which meant absolutely reliable.

Which meant that as a bright-eyed but sleepy Grace Alysia Quinn wandered off to bed, and to sugarplum dreams, she didn't remind Jace of his promise, made hours before, to go to bed at eleven.

To bed. It was, Jace decided, an insignificant aspect of the promise. It was simply unimaginable to Grace that he would want to go anywhere but bed, would choose to do anything but sleep during the eternity, to the eager five-year-old, between Christmas Eve and Christmas morn.

Grace had no idea how little he slept on even the most usual of nights, and that his restlessness on this special night would preclude sleep entirely. Had she known that Jace would spend the sacrosanct time of Santa Claus roaming outside in the bitter cold, she would never have exacted the promise she had.

She would have placed the cookies and carrots on the front porch, along with a carefully printed note thanking Santa and the reindeer for dropping by, but advising the Yuletide dreammaker that he needn't come inside. They were fine. This was a *perfect* Christmas already.

Perfect. Just as for Jace the past eleven months had been perfect. He'd become a shepherd for a most precious flock of two, ever vigilant, ever wary, on guard always for the whim of fate that might shatter this unexpected, never expected joy.

Frissons of worry pierced him now, sharp reminders of the precariousness he felt, as he surveyed the living room before leaving the house. The once-blazing fire had burned to ash. Not an ember glowed. But Jace saw still the dancing flames of this joyous day. Grace, haloed in gold, as she baked cookies for Santa Claus and *for him*, more cookies for him than for Santa. And Mary Beth, gilded too, as she prepared their Christmas Eve dinner. And golden beams on them all as they played Scrabble, and Grace sang, until mother and daughter went to bed.

The fire was ash, and Jace had extinguished the twinkling lights of the Christmas tree, had pulled the plug from the socket as soon as he'd heard the bedroom doors close overhead. The lights had glittered all day, and would blaze again tomorrow, and the pine needles were still so shiny, so fragrant and so fresh, that maybe, if he were careful, this beautiful tree would never die.

The hall light glowed, as it did every night, as did the light on the porch, and the thermostat was set to its nighttime low. There would be warmth and light for his sleeping flock. Unless the power went out. That had happened once already this winter, on a night of heavy snowfall and howling wind.

But it wasn't snowing tonight, and there wasn't the faintest whisper of wind. And even if the power did go out during his midnight absence, the house would hold its warmth until his return.

Jace would start the generator then, assuming Mary

Beth hadn't already done so. Which she could. Easily. Jace had filled the generator just this afternoon, and topped off the extra gas cans in the garage, and he had oiled the cord, making it effortless to pull, and adjusted the choke.

Mary Beth could start the generator. But she wouldn't, Jace realized. She would not create the roar that would awaken Grace and worse, might discourage Santa and frighten his reindeer.

Discourage Santa? Frighten his reindeer? But Mary Beth *was* Santa, wasn't she? Wasn't being Santa Claus something mothers did? Real mothers? The ones who were conspirators in the magic of Christmas . . . just as they were conspirators in the magic of every moment of their children's lives?

Yes. Surely. At any moment Mary Beth would come downstairs to this place of cookies and carrots and ashes, this pine-fragrant living room that Jace must vacate soon. Now. The mantelpiece clock was beginning its eleven o'clock chime.

It was safe.

His flock was safe.

Mary Beth would keep vigil while he was away.

Mary Beth. Santa.

Mary Beth . . . or Santa.

Jace quieted his fears, pulled closed, quietly, the front door, and descended the porch steps into the winter night.

The air was cold but calm. And bright. And clear. Like shimmering crystal. Like the crystalline brilliance that had begun on that January day, eleven months ago, when he'd arrived in Loganville.

He had been traveling for two weeks, since December twenty-first. His journey had had purpose, direction, destination. But it had meandered nonetheless, dependent as it was on hitchhiked rides. The most recent ride, offered by a moving van driver on the outskirts of Denver, had held great promise. The driver was heading north, en route to Idaho, and he would pay Jace to help him load and unload at various stops in between.

Jace had readily agreed. What money he'd had was gone, and it had been a while since he'd either eaten or slept, and he was feeling the hope of both when a call on the driver's CB radio changed everything. A fellow driver's rig had broken down a few miles up ahead, and he had cargo that had to reach Boulder by nightfall, and he and that promised cargo needed a lift.

The rig had broken down fifty feet from a junction on the interstate, a crossroads marked by a single sign: LOGANVILLE 5 MILES.

Jace walked those five miles, not knowing what he would find, but aware during the brutally cold journey that his need for food and sleep was verging on the desperate. As was, because of this wintry walk, his need for warmth.

All three of which could be found in the grocery, Loganville General, at the corner of Loganville Avenue and Crystal Mountain Road. Warmth was immediate, embracing and golden, as Jace entered the store. And food and sleep would come later, when he was alone inside.

Jace would steal food and sleep. Steal. But there was something about this golden warmth that made his starving brain wonder if this might possibly be the kind of place—was there such a place?—where the owner might give him food merely because he was hungry.

Maybe. Maybe. But, Jace realized, he needed neither to beg nor to steal. He could earn the food he needed. For in this balmy foyer was a community bulletin board where the citizens of Loganville advertised whatever they liked, were invited to do so by the ample supply of paper, marking pens, and thumbtacks on the wooden shelves just below.

Jace scanned the array of announcements before he reached, not as a thief, for a bright green marking pen and a snow-white sheet of paper.

You *know* I can clean your house better than you, and I *want* to!!!! So call me. Joanne H.

Due to unforeseen circumstances (Blanche's broken foot), the St. Stephens bake sale has been rescheduled for early March!!!

I will *grovel* for Broncos playoff tickets! Grovel and pay, within reason! Ralph P.

Here was a place where last names were initials only, and phone numbers need not be listed at all, and where broken bones were everyone's business—and concern—and where exclamation points ruled the day. But how would the good citizens of Loganville respond to a stranger in their midst? Jace didn't know, yet he felt oddly optimistic, a consequence perhaps of his starvation and fatigue.

He would make a sign, and he would stand in this embracing warmth, and maybe someone would notice. And care. Already a crowd was assembled around another sign—KITTEN NEEDS HOME—and its author, a preteen girl. The girl radiated importance. She had a treasure, a tiny gray ball of feline fluff, which she was empowered to give away. She beamed with confidence, too. And why not? There seemed no doubt the kitten would find a home. Indeed, a cluster of children, on Christmas vacation still, formed an eager circle around kitten and girl.

Was it a girl-kitten or a boy-kitten? a Loganville child wanted to know. A boy, the treasure-holder, whose name was Bridget, replied.

Was he healthy? *Of course*, came the officious response. Why was he being given away? Because their momma cat had had six kittens, and Bridget's mother said they could only keep one, and all but two had been given away as Christmas gifts, and of the two that remained *he* had to go, because he and the mother cat didn't get along.

"His mommy doesn't like him?" the serious query came from a blond blue-eyed girl.

"No, Grace," Bridget asserted. "She doesn't."

"Why not?"

"Because he's too wild."

"Wild," the girl named Grace echoed softly and with a

frown. The kitten, asleep despite the commotion surrounding him, didn't seem wild now. "What's his name?"

Bridget gave an exasperated sigh, impatient with the dumb questions of the very young. "He doesn't *have* a name, Grace. Whoever gets to keep him gets to name him."

"His name could be Sam," Grace murmured thoughtfully, as if she were quite certain that the kitten did have a name, *that* name, even though the humans in his universe hadn't yet tumbled to it. "I wonder if it is."

"He *can* be Sam, Grace, *if* he becomes yours. But Dinah already has first dibs. She's checking with her mom right now." Bridget brightened as she realized how to rid herself of Grace and her little-girl questions. "You could check with your mom just in case."

Even before Bridget punctuated her suggestion by pointing in the direction of Grace's mother, Jace had decided who that mother was. It seemed obvious, felt obvious, even though nothing in Jace's life qualified him to identify a loving mother.

But Jace had identified Grace's mother correctly. She was the pretty blonde who wore a nurse's uniform beneath her bulky winter parka, and who was talking sympathetically to an older woman, a patient's relative perhaps, all the while keeping a watchful eye on her daughter.

A loving eye.

Would this watchful, loving mother say yes to the kitten named Sam? Jace didn't know, couldn't tell. But whatever the decision, it wouldn't be an arbitrary, "No, you can't, because I say so."

And it most certainly would not be what Jace himself had heard when he'd asked permission to keep a dog he had found, a cold, tired, hungry stray. "A dog? Are you *kidding*? I can't afford *you*, much less a *dog*. Besides, I've already had a dog, remember? Your *father*."

Jace had hidden his orphaned stray, and he had stolen for the first time in his life, stolen food for his dog, and when the unwanted dog—but not the unwanted boy—was hungry no longer, Jace had given the beloved orphan away. DOG NEEDS HOME, his sign had read. And he had screened the applicants carefully, rejecting several, many, until a girl appeared whose only credential was that she curled her young arms around the scruffy yellow neck.

A girl like this girl who wanted Sam.

A girl like Grace, to whom Jace had already given the wild unwanted ball of fluff.

But now there was another girl, Grace's age, and she was galloping toward the table. She was Dinah, who had first dibs, and who would love this kitten, too. Her beaming freckled face promised that she would.

"She said yes! My mom said *yes!*"

It was a happy ending for the kitten.

But what of Grace? She patted the kitten a final time, a thoughtful time, as if debating whether to share with Dinah the kitten's name. In the end, however, she said nothing at all.

Jace expected Grace to scamper to her mother, for the comfort which he knew—without experience—was awaiting her there. But Grace looked instead at him, *at him*, her interested young gaze forthright, earnest, and bright, bright blue.

She walked over to him, studied the sign he had finished creating but had yet to display, and touched each green word as she read. " 'Will Work For Food.' What does that mean?"

"That I'll work for food."

"Are you hungry?"

"A little."

"You *are*?"

It was as if, to her worried blue eyes, his sign read, KID NEEDS HOME. "A little."

"What's your name?"

He was Jason—Jace—Colton, in bitter memory of his father: liar, impostor, thief. It was a name, like the man he had never known, the son and namesake had come to loathe.

But what if Jace told this bright-eyed elf that *his* name rhymed with *hers*? Would Grace embrace the hated name, transform it from tarnished to glittering with a sudden brilliant smile?

Perhaps. *Yes*. But it was such a selfish wish—his—and there was that other wish, hers, so soft and pure.

"Sam," he said. "My name is Sam."

"Really?"

"Really."

The girl who had patted the fluffy gray kitten a fond *adieu* grabbed the imposter's hand and tugged. "Come with me."

Grace's mother was still engaged in sympathetic reassurances, and Grace halted their journey a discreet distance away.

"We have to wait a minute," she explained.

Jace would have happily waited forever. He had never been wanted, welcomed, like this. He would savor the remarkable moment for as long as it could last. Which wouldn't be long. Grace's watchful, loving mother was very aware that her daughter was clutching the hand of a teenage ruffian. She offered some final words of assurance to the older woman, then politely but definitively brought the conversation to a close.

Grace spoke the moment her mother's questioning gaze found hers.

"Mommy! Guess what? This is Sam. I found *Sam*."

Mary Beth Quinn's smile was easy to suppress, for there were the obvious worries: the stranger attached to her daughter's hand . . . and Grace's own determined search for a Sam. It was a search that had begun six months ago, when Grace had heard for the first time her father's given name.

He wasn't just *Daddy*, the wonderful father who died just days before her birth, but he was *Samuel*, too. Sam. It was not a whimsical search. Nothing Grace did was whimsical. She believed, truly and determinedly, that there was a Sam out there somewhere that she was destined to know, and who would become her very best friend.

Mary Beth had assumed that eventually Grace would create her own Sam, an imaginary playmate. But there was nothing imaginary about this teenage boy. *Boy*. Mary Beth used the word advisedly. Her work as a critical care nurse had reinforced her view that teenage males were boys not men, and Grace's Sam was clearly in his teens.

And yet this boy seemed more man than boy. Tall, defiant, proud.

And pale, Mary Beth thought. And weary and thin. When, she wondered, had he last eaten or slept?

"Hello, Sam." Mary Beth extended a hand, which Jace Colton took with strength. And his dark green gaze did not waver. "I'm Mary Beth Quinn."

"He's hungry, Mommy!"

"A little hungry, Mrs. Quinn."

"Do you live around here, Sam?"

"No."

"Where do you live?"

"Nowhere, ma'am. Not at the moment."

"And before this moment?"

"Savannah."

During her years in nursing Mary Beth had met plenty of teenage boys who would have seized upon her first name, especially ones under the mistaken impression that drinking made them men. But this man-boy addressed her as Mrs. Quinn, and as ma'am, and he had a faint but definite Southern accent.

Mary Beth Quinn believed he was from the South. And that he was hungry. And that his name was Sam? Maybe. Or maybe it was her own nostalgia for the husband she had loved so much and whose memory had been so strongly, so staggeringly, evoked by the solid handshake and rock-steady gaze of this starving Southern teen.

"Mommy," Grace whispered. "This is *Sam*, and he's *hungry*."

Mary Beth had more questions, lots of them. She posed them later that night, after dinner and laughter and the offer of a place to sleep, and after the bedtime, long past the usual bedtime, of the little girl who had found her Sam.

Was he in trouble with the law? Mary Beth wanted to know.

No, ma'am.

Had he ever been?

He had stolen food, he admitted. A few times. But he'd never been noticed, much less caught. He was thirteen, he said, to her obvious surprise. But it was true. Yes, he knew, he looked older. The Savannah school system in fact, its teachers and its students, believed him to be fifteen. He had made the leap on his own when he was ten, had simply abandoned the final two years of elementary school and enrolled in junior high. He didn't always go to class. Too boring. But he liked to read, and his grades were good.

His custodial parent, his mother, knew of his decision to set out on his own. Knew and approved. She wasn't searching for him and never would.

His name wasn't Sam, Jace confessed. But he liked Sam and would like to keep it, if Mrs. Quinn didn't mind, for as long as he was here.

Mary Beth didn't mind, although her actual reply was preempted by the arrival of a visitor.

Troy Logan was unexpected on this night. But he was welcome. Always.

To say that Troy had been born on the right side of the tracks would have been an understatement. His family owned the tracks, and most of the town on either side. Loganville had been founded by Troy's great-great-grandfather and named, *re*named, in his honor.

The Logans were authentically beloved by the residents of their town. Generosity flowed in the veins of every Logan ever born, as did civic responsibility, a strong work ethic, and an unwavering commitment to family and friends.

Troy had been Mary Beth's first love, and she had been his. They began dating during their sophomore year at Loganville High, and they were the perfect couple, everyone agreed. It was true love not puppy love.

Until Troy broke her heart, in spring of their senior year, when Carolyn Johansen moved to town. Troy was intrigued by the new girl at Loganville High, all the boys were, a fascination that became infinitely tempting, and irresistibly challenging, when it became known that Carolyn had a *college* boyfriend in LA to whom she was virtually engaged.

Troy wanted to spend time with Carolyn, needed to, and it had nothing whatsoever to do with his feelings for Mary Beth. So he said. And so, perhaps, he believed.

The high-school sweethearts broke up, and Mary Beth was brokenhearted. But she was not alone. Rawley Ram-

sey was there for her, as he had been when her father
died, when both Rawley and Mary Beth were ten. And as
he had been there for her ever since. Rawley was her dear
friend, and had remained so, even though since freshman
year Rawley had secretly, achingly, wished for more.

Rawley was from the wrong side of the tracks. But his
talents on the football field had made him a Loganville
hero and had earned him an athletic scholarship to whatever college he chose. Rawley had chosen Notre Dame,
where he was scheduled to enroll in the fall. But that lifelong dream might change, Rawley would happily change
it, now that Mary Beth was free and had greeted Rawley's confession of love for her, yes, *love*, with surprise,
amazement, and eventually a return confession in kind.

Rawley took Mary Beth to the senior prom, and Troy
took Carolyn, and what happened that night was a bell-
wether for the Loganville summer, that growing-up summer, that lay ahead.

The vote for prom king and queen had taken place after
Troy and Mary Beth had broken up, and it wasn't that
their classmates didn't like Rawley, they did, although
there were distinctly negative feelings about Carolyn. But
Mary Beth and Troy belonged together, and if a romantic
prom-night reunion could be orchestrated, why not?

King Troy wanted such a reunion, was ready for it, and
when Queen Mary Beth joined him on the stage, Troy
kissed her in a way that told the applauding audience that
Mary Beth was his, always, and which evoked in Rawley
a surge of sheer rage.

Rawley rushed onto the stage even as Mary Beth was

pulling away from Troy's embrace, trying to. Troy released her when Rawley appeared, and in the ensuing fight between the two suitors, the fleet-footed football star stumbled over the microphone cord and twisted and fell. The ligaments in his knee tore. Shredded. As did, in that sudden burst of anger, all his gridiron hopes.

Mary Beth wanted nothing more to do with either of them. She couldn't go back to Troy even if she wanted to, which she didn't, not after what had happened to Rawley. And the violence she'd seen in Rawley both stunned and frightened her.

Rawley wanted her still. Desperately. Mary Beth was his only remaining dream. They could attend college in Boulder, and get married after their junior year, and Mary Beth might have acquiesced despite her newfound wariness because of her own sense of guilt.

But Mary Beth had another best friend, her mother Louise. Forget *both* Troy and Rawley, Louise advised. You're young, and so bright, and you have your entire life ahead of you.

It was welcome advice, wonderful advice. And there was more advice from Louise. Forget all boys, she counseled, for this summer before college. Spend this special time with the girls.

Mary Beth followed her mother's advice. She spent time with her friends from school, and most importantly with Louise.

Mary Beth was with her classmate friends, at a slumber party on Lake View Drive, the night her mother died. Louise had been smoking in bed, one of the last cigarettes she had ever planned to smoke. She had promised her daughter, future nurse Mary Beth, that she would quit, and they had designed a program, a gradual taper, and in another week their small house would have been smoke-free.

Their small house. It was engulfed in flames in moments.

Both Rawley and Troy were there for Mary Beth during that impossible time following Louise's death, their enmity forgotten, discarded, a triviality compared to the tragedy that had befallen the girl they both loved. And both Mary Beth and Rawley were there for Troy, supporting him, when his father was diagnosed with cancer. The outcome was hopeful, however, for Troy's father. The malignancy had been caught in time. Troy need have no qualms about attending Harvard in September as planned.

Only Carolyn escaped the summer unscathed. But by fall, when Troy and Rawley and Mary Beth went their separate ways, Carolyn left too, grew up, too, marrying at eighteen her twenty-two-year-old boyfriend in LA.

No one believed that Mary Beth would ever return to Loganville. But she did. With her cardiologist husband Samuel Quinn. The entire town fell in love with Mary Beth's Samuel and awaited like eager grandparents the baby the doctor and nurse were going to have.

It was Rawley, Loganville's recently appointed chief of police, who discovered Dr. Samuel Quinn's mangled body on that winter night a week before Grace was born. The doctor had apparently lost control of his car on a curve of pure ice and had careened into a snow-frozen tree.

Rawley broke the devastating news to Mary Beth. Then he waited patiently for the time when the woman he loved would be able to see him, *him*, beyond her grief.

It was three and a half years before Mary Beth could see anyone but her precious Grace. And when at last she could, it was Troy that Mary Beth saw. Troy, not Rawley.

Troy had returned to Loganville with neither hesitation nor complaint when his father's health had begun to fail. The Harvard-educated journalist who'd been well on his way to Pulitzer-prize stardom on a national scale became instead the editor-in-chief of the *Loganville Star*. Troy fell in love with Mary Beth again, and he was thoroughly charmed by Grace, and although nothing either official or unofficial had been announced, all of Loganville was predicting a wedding in June.

And now Troy was here, unexpected but welcome.

"I should have called," he said. "But I missed you, and I just happened to be in the neighborhood, and—you're not alone."

"No. But please come in. There's someone I want you to meet. This is Sam, Troy. Sam Quinn. He's Samuel's brother's son. Sam just arrived today and may stay for a while."

"Oh?" Troy's query was polite. And surprised.

"We hooked up at Loganville General. Sam had stopped to get directions to our home and by sheer chance spotted his cousin Grace." Mary Beth's smile indicated that the arrival of her nephew, be it at the town grocery or on the doorstep of their Bluebird Lane home, had been a surprise to her as well, and that there was more to the story—a teenage son at war with his parents—and that she'd explain it further when she and Troy were alone. Some *other* time. Troy got that smiling message too. As happy as Mary Beth was to see *him*, this evening needed to be devoted to acclimating her possibly troubled nephew to his Colorado home.

"Well," Troy said, "I just stopped by to say good night. I'll call you tomorrow, Mary Beth. Welcome to Loganville, Sam."

"Thank you, sir," Jace managed even as his thoughts swirled. The relationship between Mary Beth Quinn and Troy Logan was clearly important, *significant*. Yet she had outright lied to him. Why?

Mary Beth answered Jace's unasked question as soon as Troy was gone.

"Troy's a newspaperman," she explained. "A good one. A terrific one, actually. If I told him what you'd told me, he'd feel obligated to check every fact."

"What I told you is true."

"I know," Mary Beth confirmed as she led Jace to the room that would be his for as long as he wanted it to be. The first-floor den had been her husband's study. Its walls were bookshelves filled with medical and nursing texts, and its green-plaid couch folded out into a bed. "But just because it's okay with your mother doesn't mean the authorities wouldn't intervene."

Jace couldn't care less about the intervention of authorities. But what stunned him, and what mattered so much, was that Mary Beth, this mother, had intervened on his behalf. She had lied for Jace. *Lied* to protect Jace.

"Why are you being so nice to me?"

Mary Beth heard both man and boy in the quiet query. The boy, disbelieving yet so hopeful, and the man, worldly and wise—and quite certain that there was no reason, none whatsoever, to be nice to him.

"Because you're so nice to Grace. Do you have a little sister?"

"No, ma'am."

"Well, you do now. If you're planning to leave, Sam, do it soon, in the morning, before she wakes up."

"I'm not planning to leave." *I'd like to stay. Please. Forever.*

Jace lay awake that first night, sleep-starved but unable to sleep, fearful that this wide-awake dream would vanish if he so much as closed his eyes. He thought instead about the jobs he would get, the ones that would pay for his room and board and which would be worked before and after school.

As she'd handed him the soft stack of sheets for his fold-out bed, and pillows and blankets and towels, Mrs. Quinn—Mary Beth—had made it very clear that if he stayed, and he *was* staying, he would have to go to school. Yes, high school if he wanted. And he could, if he wanted, pretend to be fifteen.

The issue of his working, of his paying for anything at all, had not been mentioned by Mary Beth. And when he discussed it with her the next day, and the next and the next and the next, she always said no.

At the end of his first month in Loganville, however, Mary Beth told him that he could help, if he liked—as she knew he would—by watching, baby-sitting, Grace. Mary Beth worked days only, and weekdays at that, preferential treatment generously offered to the woman all of Loganville had known and loved since childhood, the girl who'd lost her father at ten, and her mother in that horrific fire, and who herself had so tragically become a single mom.

"But with you watching Grace," she explained, "I could work evenings, weekends, and maybe even nights. It wouldn't be every weekend, of course, or every evening or night. You'd have plenty of time to spend with friends."

There was as promised ample time for Sam to spend away from the Quinn house on Bluebird Lane. But he never did, never wanted to.

He was at home, with Mary Beth and Grace, all the time.

And he was welcomed, by both of them, all the time.

And was Sam Quinn welcomed by the citizens of Loganville?

Yes . . . although there were those, even in the charitable and idyllic Colorado town, who found a little odd, a little troubling, the notion of the dead husband's nephew turned baby-sitter. There were even those, refugees from the less-than-idyllic realities of the big city, who wondered if there might be unspeakable reasons to worry about an innocent little girl and a far-from-innocent teenage boy.

But Grace was Mary Beth's life. By entrusting Grace to Sam, Mary Beth was entrusting him with her life. Besides, Sam was Dr. Samuel Quinn's nephew, and if genetics meant anything at all . . . which they did, because there it was, the Samuel Quinn essence, the kindness, the compassion, the strength.

Grace and Sam wandered around town together, and eventually the duo of cousins became a small tromping parade. Grace had a circle of friends with whom she played, and whose parents concluded that it was all right if such playtimes happened while Grace's cousin babysat. *More* than all right. For the more those parents watched, the more they saw the happiness of the children, and the care, such exquisite caring, provided by the alarmingly sensual boy.

The parents saw that as well. The alarming sensuality. It was impossible to miss. The teenage girls of Loganville didn't miss it either, the fifteen-year-olds lucky enough to be in his classes and older girls, too.

And was Sam—Jace—attracted to those teenage girls? Of course he was. He was a young, healthy, stunning male. His hormones raged, restless and precocious. But he was unwilling to do anything, anything, that might jeopardize the astonishing, precarious joy.

Only two people on earth mattered. Mary Beth and Grace. The son of a thief stole not a kiss, not even at school, nor did he date, not a single Saturday night, even when Mary Beth was home.

As winter became spring, the parade became even larger. Teenage girls, forsaken by Sam but drawn to him still, joined the processional. Which was fine. These were nice girls, these Loganville teens, girls like Mary Beth had been.

They played together, Sam Quinn's young charges and his fascinated female entourage. But Sam's watchful gaze never strayed, not for a restless reckless moment, from the children in his care.

Mary Beth Quinn did not marry Troy Logan that June, nor was a wedding date set for fall. Indeed long before June, Mary Beth realized that she was happiest when she was with Sam and Grace. Sam might have been her son, and her daughter was learning from Sam what Grace would have learned from Samuel—that there existed in this world kind and gentle and caring men.

Like Sam. Like Samuel. But not like Troy? No, *of course* Troy would have been a wonderful male role model for Grace. He already *was*. But Troy wanted other roles as well. Impossible ones. Husband. Lover.

Troy had never officially proposed. But the inevitability of marriage had floated between them from the start. So Mary Beth told him, on that night in early May, "I can't marry you, Troy. Not now. Not ever."

It was the simple truth offered gently and lovingly, and received that way. Gently, lovingly, but with great sadness.

The entire town was sad for Troy. But remembering the prom-night reunion that had gone so terribly awry, the citizens of Loganville clamped down on every urge to get the high-school sweethearts back together again ... which made this Loganville summer, unlike that long-ago one, an idyll of clear blue skies, balmy breezes, and a tromping, laughing, happy parade.

It was also the azure summer during which Carolyn Johansen, childless and divorced, returned to Loganville. And maybe this was the way it was meant to be, for the attraction between Troy and Carolyn shimmered still.

By early August Troy and Carolyn were a couple. A December wedding was being planned. In late August Rawley at last spoke once again from his heart to Mary Beth.

And Mary Beth replied to her dear friend from hers.

"Oh, Rawley," she whispered as gently and lovingly as she had to Troy. "I'm still in love with Sam, still married to him, still—"

"Which Sam?" Rawley's harsh question shattered the gentleness.

"I can't believe you asked that."

"I can't either. I'm sorry, Mary Beth. Please forgive me."

She did forgive him. Of course. By the time autumn turned the billowing oaks the color of harvest fires, there was gentleness again with Rawley, a careful friendship, a quiet truce. The only pressure Rawley exerted on anyone in the Quinn household was on Sam. Loganville's chief of police was also the high school's football coach, and Rawley saw in Sam the natural athlete, and natural leader, who could catapult the Loganville Wildcats to the state championships, where they hadn't been since Rawley himself had led the team to such gridiron glory.

But Sam didn't turn out for football. He had other

after-school responsibilities, ones that began precisely at three, when Loganville Elementary—Grace started kindergarten that fall—let out.

Sam collected Grace and Dinah and whatever other little friends were joining them that day. There were on some days eight children in his charge. Sam watched them all, protected them all. And he paid attention to them too, kneeling before them as he listened *and heard* every earnest pronouncement each wanted to make.

But Sam only truly cared about Grace. It was a ferocious caring, love edged with fear, for what if despite his vigilance something happened to her?

It scared the hell out of him. Every minute, every second, of every day. Had it been left to him, the worried shepherd would have guided his flock to the library— *every day*—to listen to the wonderful stories read aloud by the town's librarian Mrs. Bearce.

Sam could have set that safe and certain agenda. His little charges would have followed him anywhere. But these were lively, imaginative children, and there were so many *other* fun things to do. Sam permitted his young enthusiasts to set the agenda, within reason. And he watched. And he worried.

The obvious dangers were fearsome enough: the jungle gym in the park, the traffic on Maple Avenue, the cracks in the sidewalk on which scampering feet might stumble, and the lake. *The lake.* He saw danger everywhere, and feared most the dangers he did not, could not, see.

Summer at the lake came and went. Safely. As did the

burning of autumn leaves. And even Halloween, including the afternoon of October 25 when there were smiling orange pumpkin faces to be made. It was an afternoon of laughter and candles and knives. But the only hands that were carved, that were nicked in any way, were his.

Something did happen. Finally. On November 11. His birthday. The day when Loganville believed that Sam Quinn, who was really Jace Colton, turned sixteen . . . but who on that November day was celebrating merely his fourteenth year on earth.

The near tragedy didn't happen to Grace, or even to a child in his care. It happened instead to a teenage girl in charge of another child, a boy whose parents, from the city, suspected a perversion even the most savvy citizens of Loganville hadn't imagined—that little girls were safe with the sensual Pied Piper because it was little *boys* that Sam preferred.

The boy's parents kept their suspicions to themselves. Their suspicions and their son. But both the six-year-old boy and his seventeen-year-old baby-sitter, a Loganville High School cheerleader, wanted to spend this November twilight with Sam and his entourage. When they saw their chance they took it, an impulsive dash across Sycamore, a quiet road where traffic was rare.

But it only took that rare car.

The girl was struck, a collision of unyielding metal and teenage thigh, a shattering of femur that severed the femoral artery as well.

The bookshelves in Jace's first-floor bedroom, Dr.

Samuel Quinn's study, held a comprehensive collection of medical texts.

Jace had begun with the chapters on first aid. But he didn't stop there. Couldn't. For the shepherd who feared most what he could not see, or did not know, needed to learn about every pediatric emergency there was—and the signs and symptoms that could be lethal if missed.

Such trivial symptoms: hoarseness, belly pain, a young head beginning to ache. Such terrifying possibilities: epiglottitis, an appendix near rupture, inflamed meninges encasing the brain.

The emergency that lay before him, the compound fracture on Sycamore Street, was straightforward in both diagnosis and management.

Stop the bleeding. It was the sine qua non of first aid. And if the bleeding site happened to be a limb, the approach was easy. Tourniquet the injured limb at the most readily accessible site between the escaping blood and the pounding heart. A tourniquet could be anything, a belt, a strip of fabric, and even, in the case of a bleeding finger, a rubber band.

Jace used his hands. He curled them tight around the girl's upper thigh, a viselike grip that stemmed the crimson flow . . . but did not impede his ferocious worry.

"Grace?"

"Yes?"

"Are you standing on the sidewalk? *Grace?*"

"Yes. Now I am."

"Okay. Stay exactly where you are. *Don't move.* That goes for everybody. Okay?"

There was a scurrying sound, the rapid dance of young feet, and then a chorus, the joyful sopranos of children.

"I'm on the sidewalk, Sam."

"So am *I*."

"Me too, Sam."

"Me *too*!"

The teenage girl would have bled to death were it not for the tourniquet-tight clench of powerful hands. All of Loganville knew it. The pretty young cheerleader survived because of Sam Quinn's incredible calm amid the raging crimson storm.

"I didn't feel calm," he confessed to Mary Beth.

"The good ones never do. Not inside." Her Samuel hadn't, not inside, not ever. "Calm is arrogant. You'd be a good doctor, Sam. You should think about it."

He thought about it only to exclude it. Taking care of Mary Beth and Grace was responsibility enough. Too much. Couldn't they see that?

No. Apparently not. Because with eyes wide-open and without a flicker of doubt, Grace and Mary Beth were quite convinced that he—the son of the liar, the impostor, the thief—could be whatever he wanted to be. Anything at all.

They trusted him, believed in him, and knew without question that he would keep the promises he made. Including the promise made on this Christmas Eve to give Santa Claus unobserved access to the fireplace, the cookies, the carrots, the tree.

As Jace walked away from the house, too restless, too

churning to sleep, he felt something new in the cold
bright air.

Peace. Calm and true and pure. As if he were an impostor no more. As if he was deserving of every trust.

And now something else was happening. He was listening. *Listening*. For what? A sound, apparently, beyond
the crunch of his footfalls on the snow. For now he was
halting those footfalls, stopping abruptly, and he was
holding his breath. And even his heart seemed to still.

So that he could listen, truly listen. For what?

The ringing of sleigh bells.

The flutter of flying reindeer overhead.

And did Jace Colton hear the soaring flutters, the fanciful chimes? Could he believe in such magic? Did he
*dare*?

For a shimmering instant the answer seemed to be
maybe.

Almost.

And then no.

No.

But it wasn't a shattering no, for the brilliant night glittered still. The peace. The purity. The calm.

Jace walked to the lake, the site of such splashing fun
for the children in summer and such terror for him. The
lake was comparably terrifying in winter. The ice was
frozen solid, Mary Beth assured him. Solid and thick. But
as he watched from shore his precious ducklings, accomplished skaters all, he readied himself to dive into the icy
depths.

The ice on this midnight clear was a mirror of the

heavens, the golden moon, the silver stars, the lush black-velvet sky.

And now his memory conjured a sound, a remembrance both magical and real, the enchantment of Grace Alysia Quinn singing Christmas carols.

Her voice was quite beautiful, a startling voice for a little girl, as clear and pure as this Christmas Eve sky. Grace knew every carol there was, every lyric of every one, and for the past three weeks she'd been singing them all.

Jace heard her, his memory did, as she sang his favorite.

*It came upon a midnight clear.*

Like this midnight clear. Starlit. Moonlit. Shimmering with peace.

*That glorious song of old.*

*From angels bending near the earth.*

Angels. The avenging one, Mary Beth, so fierce in her belief in him, and the little one, the precious golden one, the grace note in his life.

*To touch their harps of gold.*

Jace heard another sound then, soft and low. And real, *real*, not imagined. What if, could it possibly be, the exquisite pluck of a celestial harp? Could he believe after all? *Would* he?

The mirror of ice shone bright gold, as if in glorious reply, a glittering yes from the heavens, from Heaven itself. And a sudden flash of red danced amid the gold. A shooting star, colored crimson, on this Christmas night?

Perhaps. Or maybe the bright red streak was even more magical. Santa's sleigh soaring overhead. In another moment, any wondrous moment now, he would hear the sleigh bells.

But there were no sleigh bells for Jace Colton. No sweet, sweet magic from the winter sky.

The golden brilliance was earthbound not celestial, a reflected inferno from the flames that engulfed the house on Bluebird Lane, and now sirens were screaming in the frigid night air—such trivial screams compared to the ones within as Jace ran toward the searing blaze.

Taunting screams in his brain . . . and frantic prayers in his heart.

Go to bed. This was your promise. And instead you went for a restless, *reckless* walk.

But it will be all right! Santa has fireproof boots, *Grace said so*, and he's an expert on dousing flames.

There *is* no Santa, remember? No Santa. No magic. No peace. You couldn't hear the sleigh bells when you had the chance, couldn't believe enough, *did not dare*.

But there's Mary Beth! *She* is Santa. And she will have been awake, filling Christmas stockings and eating Christmas cookies and hiding the freshly washed carrots to give to the horses in the Hansens' barn.

And what of the sound you heard? The one that was soft and low and real? Are you praying it was something *other* than the explosion of undetected fumes and unseen sparks, the sort of invisible menace you've always feared and on this night of all nights you just happened to miss?

Yes. *Yes*.

That was his prayer, that Grace and Mary Beth would be outside watching the flames, and they wouldn't even be cold because the fire was so hot, and Christmas would be perfect still because they were safe, and—

And Jace Colton knew the truth. His prayer like his promise, *like him*, was a lie.

# CHAPTER ONE

*O'Hare International Airport*
*Chicago*
*December 23*
*Present Day*

It was one of those Yuletide weather patterns dreaded by airlines and travelers alike, storms in strategic hubs resulting in a systemwide chaos of cancellations and delays. By the third day of rain tempests and snow flurries, airports coast to coast were cluttered with weary travelers, their tempers frayed, their clothes crumpled, their luggage who knows where?

The nomads camped at United Airlines Gate C18 were journeying to London, hoping to, and, despite a soft fall of snow, it seemed that a break in the weather over Chicago would permit Flight 1147, the morning's nonstop, to depart right on time. Indeed, the first-class passengers had been invited to board, as had those travelers needing a little extra time.

General boarding would commence soon, the gate agent announced—a remark greeted by sudden commotion in the boarding area. Confirmed passengers, as well as displaced but hopeful ones, stood, stretched, and moved as one toward the jetway, as if proximity to the plane might improve the chances of getting on the flight.

Julia Anne Hayley did not move, not at all, not even a sigh. At least not one that could be perceived. She remained where she had spent the night, seated cross-legged on the floor beside a wall of windows that was far removed from even the most peripheral of other travelers.

Julia was alone, distant, remote. She needed to meet people, she knew. A good start would be to engage in light pleasantries with nonmenacing strangers, an impressive number of whom were congregated right here.

She would engage in such face-to-face exchanges. She would. Beginning next week. Or the week after.

One step at a time, she had promised herself. And she had just taken a most monumental one, away from everything she had known and loved and over a metaphorical bridge that had burned behind her. That she had so bravely burned.

What loomed ahead, far more immediate and daunting than the specter of eventual chats with strangers, was this journey to London.

To Christmas.

*Christmas*. The word and its memories evoked sudden panic, a fury as chaotic and fierce as the Yuletide storms. She couldn't do this. Could not. What had she been *thinking*? How had she managed to delude herself so?

Well. She was deluded no more.

She would simply go home. To Kansas.

But there was no home. Not anymore. She had sold the house, the home, where she had lived for twenty-eight years. Her entire life. It had been her great-aunt Anne's home. *Oh, Gran, what have I done?* And then her home. And Winnie's. *Oh, my little Win.*

Pain joined the panic, a twist of loss that stole her breath even as her anxious heart continued to race.

What had compelled this decision to start a new life? What had been so wrong with her old one?

*Nothing.*

It had just been different, that's all. More reclusive than most. But for so many years, those years with Gran and Winnie, it had been happy, joyous.

And for the past seven years? Not happy, not joyous. But after that first devastating year, she had been content. Her life had been safe. And until her decision to take these monumental steps, she'd never felt even the slightest frisson of panic.

And she *did* talk to people. Yes, admittedly, mostly over the phone. But that was human contact all the same, and worthwhile contact, too, for Julia helped the worried voices that called in the night.

And as for the rest of her life? She ran eight miles a day, and followed the news. She was very well informed. And, yes, she watched the soaps. And sometimes, yes, she thought about the soap-opera characters and their plights after the daily telecast was over.

But it was not as if she had any confusion about what

was real and what was not. Her mind did not blur the distinction between the characters in the fictional stories and the real-life actors who played the roles.

Indeed, at this very moment, even as pain stole every molecule of air from her lungs and panic flogged ever faster her racing heart, Julia recognized as actress not soap-opera heroine the woman emerging from the jetway.

Alexis Allen. That was the actress's name. Julia knew the character name, too. Who didn't? Actress Alexis Allen played Dr. Veronica Hastings on *Windy City*, the soap that critics and fans alike heralded as daytime's captivating answer to the sudsiness of *Dallas* and the medical edginess of *ER*.

As Julia looked at Alexis, her so-familiar face, she felt a flicker of calm amid the panic . . . the soothing memory of watching television in the safety of her home.

Her *home*.

*A*lexis Allen was furious. How *dare* he? Well. He would pay. Big-time. The price which Dr. Jace Colton, *bastard*, would eventually realize was the cost of losing her. Because no matter what, Alexis was through with him.

Through. No matter what. No matter how desperate Jace was for her after his two months of celibacy, not to mention *lunacy*, in war-torn wherever.

The arrogant surgeon *would* want her on his return. Wouldn't he?

Alexis had the confidence, and the experience with

men, to offer herself a reassuring and resounding *yes*. But Jace was unlike any man she'd ever known. In so many ways. Breathtaking ways in bed and annoying ways, ice-cold and dispassionate ones, when the passion was spent.

It was pure ice that had greeted her this morning as she'd started to take the seat beside his. Jace should have been surprised, perhaps pleasantly, perhaps not, but surprised nonetheless.

But there had been only the disdainful chill of his glacial gaze. And the ice-sharp contempt of his voice.

"This isn't going to happen, Alexis."

"It's a free country, Jace. You don't own *everything*. I have every right to take this flight if I wish."

"Have a nice trip," he'd said with ominous quiet as he'd prepared to deplane.

But this was her exit, not his. And although a solitary Christmas might appeal to him—was what he *chose*—such Yuletide solitude in London, or anywhere, held no appeal for her.

"I *hate* you," she had whispered, had hissed, before turning away.

Alexis's fury as she'd stormed off the plane had been filled with unfocused yet impassioned thoughts of future retribution. Jace Colton would pay for rejecting her.

Someday.

And even as she fumed upstream against the throng of bedraggled humanity, the weary travelers who were so grateful to be on this flight, her only immediate plan was to get out of the airport before some obsessed fan recognized her. Even the retrieval of her luggage from the plane's cargo hold could wait. So what if her designer suitcases filled with designer negligees made the transatlantic journey to London?

But if she simply left the airport, *fled* the airport, having already checked in and claimed her seat, she would be giving Jace precisely what he wanted most. Privacy.

Oh, it was possible, she supposed, given the holiday-destroying storms and the irrepressibility of the Christmas spirit, that her precipitously vacated seat might be reassigned. In which case, she reasoned, whoever was bumped into the luxury of first class would be chosen from the ranks of those legitimately flying Connoisseur, rather than the rumpled ragamuffins crowded into coach . . . and the lucky traveler would most definitely *not* be a boarding-area refugee, one of the myriad strained faces hoping against hope to make the flight.

Not that Jace would care what class, either in life or on the plane, his traveling companion hailed from. The bastard might be many things. But he was not an elitist, not socially, not economically, not intellectually. So why did the doctor fly first-class? Because he had the money? That was part of it perhaps, for oh did Jace Colton have the money.

Alexis guessed it wasn't luxury Jace wanted, but space—an abundance for his long, restless limbs and, most importantly, for the precious privacy he valued so.

International first class was so spacious that one need not speak to a seatmate unless one so chose. Which Jace definitely would not. Jace Colton did not engage in idle chitchat, and anything that wasn't idle, especially intimate revelations about himself, was out of the question entirely. Privacy was paramount to Jace. Solitude. Both of which were guaranteed in first class, an unspoken pact among the like-minded and elite clientele.

But if *she* chose Jace's traveling companion, an interloper in the rarefied sanctuary, a heathen who had no insight into the first-class rules . . . which she could do, and would. The ticket was hers, after all. Paid in full by her. She had every right to give it to whomever she liked. There might be some red tape involved, and perhaps even a name-transfer fee. But who cared? Whatever red tape she encountered would be a bright scarlet ribbon around this very special Christmas present she planned for Jace.

So. Let's see . . .

Alexis toyed briefly with placing a baby in seat 2B, an infant who with luck would scream bloody murder all the way to London. That had a certain *irony*, and a veritable nursery of possibilities whined before her. But babies came with parents, a loving mother perhaps, and a paragon of doting motherhood would not do.

Alexis needed someone who would talk to Jace and demand dialogue in return. Someone? A woman. But one who was so far from Jace's type that her plan couldn't possibly backfire into a transatlantic flight that was a sultry prelude to the one nonsolitary thing Jace truly enjoyed: sex.

For a too-brief and ultimately disastrous time Alexis had been Jace's type. Using herself therefore as the gold standard, Alexis needed to choose as his traveling companion her exact opposite, a woman who was meager where she was lush, sexless where she was so deliciously female, a woman without confidence, without glamour, without style.

And there she was—although Alexis's initial impression was that the creature sitting cross-legged before the distant wall of windows was a he not a she. A pale and skinny teen with a crush *on her*.

On further scrutiny, however, Alexis determined that this was neither teen nor boy. The further scrutiny was afforded by the creature, this woman of sorts, herself. She was staring at Alexis, a gawking as forthright as if she were watching Alexis on TV, where it was polite, at least not impolite, to stare.

As Alexis moved toward her besotted fan she felt a familiar thrill, the adrenaline rush that accompanied her every performance. Her audience was already enraptured. But there were challenges nonetheless, the all-important script which she herself would have to write.

No problem, the surging adrenaline promised.

How many times had Alexis Allen directed—oh yes, she was about to become a director, too—some idiot writer to make more interesting, more intriguing, her lines?

# CHAPTER TWO

*A*lexis's confidence that she had discovered the most perfect, most *im*perfect traveling companion for Jace crescendoed as she wove her way toward the wall of windows . . . only to falter as she neared. For there, lying atop the cross-legged lap, was a stuffed animal. It was a rabbit, Alexis supposed, tattered and old, its once plush yellow coat threadbare and gray.

Was this boy-woman mentally ill? If so, she definitely would not do.

She was at least in touch enough with reality to realize that Alexis was approaching her, and in touch enough with civility to begin to stand, clutching the stuffed animal as she did.

"Don't get up," Alexis instructed as she herself floated to her knees on the carpeted floor.

Alexis assessed as she floated. The woman's clothes were clean, neat, and quite possibly new. He slacks were black, her turtleneck cream, and her billowing overblouse a silvery gray. Her winter coat was charcoal, and wool not cashmere, but with a certain solemn style.

The overall *look* was solemn. And sexless. And colorless, save for the bright blue knapsack on the floor nearby.

There was a little more color, Alexis realized, as she met the woman's eyes. They were lavender, a rather extraordinary shade, and quite a bit less bedazzled by her than Alexis had imagined they would be.

"Hi. My name is Alexis."

"Alexis Allen. Yes. I know. I admire your work."

The voice was soft, mature. Womanly. Alexis would have preferred something sharp and shrill to torment Jace all the way to Heathrow. But she comforted herself that looking at this face, so far from lush and glamorous, so unlike *hers*, would be grating enough.

It was a makeup-free face, framed by short black hair, and thin and very pale. There was a certain drama to the face, Alexis conceded, the translucent skin, the surprising eyes, the bone structure that was unusually good. Drama. But no appeal.

"Thank you," Alexis replied to the compliment of her work. "And you are?"

"Julia Hayley."

Who, Alexis decided, was not mentally ill. Not mad. Merely odd, merely quirky, merely strange. Perfect. Unless . . . the porcelain skin stretched over those prominent bones was so poreless, so wrinkle-free, that Alexis felt constrained to pose another question. "May I ask how old you are?"

"Twenty-eight."

Twenty-eight to Jace's thirty-six. That worked nicely. If Julia had even a dash of female hormones in her emaciated body she would develop a major crush on Jace. Instantly.

Emaciated. Alexis reflected for a moment on the word. She herself was *not* emaciated. Not even excessively thin. She was lush, sexy, succulent. But Julia—well, *emaciated* was definitely apt. And as for the cause of the extreme thinness? If pathology was involved, some aberrant relationship with food, it was anorexia, Alexis decided. Not bulimia. No tiny lines bracketed the corners of Julia's mouth, no telltale clues that signaled the binge-purge syndrome to those in the know.

"Here's the thing, Julia. I have a problem. Actually, a friend of mine does. And I need your help."

"I'd be happy to help."

Alexis was a little taken aback by the certainty, as if Julia believed she *could* help whatever the problem, as if sympathy, empathy, were what she did best. And what, Alexis knew, Jace would hate most: a sexless, enthralled female who believed he needed her.

Perfect, Alexis thought, as her lines, her script, flowed on a river of satisfaction.

"My friend's name is Jace. And," Alexis confided in a whisper, "He's *more* than my friend. He's my fiancé. Our engagement has been absolutely hush-hush. Jace is *extremely* private. We both are. We were planning to announce our marriage only *after* it was a fait accompli. Which should have been last night." The wistful expression on Alexis's beautiful face gave an eloquent indication of the silk-and-satin fantasy her wedding would have been. "And today we should have been flying to London for our Christmas honeymoon at the Eden-Knightsbridge Hotel."

"The Eden-Knightsbridge?"

"You may not have heard of it. It's quite new. But it's spectacular, Julia. *Perfect* for a honeymoon. And should the newlyweds choose to leave their bridal suite, not that *we* would have, Hyde Park is right there, as are Mayfair and Knightsbridge, and the fabulous department store Canterfields can be accessed without even going outside, by way of a glass skybridge for hotel guests."

"Canterfields."

Julia's echo this time was a faraway murmur, and suddenly the anorectic herself seemed terribly far away. Where? Alexis wondered. Lost in some fantasy shopping spree? Making ever more somber purchases in shades of gray?

Wherever Julia was, Alexis wanted her back and focused *now*.

"Are you traveling alone, Julia?"

"What? Oh. Yes."

"But meeting someone in London."

"No."

"No?" Alexis echoed with what in her estimation was Emmy award-worthy surprise. *Of course* this strange translucent creature wasn't meeting anyone. "Well. It would be too much to ask you to look after Jace once you reach London, even though you'll both be alone. But looking after him *is* what I need to ask you to do en route."

"Look after him? Is he ill?"

"No." *Just terminally arrogant.* "And once you lay eyes on him you'll decide that *I'm* the one who's in desperate need of intensive care. I'm the one, you see, who called off our wedding. Everything was happening so fast. *Too* fast. I felt overwhelmed, and even a little *frightened*, I suppose, to be loved *so much*—treasured and cherished and adored—*especially* by a man like Jace."

Alexis's breathless soliloquy had been delivered to her beautifully manicured hands, during which the tapered fingers of her right hand touched the ring finger of the left, as if in remembrance of a perfect diamond, a treasure from the man who treasured her so.

Soliloquy completed, Alexis looked up and met uncomprehending lavender eyes. Julia Hayley did not understand, or perhaps she did not believe, that it was possible to be loved *too* much. And was there a little disapproval as well? Was Julia having trouble feeling sympathy for her, for *any* bride who called off her wedding once the solemn commitment to marry had been made?

Okay, fine. It wasn't sympathy for herself that Alexis needed anyway, but for Jace, the man who—in Julia's mind apparently—had been so grievously wronged.

"Look. I may not deserve Jace. In fact the more I tell you about him, the more you'll be convinced that I don't.

But *he* deserves happiness. *He* deserves to spend his life with the woman he loves, who for better or worse is *me*. Let me tell you about him, all right? So you'll understand his passion, his *intensity*. How amazing he is."

Alexis paused to regroup, to await the adrenaline rush, for now came the true acting, the authentic actressing, the talent required to make the ice-hearted bastard sound sympathetic.

Of course on paper, as in the flesh, Jace was pretty sensational.

"Jace is a trauma surgeon," Alexis began. "One of the best of the best. But despite his surgical expertise, Dr. Jace Colton spends more time in the ER than the OR. He *chooses* to. He wants to be on the front line, you see, *in the trenches*, greeting the sick and the mangled as they arrive, during those crucial moments when what he does or doesn't do will make the difference between life and death."

Jace had not told her this, of course. It was far too private, but probably true. Alexis's source was an ER nurse with whom Jace worked and who had made the admiring revelation based not on a confession from Jace but from what she had personally observed.

"Jace works at Grace Memorial Trauma Center, which is *the* trauma center of Chicago and probably of the Midwest. Jace has made it that way. Yes, GMTC is his. He owns it, directs it, and runs an incredibly tight and uncompromising ship, all in his *spare* time. He works the same number of in-the-trenches hours as the other docs, at least *eighty* per week, and he manages the administrative aspects on his own time . . . even though every second of his life *could* be spent doing nothing at all. Except, of course, spending money."

Jace Colton wasn't merely trauma-surgeon rich, a plush stratosphere of luxury in itself. He dwelled in another universe altogether, the rarefied realm of staggering wealth.

The trauma surgeon with the Midas touch. That was the way Jace's promptly fired stockbroker had once described him. And according to Alexis's own stockbroker, it was dazzlingly true.

Alexis would have embellished on the enormity of Jace's fortune had Julia seemed interested in the least. But it seemed to be Jace's personal worth, his devotion to the grievously ill, that impressed her.

"*Not* that money matters to Jace," Alexis said. "He gives it away." *Throws it away.* "And as I'm sure you must realize, Jace's money doesn't matter to me. *He* matters. Terribly. You must get on that plane, Julia, and you must *help* him. I'm so afraid that if he goes to war in the state he's in . . ."

"Goes to war?"

"*Yes.* It isn't enough to have created the best trauma center in Chicago and to spend the vast majority of his life fighting the good fight there. Jace has to do more. So he travels to war-ravaged countries all over the globe, to care for soldiers and civilians alike. Jace had committed to his upcoming mission before we fell in love. So even though we were supposed to have married last evening, and to have honeymooned in London this week, we would have been separated *anyway* from New Year's Eve until Valentine's Day. Married, but separated. And all I asked, three weeks ago, was that we postpone our wedding until his February 14 return. That way, I told him, I could spend our time apart preparing for the monumental life change of becoming a wife. *His* wife. Jace was so *calm* when I made the request, as if it were the most reasonable suggestion he'd ever heard."

"But he was hurt."

"Maybe. I suppose. But it was hidden beneath a glassy-smooth veneer of icy-cold fury. He suggested calmly, coldly, that we put *everything* on hold until his return. Then last night, after three weeks of silence, he left a message on my machine. He was going to London as scheduled and missed me and *loved* me and wouldn't I please spend these special days of Christmas with him? So that he wouldn't be *alone*? My first-class ticket for the seat beside his would be waiting for me at check-in. I must have been in the shower preparing to go out when Jace left the message. I discovered it on my return, after midnight, at which point I threw a few negligees and my wedding dress in a suitcase, all the while fantasizing about our Christmas wedding in London."

Alexis's beautiful frown gave fair and dramatic warning that her fantasy was not to be. "This morning, even as I was taking my seat beside his, I could see that something was *terribly* wrong. And his voice, when he finally spoke, was like death. 'What,' he asked, 'no Grant?'."

"Grant?"

"Yes, you know, Grant Rogers? He plays Ian on *Windy*

*City*. Grant and I had been involved for almost six months before I met Jace. It seemed serious, felt serious, until Jace. It was love at first sight with Jace. I was entranced by him, *intoxicated*. No one else mattered. I'm ashamed to say that my breakup with Grant wasn't very kind. Grant was understandably bitter. But over the past few weeks we've become friends again. And last night, on what should have been my wedding night, I was *so* upset, Julia, so *distressed* that I called Grant. I needed a friend, you see. I missed Jace, loved Jace, and I was absolutely terrified that I'd ruined everything by asking him to give me this time. Grant took me out for drinks, and whether it was to prevent me from slipping on ice or to comfort me while we talked, he touched me. *Innocent* caresses, misinterpreted by Jace, who in his supreme arrogance had been *stalking* me."

"His arrogance?"

"*Supreme* arrogance. Make no mistake, Julia, Dr. Jace Colton is one arrogant male. I have a feeling that no woman before me has ever said no to him. Or even maybe. Jace is arrogant and proud. With reason. And this morning, when Jace greeted me with his hostile question about Grant, my initial response was anger. *Outrage*. But then I looked at him, really looked, and, well, Jace obviously hadn't slept at all last night, and even though his voice was pure ice, without the slightest slur, I'm afraid he may have spent those sleepless hours drinking . . . and that he'll *keep* drinking all the way to London."

In truth, Alexis knew full well that Jace's on-the-rocks voice was simply a measure of his glacial fury with her. If Jace Colton ever drank, Alexis didn't know it. And she'd certainly had no reason to encourage him to imbibe. His stone-cold-sober sexuality was deliciously uninhibited, *perfect*, without embellishment of any sort.

Jace hadn't been drinking. At least not yet. But, Alexis mused, if ever there was a time when he might indulge, might—given recent events—even be looking forward to such escape, it would be on this flight to London. She could imagine the scene, and his pleasure. The sensual man. The sensual pleasure. The private enjoyment of solitary drinking and solitary thoughts.

Well. *Too bad.*

"Jace is hurt, Julia. Despondent and depressed. Which is so *un*Jace it terrifies me. I *tried* to explain to him why I was with Grant last night, that it was because I missed *him* so much. But Jace wasn't listening. He'd already concluded that Grant was the real reason I'd postponed our marriage and that I'd been seeing Grant all along. Jace is in trouble. And I can't help him. He won't *let* me. He doesn't want me anywhere near him right now." Alexis hesitated, debating, then whispered in a rush, "Jace has told me that he loves me more than life itself. *No*. I can't let myself believe he'd take his own life. Cannot. But he needs to talk, Julia. *Desperately*. He needs to talk to you."

Alexis expected a frown of self-doubt—and insight— on the thin translucent face. How could she, this boy-woman with the grimy yellow rabbit, possibly help an arrogant and sensual male who was devastated by the loss of a woman like Alexis?

But there was no frown on the porcelain face, only steady lavender eyes, as if talking to Jace, comforting him, was something Julia Hayley truly believed she could do.

"Once you *do* start talking to him, Julia, you can*not* let him know that you've spoken to me."

"I can't?"

"No," Alexis replied as calmly as she could at the impossible specter of Julia telling Jace the whole truth and nothing but the truth. Which was of course a tapestry of lies. "As much as I'd like you to reassure him that I love him, he wouldn't believe it, and he'd refuse to talk to you if you did, and all would be lost. Besides, this isn't about me. It's about *him*, the wonderful man who's been put through an emotional wringer at Christmas of all times. You have to be a stranger, Julia, to both of us, a fellow traveler who just happened to get my vacated seat. Okay?"

"Yes. Okay. I'll try to help him."

"*Great.* Thank you. Have you flown international first class before?"

"No."

"Well. It's sheer luxury, and the spaces are vast. None of the other first-class passengers will overhear your conversation, *couldn't* overhear even if Jace ranted and raved. Which he *never* would. He's *so* controlled. It's important however, *imperative*, that you don't say anything to him, *anything at all*, until the plane is airborne. The image of Jace getting off and driving on the icy streets in the emotional state he's in, well, *please* don't let that happen."

Once Julia's solemn gaze confirmed her understanding of Alexis's admonition, Alexis cast an experienced glance at the jetway. Boarding was going smoothly, and the posted departure time hadn't budged, and very soon Jace would be trapped with this pathetic creature intent on engaging him in conversation all the way to London.

"I'm sure you've read in magazines, Julia—or seen shows on the topic on TV—about the confessions, the *confessionals,* that take place on airplanes? The intimate secrets shared by absolute strangers as they hurtle through space? No one knows *why* the phenomenon happens, although theories abound. But it's definitely real and remarkably pleasant. *Cathartic.* I've had it happen myself any number of times. The moment the plane returns to terra firma, however, the spell shatters to bits. You see the guy for the disappointment he truly is. A man with whom in any other setting you'd never exchange so much as a word. You've already exchanged secrets by then, *secrets,* and all you can think about is getting off the plane and far away as soon as you possibly can. Of course I've never had the pleasure, the *thrill,* of being seated next to a man as spectacular as Jace. Not even Jace himself. This would have been our first joint venture into space. Is he even *more* sensational thirty-five thousand feet above earth? It seems hard to imagine. But you, Julia, are going to have the chance to find out. And it will be easy. I *promise.* Yes, Jace *may* seem reluctant to talk at first. But don't give up! He will respond. He's extremely polite, and the phenomenon will be affecting him, too. And it will be a *relief* for him to talk. Truly. He's so terribly lonely. So deeply hurt. And Julia? If you could somehow keep him from drinking himself to death en route to London . . ."

# CHAPTER THREE

*J*ace Colton was in his seat by the window, and he was looking out, staring at the delicate fall of snow.

Was he seeing the delicacy? Julia wondered as she settled into the seat beside his. Or was he so blinded by hurt that he saw nothing at all?

Julia couldn't tell. She couldn't see his face, not even in profile. Nonetheless and suddenly Jace Colton was real, a man, *this* man who loved Alexis Allen, and who Alexis claimed to love in return—yet who, Julia thought, Alexis had cruelly betrayed.

His hair was black, the color of midnight, and his slacks were a similar shade. If there had been a tie, it had been abandoned, and the sleeves of his snow-white shirt were rolled. He might have been a bridegroom relaxing at last, the wedding festivities over, the honeymoon about to begin.

But Jace Colton had spent the night stalking not marrying, and then drinking till dawn, even though, Alexis had told her, his deathlike voice had not been slurred.

Nothing was slurred about this man. Even in silhouette he was controlled, contained. And watchful, Julia realized, *watchful of her* despite his intense gaze at the falling snow.

He knew, she decided, that it was she not Alexis who'd taken the seat beside his. He saw her reflection in the window—the window, surely, and yet it seemed, it *felt*, as if Jace Colton saw her reflected off a mirror of snow.

And it seemed, it felt, as if she was seeing him, too, in a crystalline mirror.

And what did Julia see in the eyes that glittered off the delicate prisms of ice? Fire, brilliant and green. And not dead, not dying. But disapproving? Disappointed? Wishing Alexis had returned to him after all?

No, Julia thought. Felt. This black-haired stranger about whom she knew so little *and so much* seemed satisfied, not disappointed. Relieved.

"You'll need to stow that for takeoff."

The flight attendant's voice drew Julia from the snow-crystal mirror. It was a pleasant voice and not critical in the least of Julia's turquoise blue knapsack.

"I'll put it under the seat."

"Good. And may I hang up your coat for you?"

Julia had worn her winter coat since leaving Kansas. And she'd been cold despite its woolen warmth.

But Julia was chilled no more. She was warmed, *heated*, by the relieved—and welcoming?—fire green eyes.

"Yes," she murmured. "Please."

As the flight attendant vanished with her coat, Julia

placed her knapsack beneath the seat in front of her. The space was so ample that no part of the knapsack was touched, much less crushed, and Julia had set the most precious item on top, secured gently before boarding. It, that precious item, *she*, could spend the entire flight lying on her cottony belly, as she always lay.

But it was dark inside the knapsack, like a coffin, and even before her journey began Julia had decided to permit herself this indulgence. It wasn't crazy, merely sentimental.

The beloved little rabbit had been left in her care by a dying girl. A last wish. A final gift. Had Winnie been alive, Floppy would have been on *her* lap, clutched close, not in the cargo hold below, Julia never would have done that, and not even in the just-stowed knapsack.

Floppy was a living thing.

Floppy had survived.

And Floppy would fly to London as she had flown from Kansas City to O'Hare. On Julia's lap.

Julia unclasped the knapsack buckle, which had been fastened loosely, lest there be confinement of any kind. Still, within the knapsack nest, the bell concealed within the fabric of Floppy's short yellow tail had been silent.

But the bell jingled as Julia removed the cotton rabbit from the knapsack, and jingled again as Julia secured her seat belt low and tight across her lap, and jingled a third time as Julia placed Floppy on her lap for takeoff.

It was the third jingle, that sweet silvery chime, that drew Jace Colton's attention from the dancing fall of snowflakes to her. To Floppy.

His gaze was dark. Ominous and brooding. And oddly accusatory, as if she—no, as if *Floppy*—had been in his thoughts and had caused his torment. His pain.

There was such torment, so much pain, in the eyes that stared, glared, at the floppy yellow ears and threadbare limbs.

As Julia clutched Floppy protectively, reflexively, the tiny bell tinkled yet again. And Dr. Jace Colton looked from the rabbit to her. His dark green gaze was quite unreadable, its deep anguish hidden far away, and in mere instants the gaze itself was gone, returned to the swirling snowflakes and desolate sky.

But Julia read so much in the fleeting glimpse, an interpretation that came with ice. A glacier of it. She was freezing now, again. Far more cold than before. She had been *so wrong*. There'd been *no* relief in the snow-crystal mirror. No welcome, no warmth.

Jace Colton didn't want her here. Didn't need her here. He needed, wanted, no one. Julia might have acceded to his wishes, might have fled. But it was too late. Already the jet was racing down the runway.

Julia pressed deeper into her seat and found a moment of solace. This first-class seat, so spacious and soft, felt like home, the place that had been home, the armchair that had been Gran's. The beloved chair, that touchstone of love, was a rare refugee from the blurry time when so much had been lost—when in that blur, in that slur, Julia had given so much away.

But Gran's chair had survived that time of careless impulse and devastating loss, and was en route to the city where Julia had chosen to begin anew. Seattle. Her new home.

*Home*. Panic quivered, rushed, roared, even as the jet engines did. What if Gran's chair was lost, as everything else had been? And what if there was no place anywhere that could ever again feel like home?

It didn't matter, Julia realized as the racing wheels lost touch with earth. She was going to freeze to death long before she reached Seattle . . . long before, in all likelihood, she even reached London.

The bell, that sweet sound of joy, had chimed at the precise place in his reverie when he had been listening for sleigh bells overhead—when for that fanciful moment on a midnight clear he had almost heard the magic, had *almost* been able to believe.

But he couldn't. Hadn't. Had not dared.

And now, on this snowy day, there had been a chime. Delicate and sweet. And fanciful? Yes, apparently, for when Jace looked in the direction of the silvery sound, there'd been only a yellow rabbit clutched by skeletal hands.

Jace had stared at those hands, knowing he was staring and not knowing, then, that the jingle had been real. And he had wondered, an idle musing, if the Ghost of Christmas Past had decided to visit him at last, to taunt him with tinkling bells and ever more pain.

Jace needed no such ghost. His remembrance was as brilliant as that long-ago night. He had become Jace again on that night—Jace not Sam—worthy namesake *again* of his father. The liar, the impostor, the thief.

Jace Colton the son deserved to die. And he would, should have, during the week that followed that night, when he had wandered ever farther, ever deeper, into the winter wilderness northwest of Loganville. Jace had not been afraid of death. He had wanted it, welcomed it, hungered for it.

But the inferno within had not permitted him to die. It was too soon, too easy, too swift an escape. He needed to burn slowly, scream softly.

A year of remembrance was the searing sentence Jace gave himself. Then death. But even before the next Christmas Eve drew near, that wanted, welcomed execution eve, the voices began. Familiar voices, and such beloved ones. They came to him at night, in his nightmares, which—because of them—became dreams.

You're *not* to blame, Mary Beth insisted. It was an *accident*, like the accidents that killed my mother and my Samuel.

I would have been *so mad* at you—Grace shook her finger as she spoke—if you'd scared Santa away. The fire was *Santa's* fault, although he didn't *mean* it. He was probably carrying a candle, and it fell over, and he didn't notice the flames until it was *way* too late.

They wanted him to live, these beloved voices. And to suffer no more. And they implored him to become the man they believed *still* that he could be. Jace didn't want to hear the loving voices. He wanted nightmares not dreams. Deserved nightmares.

But the dreams and the voices came.

So Jace stopped sleeping.

And still the voices spoke.

They were hallucinations, Jace knew. Phantoms from his sleepless nights. But there they were. Mary Beth and Grace. Inside him. *Alive* within.

And if Jace killed himself? If he burned slowly and screaming? They too would die. He would kill them. *Again.*

Jace believed for a while that Grace and Mary Beth were truly alive within him. He had needed, for a while, to believe.

But he knew the truth. The voices within, the ones that demanded so much of him, were his own.

And Jace Colton placed far weightier expectations on himself than Grace and Mary Beth ever had. He would become the doctor Mary Beth believed he should be. A shepherd who knew no calm. He would care for his flock even as his heart raced with worry and ached with fear. It would be a special flock, the sickest of the sick, the most urgently needy, for whom the slightest misstep would result in sudden death.

The shepherd spent his life tending to that flock.

Except at Christmas. Then and alone Jace permitted remembrance of that long-ago Christmas Eve. Permitted it, compelled it, exposing every lost hope, every trust betrayed, to the conflagration that seared his soul.

Jace relived that midnight clear precisely as it had been—not, never, as it *might* have been. He forbade himself such fantasy, such joy.

But on this day, when he'd heard the silvery chime, as if from a sleigh bell, he'd wondered—as he'd gazed at skeletal hands clutching the yellow rabbit—if he was about to be taunted with joyous might-have-beens, *would-have-beens,* had only he kept his promise . . . or dared to believe.

The chime came not, however, from a long-ago flying sleigh, but from a cotton rabbit's bobbed yellow tail. And the clutching hands?

Did they belong to a ghost?

No. Although she seemed, this woman beside him, an apparition of sorts, delicate, ethereal, and shimmering. Or was that trembling he saw? Trembling from her fear of him.

Jace was a master at concealing his thoughts. But the rabbit's chiming tail had caught him in a rare unguarded moment of anguish, of anger, of pain.

Jace had looked away as quickly as possible, releasing the trembling apparition from his fearsome gaze.

But Jace had not been released from the image of her.

She was very thin. Too thin. The ravages of illness? Of madness? No, Dr. Jace Colton decided. Not of madness. Her fear of him was eminently sane. Of illness, then? Was she a cancer patient granted her dying wish, to see Merry Olde England in all its Christmas glory?

No, he decided. The doctor decided. Yes, her skin was pale, startlingly so. And translucent, as if she'd spent her entire life under glass. But the gossamer flesh was white not sallow, untinged, untainted, by the hues and shades of disease.

And her black hair, although quite short, shone with the glossiness of health.

She was pale and thin, and glossy and shimmering, and fearful. But healthy. Delicate yet strong.

A long-distance runner, perhaps.

Or a dancer. A ballerina.

An image came to him of a snow globe he had seen years after his life, and death, in Loganville. The scene within the glass ball was at once mesmerizing and improbable, a ballerina twirling amid snowflakes even as a winter moon cast its golden glow.

Mesmerizing and improbable. Like this ballerina who had so improbably—so impossibly yet so thoroughly—distracted Jace Colton from his Yuletide journey of torment, of solitude, of rage.

# CHAPTER FOUR

*T*he pilot's voice reverberated overhead within moments of Flight 1147's on-time takeoff.

"It's going to be a little bumpy for a while, so I'm asking everyone, flight attendants included, to remain seated until the turbulence has passed. The good news is that the storms have given us a tremendous tail wind. At present we're projecting an early—9:20 P.M.—touchdown. It's raining in London and a balmy fifty-four degrees. So sit back, relax, know the bumpiness will pass, and enjoy the flight."

It was fifty minutes before the turbulence had gentled enough to enable the first-class flight attendants to begin making offerings to their elite coterie of guests.

The in-flight menu was presented, an invitation to the lavish brunch, to be served soon, and to the five-star dinner that would commence ninety minutes before their arrival at Heathrow.

Then came magazines and newspapers from around

the globe, followed by an impressive assortment of movies on cassette which could be screened privately on the monitors encased within the expansive armrests of the luxurious seats.

Jace and Julia received in silence the menus, and declined with shakes of their respective heads the magazines, newspapers, and cassettes, and between those nonverbal interactions, Jace Colton gazed at storm clouds and Julia Hayley stared at the rabbit who lay, silent too, on her lap.

Eventually dialogue became necessary, at least with their flight attendant. Her name, engraved in gold and worn on her lapel, was Margot.

"Miss Hayley?" she asked after consulting the handwritten name change on the passenger manifest. "Have you made your meal selections? The choice between the omelette, the Belgian waffle, or the fruit plate for brunch, and for dinner either the salmon or the filet?"

"Nothing for me. Thank you."

"*Nothing?*" Margot's surprise was unconcealed. True, there was airline food. Something one might reasonably avoid. But this was international first class.

"No. Thank you."

"But something to drink?"

"No," Julia murmured a third time. "Thank you."

Margot looked at Jace, whose stormy gaze had been drawn from the clouds by the conversation taking place with Miss Hayley in seat 2B. "And for you, Dr. Colton?"

"No food. Thank you. But if you'll bring me a handful

of those little bottles of scotch, you can forget about me for the rest of the trip."

Margot did not want to forget about this gorgeous passenger.

"You're not a plastic surgeon, are you?"

"No. Trauma. Why?"

"I'm desperately seeking a second opinion."

She was clearly talking about herself, and there was for Jace the obvious reply—that even though he was credentialed in trauma not plastics, he couldn't imagine why she'd ever sought a *first* opinion. His surgical credential was trivial, of course, compared to his experience, and his expertise, as a stunningly sexual male.

Jace was accustomed to such casually seductive repartee. On this day, he acknowledged his half of the dialogue in silence, with a weary yet devastating smile.

Margot smiled in reply. Compliment received.

"Would you like ice, Doctor, for your scotch?"

"Not necessary."

"Okay."

Jace's scotch arrived, glowing amber in six small glass bottles—at which Julia stared, as he had stared at the fingers that clutched the rabbit who rang, a glowering as unguarded and as fierce as his own must have been. Then.

Jace was so aware of her ferocious gaze. Yet she seemed oblivious of him, so focused was she on the shimmering bottles . . . and so worried that Jace felt an astonishing urge to reassure.

He was *not* an alcoholic. That was the easy truth. He drank only on airplanes, when he was responsible for no one but himself, and only when he was in transit between worlds, from Chicago to war—or from the snowy present to the fiery past.

True, only occasional drinking did not de facto exclude alcoholism. Binge drinking, even rarely, could definitely qualify. And he did enjoy what rare drinking he did, the slight blurring of the scalpel-sharp discipline with which he lived his life. But drinking was neither essential to him, something he longed for or craved, nor was it ever even close to a binge.

Jace didn't anticipate drinking all the scotch. But even if during the transatlantic flight he emptied all six bottles, the physiology, Dr. Jace Colton knew, was quite benign. Given his height, his weight, his muscle mass, he would easily metabolize every molecule by the time the plane returned to earth.

And no matter how much he drank, the volume or the pace, the pale yet vibrant vision in seat 2B needn't worry that she'd suddenly be traveling beside a rowdy, garrulous, drunken man.

Jace's urge to reassure was eclipsed by an even more compelling wish.

"Tell me what you're thinking."

His voice was soft. Amazingly so, he realized. And gentle. Amazingly too. So soft, so gentle, that perhaps she would not hear.

But she did. She looked at him, her worried lavender eyes bright against her gossamer skin.

"What did you say?"

"I said," he repeated so softly still, "tell me what you're thinking."

Jace wasn't certain that she would. Why should she? But she did, this ferocious ballerina, in a breathless rush.

"I was thinking that you shouldn't drink when you're depressed. I mean, alcohol is a depressant, isn't it? *Can* be."

"Yes. It is. Can be. But who's depressed? Me?" A glint of amusement glittered in his dark green eyes. Then vanished. The amusement did. But the green glittered still, brilliant, solemn, intense. "Or you?"

You, Julia thought. You're hurt, despondent, depressed. Except that Julia saw none of those things. Not now. But she *had*, hadn't she? For that fleeting moment when the chime in Floppy's tail had drawn him from the snowflakes? Hadn't she seen then a dark tormenting pain?

*Yes,* and Julia knew so well what he was doing now, concealing every anguish beneath a glittering facade. Everything was fine, the facade asserted. *He* was fine. He was just going to have a few drinks to celebrate the season.

It was a dazzling facade, and so convincing that it seemed as if he truly wondered if it was she who was depressed. Wondered, and was concerned.

"I'm not depressed," he said. "So it must be you. Would you like to talk about it?"

Get him to talk, Alexis had said. And now he, this man whose glacial gaze had frozen her to the bone—as it conveyed with chilling eloquence that he neither needed nor wanted her help—was giving her her chance.

"I guess," Julia murmured. "Yes. Thank you."

"Good. I'm Jace, by the way. And you are?"

"Julia."

"Hello, Julia. And this is?" Jace gestured toward the rabbit.

"Oh," she whispered. "This is Floppy."

"Hello, Floppy," Jace greeted quietly as Julia's wistful smile tore at his heart. His *heart*? The place he so willingly seared every Christmas, and which during all the seasons between was pure ice? That was Jace Colton's heart. Fire and ice, those uninhabitable extremes. But now something else, something new, compelled him to say, "So tell me, Julia, why you're depressed."

It was an extraordinary invitation, as if he truly wanted to know, and Julia felt as if she could actually tell him why she had been despondent once, and so desperate that alcohol had seemed the only way to survive.

"Julia?"

"My boyfriend and I were supposed to be traveling to London together." The words flowed, stunning her but not him, especially the flowing way she said boyfriend. "But he met someone else."

"Another woman."

Woman—like boyfriend—was a word that Julia had never applied to herself. Even though, unlike boyfriend, during the seven years of Winnie's life—and the seven years since her death—Julia *had* made the transition from teenage girl to woman fully grown.

"Yes. Another woman. He met her three weeks ago. Our marriage hasn't been canceled, he says, merely postponed."

"You'd made wedding plans?"

"We were supposed to have been married in Chicago last evening and to have been en route for our London honeymoon right now."

*There*, Julia thought. That should do it. Jace would realize she was talking about him not her, and, despite what Alexis had warned, they would be able to talk, as they were talking now, but with truth—not lies.

Julia was a little surprised Jace hadn't seen through her improbable fiction already. It wasn't because he wasn't paying attention. He was. Intently, intensely.

And, at last, comprehension began to dawn. Julia saw the fierce aurora, dark and deep, a fury of glittering green fire.

"Do you love him, Julia? Love him still?"

Jace's query was exactly what Julia herself had wondered as she'd listened to Alexis in the terminal at O'Hare. Jace loves you *still*, Alexis? Julia hadn't posed the question. It was fair, she had reasoned, *honest* for Alexis to have confessed to Jace that she was overwhelmed by his love and needed a little more time. Fair. Honest. And not, Julia had told herself, the betrayal of love *she* believed it to be.

But now Jace was posing the question that Julia had not, and his voice was edged with a harshness that matched the smoldering darkness in his eyes.

"Still?" she echoed. "What do you mean?"

"Nothing. Forget I asked. It's really none of my business." *Just impossibly, astonishingly, my immense concern.*

"No, Jace. Please tell me. Maybe it will help. Talking helps, doesn't it?"

Did talking help? How did he know? Jace Colton kept his own counsel. Always. But it was she who was asking if talking helped, as if she didn't know, as if she were as alone as he. Alone. And lonely? Perhaps. So terribly lonely until she had fallen in love—only to be betrayed.

The solitary ballerina wanted to talk. *To him.* She needed, it seemed, to talk to the man who didn't talk, and yet who had started this conversation in the first place. Had *wanted* to. Needed to? Gently, encouragingly, that man replied, "So they say."

"I think it's true. Just telling you what I have, admitting it aloud, has helped. And if I knew what you meant by *still* . . ."

"I'll tell you, Julia. But only if you promise to consider the source."

"Meaning you?"

"Meaning me. This isn't really my area of expertise."

"This? You mean love?"

Love, Jace mused. She said it so fearlessly, as if love were a treasure still, always, despite the pain when it was lost.

"Yes, Julia. That's exactly what I mean."

"You've never been in love?"

"No. Never."

It was the truth, Julia realized. She saw it in the brilliant clarity of his eyes. Jace Colton had never been in love. Which meant the lies belonged to Alexis *and to her*.

Both truth and lies were crushing her now, for as much as they said about Alexis, they said even more about her. Alexis Allen had had an airport terminal full of people to whom she could have given her first-class ticket to London. But she had chosen Julia. To help the despondent Jace? To make certain he didn't drink himself to death on the flight to Heathrow?

No. Jace Colton was *not* despondent. And the torment she'd believed she'd seen when he'd looked from snowflakes to Floppy to her? A mirage most likely. Or maybe the dedicated physician had been thinking about a patient he had lost, a trauma victim he could not save, no one could, but about whom he felt great sadness nonetheless.

And the dark circles beneath his dark green eyes? The consequence of haunting ice-laden streets in pursuit of the woman he loved? No. This man was not a stalker, could not possibly be, and there was not, had never been, a woman he loved. He'd been working not stalking, saving what lives, what loved ones, he could.

And all Jace had wanted, and what he so abundantly deserved, was the chance to exorcise anguished thoughts of lives he could not save, and to sip a little scotch, and to celebrate in private the fact that Alexis was off the plane and out of his life.

Jace viewed with relief the banishment of Alexis. Julia had seen that glittering truth in the snow-crystal mirror.

And as for Alexis's feelings about losing Jace? Fury. Julia had seen that, too, as Alexis had exited the jetway.

The outrage had vanished so swiftly that Julia had forgotten it until now. But it had been there, fleetingly, before yielding to thoughtful contemplation as Alexis had surveyed the haggard masses—and then to supreme satisfaction when the beautiful actress had spotted her.

For there she was.

Alexis's revenge.

"Julia?"

"I just figured it out myself." *All of it.* "What you meant by *still.* You meant how could I love, still, someone who had so cruelly betrayed my love?"

That was right, of course. But as Jace had witnessed her comprehension, and its agony, the disgust he felt toward himself far eclipsed his contempt for the fiancé who'd left this lovely ballerina teetering at the altar, devastated at Christmastime.

Devastated. The word taunted and pierced. Julia had not seemed *that* devastated as she'd recounted her story of betrayal. But she was devastated now. By him. By his *still,* the single syllable that doomed all hope of future peace. Even if she and her faithless fiancé did marry, his *still* so harshly forecast, she could never trust him again. Her marriage would be forever haunted by the specter of some other woman, more intriguing than she, with whom her roving husband would need to spend just a little time.

"And you're right," Julia was saying. "I couldn't still love him. Shouldn't. *Don't.*"

"That sounds a little hasty, Julia. Too hasty. Especially

given that we've already established, and you agreed to recall, that mine was not an expert opinion."

"But it's what I believe, too. When someone shows you who they truly are, don't give them the chance to show you again. That's the advice *I* would have given *you* had the situation been reversed. I just wasn't able to give it to myself. So. Thank you."

"For hurting you?"

"You didn't hurt me, Jace. Really. You helped."

"I'm not convinced," he said softly.

"I'm *fine*. Really. I *am*. It was not a relationship that was destined to survive."

# CHAPTER FIVE

As she reached into her bright blue knapsack Julia's hand lingered for a moment on her sketchbook. She had two watercolors yet to complete, two images of happiness. But that joy was scheduled for Christmas and the day after, when she would need it so. Besides, her paintings were so unusual that her green-eyed traveling companion couldn't help but notice, and politeness would constrain him to comment, and . . .

Julia's hand drifted from sketchbook to guidebook, in which was neatly folded her personal itinerary for her six London days.

December 23: Run (see map on page 18). Mayfair &
    Knightsbridge. Eat.
December 24: Run (see map on page 43).
    Canterfields. Eat.
December 25: Paint.
December 26 (Boxing Day): Paint.

December 27: Run (see map on page 68).
   Canterfields. Eat. Read about British Museum.
December 28: British Museum. Confirm AM flight.
   (Arrange transportation to airport). Pack.

Because of the storms, she'd be arriving in London one day later than planned. So, as she withdrew the guide-book, she mentally consolidated her itinerary for the first two days. The morning runs could be abandoned. Easily. It was an acceptable deletion, and even an advisable one. During these past few weeks of metaphorically burning bridges, she'd burned far more calories than she'd consumed.

The remainder of the twenty-third was to have been spent wandering the festive streets of Mayfair and Knightsbridge, a journey designed to evoke specific memories, ones to which she'd have time to adjust—overnight—before venturing to Canterfields on Christmas Eve.

Now, tomorrow, she would have to stroll directly from the Yuletide streets to Canterfields, and the most potent memories of all. Potent, lovely, fearsome.

Julia subdued a sudden quiver of panic by focusing beyond the daunting mandates of Christmas Eve to the safety, the certainty, of painting in her hotel room on the twenty-fifth and twenty-sixth.

On the twenty-seventh, she would return to Canterfields, to bid *adieu* to the Christmas now past.

*Bye-bye Kismus*. Julia heard the echo of the beloved

voice and saw the image of her small misshapen hand waving farewell and—

*I can't do this. Cannot.* The decisive pronouncement came from a racing heart that pulsed thunder but not oxygen to her brain.

Julia clutched the guidebook, touched the folded sheet, and forced herself to visualize the twenty-eighth, the day *after* bye-bye Kismus, and her final London day. The British Museum, she'd decided. Her emotional journey to her own past complete, she would explore the grandeur of ancient civilizations, the vastness of lives, of worlds, beyond her own.

Julia's itinerary instructed her to read about the British Museum on the evening of the twenty-seventh. But storms changed even the most carefully made plans, as did intense and gentle dark green eyes, and Julia needed something to do. Now.

And for the remainder of the flight.

So she opened her guidebook to "The Wonders of the British Museum" and began to read.

Jace had carried aboard the flight a coal black briefcase from which, as Julia had retrieved her London guidebook, he'd withdrawn the packet of documents that had arrived yesterday afternoon. He'd already glanced at the cover sheet, the only page that mattered near-term, the confirmation of his whereabouts in London.

But as Julia opened her guidebook, Jace began a casual perusal of the remainder of the packet. Assuming no last-minute changes, no place on the planet more desperate, the team would be going to the Balkans. And the team itself? Some he knew, some he didn't. As always, though, a balance of specialties was represented, from trauma to obstetrics to ortho to peds.

Jace read. Sort of. Between glances at her.

And Julia? She had been reading, he decided. Sort of. In the beginning. Dutifully and thoroughly. She glanced away from the text when so directed to consult the relevant diagrams, photographs, and maps.

But for some length of time, a unit measured in pure pain, she had been staring at a diagram of the Duveen Gallery, a gaze that had nothing whatsoever to do with the Elgin marbles housed within.

In fact, Jace realized, Julia wasn't looking at the page at all, but at the crisp fold of a snowy white sheet of paper. What was she seeing? he wondered. The stark white loss of love? The ice-sharp edge of betrayal? The unrelenting emptiness when hope was gone?

Julia had said the words: She shouldn't, couldn't, wouldn't *still* love a man who had betrayed her so.

But it was Jace who had provoked the confrontation with the truth. Jace who had caused her pain. He would so gladly have transferred that anguish to himself.

Where it belonged.

Julia's heart ached thanks to him, and Jace worried about other agonies as well, physical ones. Every muscle in her body was clenched, a clasp so taut that the physician found himself thinking disturbing words. Acidosis. Necrosis. Death to tissue denied the essential nourishment of oxygenated blood no matter how the suffocating tissues pleaded and screamed.

Julia seemed deaf to such frantic pleas. Was deaf. And as motionless as the marble statues she did not see. Except, that is, for the merciless devouring of her lips.

Dr. Jace Colton spent his professional life touching other human beings. Patients. His touches were sometimes quite aggressive—a trochar to a subclavian vein, a sixteen-gauge needle to a hemorrhaging chest, and other needles, smaller but comparably invasive, to the heart, the spinal canal, the eye. And sometimes, the physician touched simply to reassure.

And in his personal life, such as it was? Jace Colton's touches were sensual intimacies of hands, of lips, of mouth. Breathtaking, his lovers proclaimed. Innovative. And generous.

In bed. But out of bed, away from passion, Jace never held his lovers' hands, nor did he touch an affectionate finger to a beautiful cheek, nor plant a farewell kiss on a porcelain brow, nor drape a proprietary arm around a feminine curve.

Jace touched his lovers with purpose, with passion, for pleasure, and nothing else. Because there was nothing else. Not affection. Not caring. And most certainly not, never, love.

So what impulse guided his hand now?

Some astonishing impulse that did not bother to consult him before making its move.

But there it was. His hand, his fingers, touching her lips.

They were damp, those ravaged lips, and bruised and

warm, and being devoured still, a different kind of hunger, by his searching eyes.

Jace wondered, as he caressed the bruising, about a gentler ravaging, a most gentle one, and that other hunger, its warmth, its trembling, its taste.

"Sorry," he murmured as he compelled his rogue and ravaging thoughts to cease, and his renegade fingers to fall away.

"Sorry?" Julia echoed, bewildered, then apologetic, too. "Oh. I was chewing my lips, wasn't I? I do that sometimes. It's a terrible habit. I'm sorry if it bothered you."

"Julia," he said softly, "I'm the one who's sorry."

"For what?"

Her question came with such wonder that Jace didn't answer at once. He couldn't. For it seemed as if she could not possibly imagine a reason for him to be sorry. For touching her lips? No. For caring about her pain? No. For his rogue, renegade, ravaging thoughts? No. No. No.

"For hurting you," he said at last.

"But you *didn't*."

"Yes, I—oh." Jace's attention was necessarily drawn from Julia to Margot.

"Just checking," their flight attendant said, "to see if there's anything either of you need."

Julia answered "No, thank you," even as—returning to Margot the never-opened bottles of scotch—Jace replied, "Food."

"*Food*, Doctor?" Margot's mock exasperation was a flirtatious tease. "Just as we've finished *putting away* brunch and won't be opening the dinner service for hours? It's not that there's *nothing* available, but . . ."

"Any calories will do."

Margot smiled. "I think I can scrounge up some calories."

"Great." Jace smiled too. "Thank you."

"You're *welcome*."

Margot gone, Jace's attention was undivided again, fully devoted to Julia.

"I realized I was hungry after all," he said. "I thought you might be, too."

"Because of my lips."

Jace gazed from her worried eyes to her ravaged lips, the warmth, the dampness, he'd so impulsively touched, as—her wonder had seemed to say—she'd wanted him to. "Your lips, Julia?"

"Because I was chewing on them."

His eyes returned to hers. "No. I just thought you might be hungry."

Because I'm so thin, Julia realized. Because I've been running too much and eating too little. "You don't need to worry about me."

"I know that." *But I do.*

"Or feel sorry for me."

"I don't." His quiet pronouncement was immediate. And decisive. But his thoughts reeled. Sorry for her? Pitying her? This woman who treasured love despite her own betrayal, and who'd made a commitment to a beloved stuffed rabbit—whose?—and . . . and Jace was fascinated, enchanted, intrigued. And yes, concerned. But *sorry* for her? Hardly. "I do, however, feel very sorry for him."

"Him?"

"Your fiancé."

"Oh."

"Oh?"

"There is no fiancé, Jace. That was a lie."

A lie? He hadn't seen it. Had not even begun to guess. "Why?"

"Because of Alexis."

"Alexis." His voice darkened, chilled. "What about Alexis?"

"She said that you were hurt, despondent, depressed, and that you needed to talk. So I promised—"

"How do you know Alexis?"

"I don't. Not really. I know *who* she is, of course, but . . . I was in the boarding area, one of many passengers who'd been on an earlier canceled flight and on standby for this. Alexis decided to give her ticket to me."

"A decision that came with a story."

"Yes. She said that the two of you were supposed to have been married last night."

"And?"

"That she'd told you she wanted to postpone the wedding because your . . . love for her was so overwhelming that she needed a little more time. She said you weren't happy about the postponement, but that you agreed. It had been three weeks since she'd seen or heard from you, she said, but last night, on what should have been your wedding night, you left a message asking her to spend

Christmas with you in London. Which she decided to do. But by this morning everything had changed."

"Because?"

"Because you'd seen her last night with Grant Rogers."

"Let me guess. I was stalking her?" Faint amusement touched his cold dark eyes. "And when I saw her with another man I became hurt, despondent, depressed?"

"Yes. And far too angry to permit her to travel with you to London."

"But needing to talk to someone. You. Alexis chose you because you looked so sympathetic."

*No.* Julia looked down, away, to Floppy. And to her own thin, pale hands. She spoke at first and silently to that boney pallor. Alexis chose me because I looked *pa*thetic, not *sym*pathetic. Pathetic, and needy, and impossible. Then to her hands still, but aloud, she said, "Alexis chose me to *bother* you, Jace. To intrude on your privacy so that you wished it was she, not me, beside you."

Jace understood. Suddenly. Achingly. And with fury toward himself. He should never have become involved with the celebrated actress. Scarcely had. But Alexis had been lush and wanting and easy, and he had indulged, had chosen to, an indulgence which until now had touched him alone.

Now his choice was touching Julia, and he should have realized at once that it would have been oddly perceptive of Alexis, impossibly insightful, to have seen the truth of Julia. Her compassion. Her grace.

That wasn't, of course, what vain—cruel—Alexis had seen at all.

"Julia?" His voice was a caress. "Of the many reasons my relationship with Alexis did not work, one of the more striking was that she didn't know me. At all. She could not, for example, even begin to guess who I'd want as a traveling companion to London. The beauty is, because she knew so little about me, she was likely to guess dead wrong. As she did today."

Julia looked from bones and rabbit to him. "But you didn't, you *don't*, need to talk."

"About Alexis? No. I don't." *But I need to talk to you, Julia. About anything.* "What Alexis told you wasn't true." A wry smile curved his lips. "Except for one tiny little detail. We were at one time supposed to have been married last night . . ."

*T*hey had met in mid-October. Dr. Jace Colton had come to the set of *Windy City* as a favor to the show's usual surgical consultant, a friend whose wife was ill.

Later Alexis would decide that the "friend" appellation was false. The bastard had no friends. Just acquaintances, just colleagues.

Just lovers.

On that October day, however, Alexis knew only that she wanted the gorgeous doctor in her bed. And had she seduced him? No. It had been a decision, his—not a seduction, hers—and made with the cool precision of surgical steel.

But he was glorious. His lovemaking was. Masterful, sensual, and edged with an intensity that both frightened and thrilled her. Sex was an escape for him, Alexis decided, a chance for Dr. Jace Colton to forget—with the carnal—the carnage of his work, and to use his gifted surgeon's hands in an entirely different way.

A necessary escape. But not a reckless one. Before Jace so much as touched her, he discussed with her the consequences of their passion and what those consequences *must not be*.

It was a clinical discussion, dispassionate, explicit, and clear. Jace Colton did not want children in a very big way. Which was fine. Perfect. Neither did she. Alexis didn't know Jace's reasons, only that they were solemn and fierce, but she knew hers. She loved her life precisely the way it was, and she'd worked long and hard to achieve what the entertainment media was now heralding as her "overnight" success.

Besides, she really didn't *like* babies, or children, or, heaven forbid, insolent teens. The biological clock that was supposed to chime lustingly every time she saw a gurgling little cherub was conspicuously mute.

Alexis had tried birth control pills, the most effective contraception this side, passion's side, of abstinence. But the hormones made her feel perpetually premenstrual. Bloated, headachy, irritable, *blah*. And tubal ligation was too permanent. She was only thirty-four. At forty-four, or fifty-four, the silent clock might sound its maternal bells after all.

Alexis used a diaphragm, a new one every six months

and refitted every time, and with her always new and perfectly fitted diaphragm, she used an abundance of contraceptive foam.

It was careful, compulsive, comprehensive contraception. But Dr. Jace Colton wanted to augment it with his own. And did.

Even though she urged him not to.

Still, Alexis blamed him, his potency, his passion, when she realized in late November that her clockwork-like period was seven days late.

True, she'd been under unusual stress. Her *Windy City* character, Dr. Veronica Hastings, had become the most captivating heroine on daytime TV. The role was demanding, long hours coupled with a physicality for which since even the movie moguls of Tinseltown were watching, Alexis declined stunt doubles no matter the risk.

A lead actress Emmy nomination was in the bag, the entertainment pundits opined. As was the award itself. And her agent was being besieged by scripts for feature films.

It was the sort of euphoric stress of which every actress dreams.

But there was that *other* stress. Dr. Jace Colton. The only male on the entire planet who seemed to have forgotten she was alive. It had been almost a month since she'd heard from him, and he was definitely in town. She'd checked.

It seemed impossible, *was* impossible, that their affair could be over. It had barely begun. Besides, it was Alexis who ended affairs. Always. No man had ever tired of her before she tired of him.

True, she'd never met a man like Jace. But he would call. He *would*. She was getting more than a little impatient, though, with the wait. Her already pressure-filled life didn't need the suspense, not to mention the disappointment, of checking for messages from Jace between every *Windy City* scene.

And now her period was late.

Alexis called Jace at the trauma center, and having already confirmed that he wasn't working that night, announced that she'd be at his Lake Shore Drive penthouse at eight and that they *needed* to talk.

And Jace's response to her phone call? Remote, detached, not particularly surprised—as if he routinely ended his affairs by simply ceasing to call, and on occasion the precipitously spurned lover would insist on a face-to-face confirmation of the obvious.

Well, she had a surprise for the arrogant doctor. She presented it the moment she was inside the luxury penthouse that was as elegant, and as stark and as private, as he.

"What if I told you I was pregnant?"

"I'd say it was impossible. At least," Jace amended calmly, "that the baby could be mine."

"If there's a baby, Jace, it's definitely *yours*."

"If, Alexis? You don't know?"

"No. But I'm seven days late."

"Find out."

"And then what?" Alexis knew the answer. *She* would

have *their* abortion. She would undergo whatever discomfort there was, plus the risk of the tabloids finding out. And what of the man whose potency had done this to her? The virile Dr. Colton would find for her the best of the best, a surgical colleague from whom she could expect utmost discretion and impeccable care.

But Jace had yet to deliver his obvious line—I'll make all the arrangements—and in the silence something else was happening.

Two things.

One to her and the other to him.

What was happening to Alexis was familiar and certain, the aching warmth in her lower abdomen that signaled her period had arrived. Cramps would soon follow, distracting but far from severe, and she would bleed, a mild to moderate flow, for the next five days.

She wasn't pregnant, merely late, and in her rush of relief she almost blurted out the wonderful truth.

But she remained silent, a voicelessness that had nothing whatsoever to do with letting Jace so easily off the hook.

Her silence had to do with him, what was going on inside *him*, a storm so captivating she couldn't have spoken if she'd wanted to. Which she *didn't*, because standing before her was something Alexis wanted more than she'd ever wanted anything in her life—him, looking at her with this fierce, raw fury of torment, of passion, of need.

Alexis wanted him to look at her like this forever, and to touch her, *make love to her*, as he did.

It was as if Jace was touching her now, she was trembling so, and suddenly it became imperative that she speak.

"Jace? What if I *am* pregnant?"

"Then," he said, "we get married."

"Married?"

"That would be my suggestion, Alexis. My choice."

*Marriage* had not existed on her wish list any more than *baby* had. Nor, she was quite certain, had it existed on his.

But Jace was asking her to marry him, wanting it, choosing it, choosing *her*. His bride. His wife. The mother of his child.

A cramp deep inside reminded Alexis that there was no child.

But there would be, *could* be. She merely needed to keep him out of her bed for the next five days. Alexis had the uneasy feeling that such abstinence would not be difficult for him, that he wasn't yearning to touch her as she was aching, how she was aching, to be touched by him.

But Jace *would* touch her again, and believing she was already pregnant, his lovemaking would be without caution, without precaution, and in no time a pregnancy would be bloatingly real.

*Or* she could start taking birth control pills, and given her sensitivity to the hormones she'd begin to look pregnant right away . . . and she and Jace would marry soon, before he went to war . . . and while the father-to-be was tending to wounded soldiers overseas, she would miscarry . . . and she would be so distraught upon his Valentine's Day return that even he would know to postpone for a while the subject of divorce.

And during that window of grace? She'd tell him she wanted to try again, as soon as her obstetrician gave the okay.

And would they try? Would *she*?

Yes—assuming she hadn't managed by then to get Jace to look at her as he was looking now, with this tempest, this torment, of longing and of need.

And if she couldn't evoke such stormy passion without bearing his child? Then she would become pregnant.

And what kind of mother would she be? The answer glittered in his fierce green eyes: a good one, devoted and unselfish. Jace would have it no other way.

"Alexis?"

"It would be my choice, too, Jace."

"Then find out, and let me know."

# CHAPTER SIX

"**W**as she ever pregnant?"

Jace's answer to Julia's quiet query was preempted by Margot's return. With calories. A lavish and seasonal display.

A candy-cane wreath haloed a red bowl of macadamia nuts, and hot chocolate with miniature marshmallows afloat steamed from shining green mugs. There was an inedible yet festive offering as well, playing cards adorned with a beribboned and smiling jet aloft in the friendly Yuletide skies.

Jace was appreciative of both calories and presentation, and assured Margot that yes he'd let her know if there was anything else they needed. There was more conversation, because Margot lingered to chat with Jace.

By the time Margot left, Julia believed her question to Jace would be long forgotten.

But it was not.

"No," he said as if there'd been no interruption at all. "She never was, as I discovered when we got together a few days later to discuss our plans. Alexis was appropriately serious about the plans we were making for our life. But she wasn't worried, wasn't . . ."

"Terrified."

"Terrified, Julia?" *Terrified*. It was the same word, *his* word, spoken when he'd confronted Alexis with her lie. "Of what?"

"Of becoming a parent. Of caring so much. Loving so much."

"Yes," Jace said softly. Caring so much. Loving so much. Losing so much. Too much. "Alexis wasn't terrified of anything except losing what she wanted."

"You."

"Yes . . . me."

"Why?"

His answering smile wasn't arrogant, merely wry, and slightly harsh. "Did Alexis want me? Good question, Julia. I honestly don't know."

"That's not my question!"

"No?"

"*No*. I meant why would you have married her?" *A woman you did not love?*

"The usual reasons," Jace said quietly. "My baby. My responsibility. And an abiding belief, I suppose, in the notion of family."

"And," Julia said, "you wanted your baby."

She was reading his heart, Jace thought. That place of unlivable extremes, of ice and of flames, where nothing could survive, he had *wanted* nothing to. Until the baby. His baby. "Did I?"

"Yes." *So much.* "Didn't you?"

His feelings had been so mixed, and so unexpected. He had not imagined, would never have imagined, the hope amid the terror. The joy.

But hope and joy had been there. As had love. And when the truth had come, the revelation of the lie, Jace had grieved for the precious little life that was not to be, as if that life had existed, only to have died.

Jace had grieved for the phantom life, the glorious lie. And ached for its loss.

Ached still.

"I'm sorry," Julia murmured. "I shouldn't have asked that."

"Sure you should have. I was just thinking about the answer, which is yes . . . and no. I wouldn't have wished either myself or Alexis on any child."

"But you would be a *wonderful* father."

Julia's pronouncement, certain and bold, was greeted with surprise. By him. And with surprising uncertainty. And, so softly, "Thank you."

"You're welcome."

Silence fell. Shimmering, gentle, intense. *Too* intense. Julia's gaze fell to the holiday deck of cards.

"Are you a card player?" Jace asked.

"I was," she confessed as a slender finger traced streaming ribbons from silvery wings. "Once upon a time."

Once upon a time, Jace mused. An invitation to a fairy tale. "Did you have a favorite game?"

"Gin rummy."

"I've played a little gin rummy myself." It was the only card game he even knew, learned from a trauma nurse during a mission to Afghanistan and played on similarly blood-drenched soil several times since. Card playing was a way to pass time between crises, an oddly sane triviality amid the insanity of war, and even though Jace would have preferred to spend such rare interludes by himself, in the spirit of camaraderie he joined in. And although it could not have mattered less, he almost always won. "Were you, are you, good?"

A glow lit her lavender eyes. "I used to be. I was taught by the best, you see, by my great-aunt Anne . . . Gran." The name, a grandmother's name, was spoken with love. "When I was little, Gran would let me win, *some*times. But once I was old enough to play well, and to understand *how* to play, there was no mercy. Which was fair of course because by then Gran had taught me all her tricks."

"Her tricks?"

"For keeping track of discards, and knowing what each means, so you can decide what to discard, to get the card you want in reply."

That sounded like skill not tricks to Jace. But he smiled. "Would you like to play?"

"Sure." Her eyes sparkled. "For the usual amount?"

Jace Colton was being hustled, and more. He was being included in a ritual—this fairy tale—that meant so very much to this unwitting seductress.

"Absolutely. And the usual amount is?"

The lips he had touched, and which had been ravaged

by her, were ravishing now. Ravishing for him. "A million dollars a point."

*J*ace won a few hands. Luck. Julia won all the others. Tricks and skill.

And enchantment. For he was enchanted by her.

"Why are you going to London?" he asked as her pale and graceful hands shuffled beribboned jets—then became motionless, utterly still, as she considered her reply.

The decision made, she looked from cards to him. "To face Christmas."

Jace waited patiently, restlessly, for more.

"My sister Winnie died seven years ago."

"I'm sorry."

"So am I. We'd known since her birth that she wasn't destined to live, but . . ."

"It doesn't make the loss any less devastating."

"No. It doesn't." Julia drew a breath, then smiled—a little. And as she spoke of her sister, her eyes shone bright and clear. "Winnie *loved* Christmas. We loved it together. Since her death I've been avoiding it, denying it. Hiding from it."

"Does London have special meaning?"

"No. Well, the London department store Canterfields does. Winnie's favorite ornaments came from Canterfields, from a mail-order catalogue we received. I've never been to London, and all of my Christmases, all of *our* Christmases, were in Kansas."

"Where you live."

"Where I *lived*. I've left Kansas." *Left home*. The thought came with amazing calm. Where was the panic?

"Are you moving to London?"

"No. I'll just be there for Christmas, to face Christmas." *Face Christmas*. And still her heart did not race.

Had there been some truth amid the lies of Alexis Allen? About the confessions between strangers on airplanes? The intimacies they so effortlessly shared? And was there a stratospheric magic that Alexis had failed to mention? A spell that banished panic and vanquished fear?

There was, Julia knew, magic in this flight through space. Magic, and a magician, a green-eyed sorcerer who was looking at her with the most improbable illusion of all—the absolute confidence that she could leave Kansas, *leave home*, and face Canterfields, *face Christmas*.

"And then?" he asked as if confident, this illusionist, that she would survive and flourish beyond London.

"Then to Seattle to live." To live *again*. To *try* to. Panic flickered at last. But briefly. Banished, extinguished, vanquished . . . by him.

"Seattle," Jace echoed. "The Emerald City."

"Yes. Where else would a girl from Kansas go?" Her reply was slightly breathless, as the remnants of panic floated away. Then she admitted, calmly, that the name Emerald City had indeed prompted her to place Seattle on her list. But the more she learned, the more it seemed right. Best. For her.

"Seattle's supposed to be very beautiful."

"If drizzly."

"If drizzly."

They drank hot chocolate in the netherworld where time zones changed so often there was no time.

And they ate macadamia nuts, and played gin rummy, and talked, and smiled.

Jace and Julia smiled, both of them did, even as they ached, both of them, when a little girl galloped giggling into first class.

Her name was Sophie, and she was three years old, and her dress sparkled with sequined snowmen, and her golden curls danced.

Sophie's father was right behind her, his long strides keeping pace with her small racing ones. He spoke to whoever was listening, as everyone in first class was, an apology—so unnecessary—laced with love for the lively Christmas elf who was his.

They'd been fortunate enough to get bulkhead seats, Sophie's father explained. And while his wife was settling the twins for naps—they were six months old, and both sleepy at once, a minor miracle—he was keeping an eye on Sophie. *Supposed to be.*

He wasn't quite certain how she'd scooted away. It happened so quickly. But, he admitted, the mad dash was *not* the consequence of a glucose rush. This was his Sophie's usual speed, and the giggling and galloping were linked always, one with the other.

She was Christmas, this sequined Sophie, and this was Christmas. Long after she leapt, giggling, into her father's arms, and was gone, smiles lingered in first class.

Her memory lingered as well . . . as did memories of other joyful little girls.

She might have been Grace Alysia Quinn, who sang like an angel and skated on silvery ponds of ice. Or Edwina Anne Hayley, Winnie, who was an angel, too, but who'd never danced, never skated, never run.

Julia saw, when she looked at the man beside her, the pain that had glittered off the snow-crystal mirror—and had not been a mirage after all—even though it vanished, he vanquished it swiftly, this time as last.

"Where are you staying in London?" he asked.

"The Eden-Knightsbridge. Like you. At least that's what Alexis said."

"She really did her homework, didn't she? Not only did she discover what flight I was taking but where I was planning to stay." It had not been, Jace imagined, a particularly difficult task. Alexis had known the date he was scheduled to depart Chicago. She merely needed to call the obvious airlines and the obvious hotels, pretending to confirm, as a secretary might, the busy doctor's travel plans.

"You weren't going to spend your honeymoon at the Eden-Knightsbridge?"

Jace didn't answer at once. His expression became solemn first, serious and intense. "Once, Julia, and for a very brief period of time, Alexis and I planned to marry last night. After which, and alone, I was going to London."

His eyes, so serious, were unshadowed. Glittering clear. But Julia recalled the anguished shadows when

Floppy's chiming tail had drawn his gaze from snowfall to her, and when Sophie, radiant with Christmas, had galloped and giggled with joy.

Julia spoke to him, and to those memories of such darkness.

"To face Christmas," she said quietly. "Alone."

"To face Christmas," Jace Colton conceded softly. "Alone."

# CHAPTER SEVEN

*A*lexis Allen was a proficient liar. But she was a truthsayer, too. She had been so right about the phenomenon of hurtling through space, the stratospheric magic that shimmered here.

The actress had proclaimed with comparable certainty that the spell shattered the moment the plane returned to earth. The disappointing reality of the guy—or, a reality Alexis did not contemplate, the girl—came crashing down and there remained, according to Alexis, only the urgent wish to flee.

Jace Colton could not flee. He'd already suggested, politely and miles above earth, that they share a cab to their hotel. But after that . . .

The plane's turbulent descent into London, a ferocious battle between wind and steel, mimicked the feelings that swirled within Julia. Magic sparred with physics, and illusion waged all-out war with Earth's gravitational pull.

She wanted, impossibly, to defy gravity still.

Impossibly . . . and yet at the precise moment the jet gentled onto soggy tarmac, Jace said, "I demand a rematch."

The magic shimmered during the rainy cab ride into town and as they joined the queue of weary travelers— passports and credit cards in hand—assembled in the hotel's reception area amid a path of purple ropes.

The couple ahead of Jace and Julia were stylish, American, and, as their conversation with the reception clerk echoed off Florentine marble, increasingly upset.

"Your room *was* held for you, sir," the clerk insisted. "*Last* night, for which your reservation was guaranteed."

"We had reservations for *four* nights."

"Yes, madam, I know. But only the first night was secured by credit card, and when you didn't arrive and we didn't hear from you—"

"Don't you Brits watch the world news? Winter storms have wreaked havoc with air travel throughout the United States."

"Which has had a profound ripple effect in the UK," the clerk asserted. "Canceled flights have left thousands of holiday travelers stranded in London, some of whom have been accommodated at this hotel when rooms have become available, as yours did today."

"So you have *nothing*?"

"I'm afraid not. Except, naturally, for those guests whose reservations are guaranteed for tonight. We must hold those rooms for them just as we held yours for you. Our concierge will be happy to assist you in finding other lodging."

"Damn right he'll assist us."

"Oh, dear," Julia whispered as the infuriated travelers stormed away from the reception clerk toward the comparably beleaguered concierge.

"Ugly Americans?"

"Well, yes. But my guaranteed reservation was for last night, and it didn't occur to me to call. I'd better just go stand in the concierge line."

"No, Julia, stay here with me. My reservation is for tonight, so presumably my room will be waiting, which is where you'll sleep."

"Oh, Jace, no, thank you. I couldn't."

"Yes, you could." Jace plucked her passport, but not her credit card, from her thin white hand. "And can." *And will*.

"But what about you?"

Her question was as innocent as their sleeping arrangements could be. As chaste. True, Jace had reserved a single room. But even a single in this luxury hotel would have a king-sized bed, or maybe two queens, and there'd undoubtedly be a couch as well.

The thought that they would share his room, however chastely, had not occurred to the exhausted woman who stood beside him . . . and whose eyes had shone with wonder when his fingers had touched her ravaged lips . . . and who needed sleep on this night, for she had Christmas to face tomorrow.

Jace would not do anything, of course, to impede such sleep. But Julia wouldn't sleep well, and perhaps not at all, with him in the room. The situation would be too foreign to her . . . and too wondrous, too?

"I'm fairly familiar with London," he said. "I'll be able to find a place without even needing to bother the concierge."

"But I could do that, too. You could tell me where to look."

"I could. But I'm not going to. I'm not going to let you wander around London in the middle of the night looking for a room."

"But . . ."

Jace smiled. "Forget it, Julia. I'm not. If it will make you feel better, I could ask you to tear up my marker."

"Your marker?"

"For the countless millions I owe you from gin rummy."

"But that was just . . ." *wonderful, magical.* And there had been that promise of more magic, that defiance of gravity still.

"I still demand a rematch, Julia. If you want."

"I want."

"So do I." *I want to make every sadness vanish as swiftly as that one did.* "So. Tomorrow night? We'll have dinner followed by—"

"Next, please."

The clerk's polite but weary request interrupted Jace's words. But not his thoughts. He was making plans for Christmas Eve, such different plans, so very far from the searing solitary journey he always made.

But Jace Colton could conjure his own private inferno

anytime. Some other time. All the time. And Julia might need to talk after her day at Canterfields. Might want to.

*I want.*

"Your suite is ready and waiting, Dr. Colton," the receptionist announced with relief as the name on the credit card Jace handed him summoned a reservation, and a room, on the computer screen.

"My suite?"

"Yes. The Azalea Suite. Nonsmoking, two-bedroom—oh, I see from the record that you had hoped for our bridal suite. I'm sorry to say that hasn't become available. But the Azalea Suite is really quite spectacular."

"And has two bedrooms?"

"Yes, sir. Two of our most luxurious, each with its own bath, and there are splendid views of both the city and the park, and the central parlor is really *most* attractive."

"Sounds perfect." Jace handed the clerk his passport and Julia's. "It was Alexis, I assume, who changed the reservation to the two-bedroom suite?"

The clerk consulted the reservation record. "Let's see. The change was requested by Mrs. Colton on December 18. Oh yes, it does give her first name as Alexis."

The clerk stole a furtive glance at Julia.

"My mother," Jace clarified with a reassuring smile. "Alexis, that is. She's an incurable romantic."

*T*he Azalea Suite was as luxurious as promised, a pastel splendor of mauve, of cream, of teal, and so spacious that Jace and Julia might have been staying in the separate rooms they had each reserved, with any number of other hotel guests housed between.

The furnishings were elegant, the decor sublime, including the adornment in the central parlor, fragrant and sparkling and twelve feet high.

The Christmas tree was blue spruce. Chosen, Jace imagined, to complement the shades of teal. And the decorations on the tree? Tiny white lights, perfectly spaced, with hand-cut-crystal snowflakes and silver-satin bows.

Jace frowned at the magnificent tree, a frown for Julia, fearful such an imposing confrontation with Christmas might be something she was far too fatigued to face.

But Julia wasn't frowning, merely fatigued, and so willing to be guided to the bedroom that was hers, the lavish mauve sleeping chamber which was a mirror image of the faraway teal that was his.

Jace bade her good night at her bedroom door and offered the gentle wish that she sleep well . . . which Julia echoed in kind.

*J*ace didn't sleep well. At all. He neither expected to, nor did he try.

He watched the city go to sleep, and stared into the vast blackness of the winter night, and at dawn, after he'd showered and changed, Jace watched the world awaken to this Christmas Eve day.

This Emerald City day. Rain fell, a most gentle drizzle, from the polished pewter sky. Maybe this would be a good day for the girl from Kansas, not as difficult as she feared, and in celebration at day's end a Christmas rainbow might appear.

Jace's reverie of a twilight rainbow for Julia gave way to a reflected image of a rainbow now. Julia herself.

He smiled as he turned. Smiled. Despite what he saw. Fatigue. Exhaustion. Still.

"Good morning."

"Good morning."

Her lavender eyes shone brightly above the dark purple smudges of her sleepless night. And her cheeks flushed pink. The jumper she wore was forest green, her blouse burgundy, and pearls gleamed at her neck and ears.

Julia had dressed for this monumental day. Dressed up. As tired as she was, as worried and as wary, Julia Anne Hayley was going to face this Christmas with reverence, with dignity, with grace.

Precisely, Jace thought, as she would have faced a firing squad.

"Well, wish me luck."

"I will," Jace replied. "During breakfast."

"Oh, no. Thank you. I ate so many macadamia nuts last night that if I never eat again I'll be fine." Then, as if they were still in that place of macadamias and magic, she confessed to the intimate stranger, "Besides, I'm really too apprehensive to eat."

"What do you fear, Julia?"

It was a simple question, and so gently posed. But Julia had no answer. She had never put her fear into words. She had not even, she realized, permitted her fright to come into focus in her mind.

The fear was simply there, amorphous and ominous and dark, like a storm on the horizon, the kind of gray-black rampage that might give rise to tornadoes—the whirlwinds, the twisters, that devastated and destroyed.

The girl from Kansas had never defined the vortices of those swirling funnel clouds. But in response to Jace's query, her mind whirled possible replies.

What did she fear? Well, hurting so much she couldn't breathe, would never breathe again . . . and screaming a scream that wouldn't stop, could never stop, once she permitted the keening anguish to spill from her heart to her lips . . . and drinking again.

Drinking forever.

"Julia?"

"Going crazy, I suppose."

"You won't."

"You can't know that."

Jace smiled. "But I do. Talking helps, Julia. So they say. Maybe if you told me about Winnie? Can you?" *Will you?*

Jace Colton was asking for her trust on this day of all days, twenty-two years—to the day—when he'd broken a promise to a five-year-old.

And, as he awaited her reply, Jace felt a ferocious war within, a savage battle between wishes and reason. Trust me, Julia. *Don't you dare.*

But she did.

She did.

"I don't know where to begin."

"The beginning?"

Julia answered with a nod, half a nod, a graceful tilt that left her eyes downcast. "I was fourteen when Winnie was born."

"Julia?"

She looked up, graceful still. "Yes?"

"Begin with you."

"With . . . ?"

"You. Your great-aunt Anne," Jace prompted softly. "Gran. And your parents. And your childhood in Kansas."

They stood apart, separate dancers on a luxurious stage. Jace was by the window, backlit by drizzling pewter, and she was across the parlor behind the plush mauve couch.

But the courageous ballerina was solitary no more. It was, this faraway ballet, an exquisite pas de deux.

"My mother was born to great wealth. And propriety. Generations of it, against which she rebelled in every way, including with her choices of the most unsuitable boys. When she was seventeen, and inevitably I suppose, she became pregnant. The pregnancy had to be hidden. And where better than a small town in rural Kansas? Gran, who was my grandmother's cousin, had just moved to such a place. Tierney. Gran didn't know a soul in her new town. She and my great-uncle Edwin had lived in Kansas City for over forty years. But they'd discovered Tierney on a drive one day and decided it would be a lovely place to retire. Which is what Gran did six months after Edwin died. But he was with her still, she said. *Always*. She was a happily married widow."

Julia's hands lifted and opened, like petals of the whitest flower. "Gran and Edwin had wanted children, but had had none, so when Gran's cousin asked if she'd mind providing sanctuary for a wayward pregnant teen, she readily agreed. The hidden pregnancy was supposed to be followed by an even more hidden adoption. But Gran . . ."

"Wanted you."

"Yes," Julia whispered. "Gran wanted me."

The ballerina moved then, from behind the plush mauve couch to the teal blue tree. And was there fear as she beheld its grandeur? No. None. And no trembling as she illuminated the tiny white lights, a glow that created myriad rainbows within the crystals of snow.

"My mother named me Julia, her name, but my middle name, which I gave myself when I was four, was Anne, Gran's name, and eventually my last name became Gran's, too. Within a week of my birth, my mother was gone. She didn't return until I was fourteen. Gran had given me a gentle version of the truth, that my mother was far too young to have a baby and that she, Gran, had wanted me so much. My mother provided the edgier version when she showed up pregnant with Winnie. It didn't matter. Nothing mattered except that I'd gotten to spend all those years with Gran. And Edwin. He was with us, sharing his wisdom through Gran, not to mention *his* gin rummy tricks."

Julia touched a snow crystal, a delicate caress that sent the light shimmering, casting rainbows on her face. On her smile. "We had such fun, the three of us. There weren't enough hours in the day for everything we loved to do, and when the time came for me to go to school, I just . . . couldn't."

Jace imagined the scene between the abandoned little girl and the great-aunt she loved. A temper tantrum? No. Just a forthright confession of the truth. I can't leave you Gran. I *can't.*

"What did Gran say?"

"That she could teach me at home, as she'd been doing already. I'd go to school *sometime*, we agreed. But that time never came. I didn't care about making friends my own age because I had Gran, and she didn't care about making friends her age because she had me. And Gran had learned from her life with Edwin that even forty years wasn't nearly enough. They'd been careless with some of that time, not intentionally, just unwittingly, believing they had forever and forgetting to treasure every minute, every second, of what time they had."

Julia stared at a snowflake as she spoke, a crystalline imitation of the real thing but with advantages of its own. Yes, the delicate ornament might shatter. But with care it need not. And with such care its glassy perfection would never vanish, never melt.

Her expression embellished the words she'd just spoken, the admonition to treasure each and every moment of life, and it forecast the sadness that inevitably came.

"When I was thirteen, Gran had a stroke. She was seventy-eight and had always been in wonderful health. The stroke was quite mild. She recovered fully, and needed only to take two aspirin tablets every day. Nothing changed, really . . . and yet in a way everything did. But we still took the long walks we loved, and Gran routinely won at rummy no matter how cleverly I played. We had just celebrated her seventy-ninth birthday when my mother appeared with another pregnancy to hide. She'd married the right man, socially speaking. A good marriage, but not a happy one. Her realization that she was pregnant came, in fact, as she and her husband were beginning to discuss the possibility, the probability, of divorce. Her pregnancy needed to be hidden though, and all decisions postponed, until the baby was born."

"Because paternity was in question?"

"Yes. It was critical in her estimation that she know whether the baby was her husband's, in which case the price tag on her divorce would go way up, or her lover's—a married politician for whom a love child would spell disaster. Neither man knew of her pregnancy. She simply told each that she needed to get away to think things through and that she might be gone for a while. Months. She believed the baby's blood type would provide the information she needed. She was type O, as was her husband, and the congressman was A. So, she reasoned, O meant heir and A meant adoption. Her reasoning was faulty of course, as both Gran and I knew. We had read, just that year and together, Tierney Junior High's biology text. We knew that either man could father a type O child. But we didn't tell my mother. She was a wreck, both physically and emotionally. She needed a place to rest, to recover, to heal."

"As did her baby."

"Yes," Julia murmured. "But, for Winnie, it was far too late. The damage to Winnie had already been done . . ."

# CHAPTER EIGHT

"*D*amage," Jace said, so softly.

And Jace saw, so clearly, the shadows on her face, the darkness where there had been rainbows, as if the faux snowflakes, the crystalline perfection that would never melt, nonetheless chose no longer to spin the light.

And Jace heard, so clearly, the bitterness in Julia's voice.

"Skeletal anomalies," she said to crystal as cloudy as her eyes. As gray. "And neurological ones. And her internal organs were damaged, too. The malformations were developmental not hereditary, a consequence of her life in utero not her genes. The anomalies didn't point to any specific syndrome, the doctors said. Not even fetal alcohol, despite the fact that prior to her arrival in Tierney, my mother's diet had consisted of alcohol, cigarettes, and a pharmacy of prescription drugs."

"But," Jace said quietly, "the findings might have been a combination of all three."

"Yes. Or maybe," Julia whispered to a perfect snowflake, "the damage to Winnie wasn't my mother's fault at all."

The bitterness vanished from her voice, as did the dark shadows on her translucent face. Vanquished by a burst of reflected brilliance from crystal? No. The shadows, like the clouds that had shaded her eyes, were conquered by a glow deep within, an illumination that was pure and gold.

Pure gold.

Was it generosity shining through? Julia's willingness to be fair to her mother despite what she had done?

That was part of it perhaps.

But mostly, Jace thought, the glow was for Winnie, a shimmering acknowledgment that the damaged little girl was who Winnie was—and had always been meant to be.

"The doctors didn't expect her to survive beyond the first few days."

"But she did."

"Oh, yes, she did. She was a fighter, our sweet little Win. She wanted to live, to be with us."

"With you and Gran."

"Yes. With us . . ."

*T*he mother who gave birth to the damaged infant wanted only to give her away. Or send her away. There were people who adopted infants like this one, and institutions for such catastrophes of nature, and money was no object, and the issue of whose baby she was no longer mattered.

Nothing mattered except putting the imperfection behind her. And if Gran and Julia wanted to keep the malformed baby? Fine. As long as they told no one the truth.

Gran and Julia knew only one truth. There was a little girl who needed them. They named her Edwina, after great-uncle Edwin, and her middle and last names, like Julia's, were Gran's, and when Edwina Anne Hayley was released from the hospital on the tenth day of her life, her doctors warned very gently that Winnie might not do well at home. Not well at all. Gran and Julia shouldn't hesitate to bring her back to the hospital at any time.

Back to the hospital. To die.

Winnie's doctors offered no forewarning that the baby girl would never crawl, much less walk. Winnie's physical limitations were obvious, and there was no reason to believe that she would live to an age at which such ambulatory milestones would typically occur.

Winnie's physicians did share their concern that the infant girl would neither see nor hear. Which meant, they explained to Julia and Gran, Winnie would seem unresponsive to her surroundings . . . and to them.

But Winnie *did* hear the loving voices that spoke to her. Gran and Julia were certain that she did. And she did respond. Her misshapen hands patted their mouths, the source of the sounds of such love, and when Julia held Winnie in her arms, the baby fingers tangled themselves in Julia's long black hair, grasping the silken strands as if Winnie were holding Julia, too.

But Winnie did not see, even though her eyes, so blue, closed only when she slept. They were awake when she was, and open wide, as if straining to see beyond the darkness.

Winnie's searching blue eyes were in constant motion, too. Nystagmus, it was called, the rhythmic pulsing that could never be cured, could never be stilled, because it—the steady beating, the ocular metronome—was caused by neurologic damage impossible to reverse.

For six months Winnie did well, not *very* well but well enough, and far better than her doctors had forecast. Her survival itself was a stunning surprise.

Then came that December day, three weeks before Christmas, when Gran awakened feeling "punk." It was just a virus, Gran insisted. Nothing worse. Certainly *not* the prelude to another stroke.

A virus that might respond, Julia wondered, to Gran's favorite dessert?

Tapioca pudding had been a staple in the house on Willow Road for Julia's entire life. It was Gran's favorite, and hers and Winnie's, too. Which explained, on that December day, why they were out. Julia had been planning to restock the beloved item on Monday, three days away, when she made her weekly trip to the store. *Tap pud* was already at the top of her shopping list.

But Gran was under the weather today, and the weather outside was cool but clear, and even though snow glistened on lawns and clung in cottony tufts on shrubs and trees, the streets and sidewalks were dry and bare.

Julia bundled Winnie warmly for her first outing into

Tierney, this mile-long walk to the grocery, and she described as they walked the sights her baby sister could not see.

Julia spoke of sun-caressed snow, and azure sky, and the seasonal decorations that were everywhere. Here was a holly-and-candy wreath. And here a family of plastic reindeer grazing in the snow. And here a lighted eave, a stenciled sleigh, a Santa, a snowman, an elf.

And here, in front of the white-steepled church, a crèche. Julia would have paused before the church even had its snowy lawn been bare. Edwin was here, in the immaculately tended cemetery, in a grave beneath a majestic tree.

It was all right—safe—to pause before the nativity scene. Winnie was warm in Julia's arms. Her face, and her sightless trembling eyes, were cuddled against Julia's chest, protected from the chill.

Julia whispered to Winnie of Edwin, for whom she was named and whose grave they would visit in spring, when it was warmer, but who was with them even now. And Julia whispered to Winnie of the life-sized figures in the manger, of Mary, of Joseph, of shepherd, of lamb.

And of child.

"There's a precious little baby," Julia whispered. "Like you, my precious little Win."

When they reached the grocery, Julia whispered still.

"This is where I do all our shopping," she explained to the six-month-old who heard her sister's voice, loved it, seemed to, but who could not possibly understand. "Always before I've left you at home with Gran, so I'd have both hands free to carry the groceries. But today I have you, which is *much* more fun, and we only have one little tiny item to get. Let's see. It's down this aisle."

"Oh look!" The exclamation came from a woman Julia did not know. She and Gran knew no one. This woman was a mother. Her son was with her, a child of three. "Look, Cody, it's a *baby*. Can we see?"

"Of course," Julia said as her own words, whispered so recently, echoed in her mind. *A precious little baby, my precious Win, just like you.* Julia smiled, untangled Winnie's misshapen hands from her own long hair, and told her sister as she turned her, "There's a little boy, Winnie, who wants to meet you. His name is Cody. Cody, this is Winnie. Edwina Anne—"

"How *dare* you?" The incensed demand came from Cody's mother.

"What?" Julia's heart began to ache, to weep, to scream.

As the woman was screaming even as she was backing away, *running* away. "How dare you bring that *thing* in here? Where there are *children*? It's disgusting, *indecent*. You should be *ashamed*."

Ashamed of Winnie? Of her lopsided skull and trembling eyes? As if she were a *monster* not a precious little girl?

Julia curled that precious little girl tighter in her arms and tried without success to stop her own spill of tears. Julia kissed Winnie's beloved head in all the places where the teardrops fell, concealing from Winnie the anguished dampness with loving warmth.

Julia tried not to shiver. But that was so difficult, impossible really, for she was so cold.

And then suddenly warm. It was an embracing warmth, and it came from without not within, an encircling halo of heat.

She was being hugged, *they* were, by a long-armed stranger, a tall, red-haired, teenage girl.

"I'm Galen," the willowy halo greeted as she released her physical embrace. But not her emotional one. "Hi."

"Hi. I'm Julia."

"And this"—Galen's long fingers gently caressed the dampness of Winnie's hair—"is Winnie. Edwina Anne. May I hold her? Would she mind?"

"No," Julia said. "She wouldn't mind."

It was probably the truth. From time to time Winnie was held by her doctors and nurses at the hospital twenty miles away. She registered no protest to such foreign arms. Perhaps she couldn't protest, or maybe she didn't care.

But Edwina Anne Hayley definitely *knew* when she was being held by Julia and by Gran, who loved her so, because she touched, she grasped, in reply.

As Winnie touched, grasped, Galen. Her tiny fingers patted the mouth that greeted "Hi, Winnie" then clung determinedly to the long red hair.

"She likes you," Julia whispered.

"And I like her." Galen smiled. "Why don't I hold her while you finish your shopping?"

There was just the tapioca pudding, which was all Julia bought, and as they left the grocery store, the girls who were to become best friends learned a few details of each other's lives. Their houses, they discovered, were as far apart as houses in Tierney could be, and Galen was sixteen to Julia's fifteen, and the reason, Julia explained, that they'd never seen each other at school was because she'd been schooled at home by Gran.

Galen was holding Winnie still, and Winnie was holding her, a tangled grasp, as they walked toward Julia's home on Willow Road. Galen chose the route down Central Avenue, not the residential side streets along which Julia and Winnie had come.

Had Julia chosen that less-traveled route because of Winnie? Because she had known that people might ask to see the baby only to shriek, to scream, *to hate* when she complied?

No. Julia hadn't known, had not imagined, such cruelty. She'd simply chosen her usual route to the store, the prettiest journey, past homes adorned for Christmas and the white-steepled church.

There were Christmas decorations along Central Avenue, too, dazzling and brilliant, and illuminated as the approaching twilight grayed the winter sky.

Galen held Winnie's face against her chest, as Julia had, a sheltering embrace. But when they reached the brightly lighted tree, Galen turned the protected bundle so that Winnie could see.

"Look, Winnie. Look at that beautiful tree."

"Galen, she can't . . ." *see.*

Julia's quiet admonition floated away in the suddenly balmy twilight air. For the words were no longer true. Her little sister *did* see the Christmas tree. Her small hands reached toward the twinkling lights as if to touch, to tangle, and her lips curved in a way that had been only a shadowed promise before, a glorious hope, but was a true smile now. Radiant and aglow.

And something *else* happened that Winnie's doctors would never be able to explain, didn't even try. Winnie's nystagmus disappeared completely and forever, the irreversible nerve damage reversed after all.

By Christmas? Because of Christmas?

Perhaps. For it seemed as if Winnie had been an embryo still, touching yes, and patting and grasping, but not fully formed, not as formed, fully, as her small damaged body could be.

Until Christmas. She awakened then, was born then, reaching toward Christmas as a delicate springtime flower reaches toward the sun.

Was it the twinkling lights that awakened her? Or the ribbons of tinsel that fluttered bright, bright silver against the winter-gray sky? Or was it perhaps the spirit of Christmas, the celebration of all that was good, that was pure, that was true?

They didn't know. They would never know. Even though the Christmas that brought sight to Winnie's eyes brought sound as well to her newly smiling lips. Sound, and in time speech.

Edwina Anne Hayley would never chatter. Her damaged nerves would not permit it. But her words were eloquent. *Raydee*, reindeer. *Aynga*, angel. *Ju-Ju*, Julia. And *Gayla* and *Froppy* and *Kismus* and *Gwa*.

Ju-Ju and Gayla and Gwa had no idea how many real-world Kismusses, how many December twenty-fifths, their little Winnie would have. But Winnie could and did have a new Christmas every few months. Needed to.

Winnie's loved ones would so happily have given Winnie Christmas year-round—would have kept the decorations up always—had it not been for Winnie herself.

The joy for Winnie was the renewal, the welcoming of the ornaments she loved, so happy to see them again, and the sparkling lights, the familiar tree, the shimmering spun-glass snow.

And the Christmas presents? Winnie could have had so many. Julia and Gran and Galen would have given her all there was to give.

But for Winnie Christmas was the gift. The only gift she ever wanted. And after a few weeks of each new Christmas, Winnie would say *Bye-bye Kismus*.

Christmas would be put away until her loved ones sensed that it was time to welcome Christmas anew, because their lovely Win seemed a little lost, her luminous glow not so bright, and her once-unseeing eyes were straining yet again, as if searching for her angels, her reindeer, her tree.

Gwa became an angel when Winnie was three. Julia was seventeen, and Gran was almost eighty-two. Gran died in her sleep without warning, and with blessed peace.

Gran hadn't known on that night in March that she was going to die. But it would happen sometime, she knew, and Gran had learned from her beloved Edwin's unex-

pected death—too soon, too young, only sixty-seven—
that coping with the loss was difficult enough, impossible
enough, without having to make the myriad decisions
that accompanied death.

So Gran made those decisions in advance, detailed
clearly and precisely in her will. And Gran's Kansas City
attorney, who'd been so helpful to her with Edwin's estate, would be there for Julia as well.

Anne Hayley was buried beside her Edwin as she
wished, as she willed. She had even chosen the words,
and the type of script, that would be engraved on the marble headstone that would be theirs.

Gran's estate became Julia's. The house and its contents, and the money. So much money. Julia had always
known, Gran had told her, that there was *plenty*, more
than they could possibly spend. Julia could have whatever her heart desired, Gran had always said.

But Julia already had everything she wanted, and
they'd lived frugally, because that was who Gran and
Julia—and Edwin—were.

Winnie's hospital bills had always been promptly and
gratefully paid, and in the discussions of the surgeries
Winnie might undergo cost had never been an issue.
None of the various surgical procedures would, however,
prolong Winnie's life. Nor would they improve the qual-
ity of living she already had. The surgeries would be cos-
metic interventions only, accompanied by lengthy
hospitalizations and postoperative pain.

Winnie had no surgery. But if she had? If she'd under-
gone every painstaking and expensive procedure that

medical science could contrive? The costs of all those surgeries would have been effortlessly covered by Gran's fortune *or by Winnie's*.

Julia learned of Winnie's wealth only after Gran died. At Gran's insistence monthly deposits had been made directly into Winnie's account, a transaction by personal check, personally written, by Winnie's mother, *their* mother, to Edwina Anne. It was blackmail of sorts, recompense for Gran's promise of silence regarding Winnie's parentage. But this blackmail, although monetary, was about emotion not finance. Gran believed very strongly that the mother who had abandoned her damaged daughter should be reminded of that abandonment each and every month.

Life following Gran's death would go on comfortably, lavishly, if that was what Julia chose. Gran had made certain of it. But what of the immense void? The staggering loss?

It was Galen who realized that what Winnie needed, what they *all* needed, was a new Christmas, even though it had only been two weeks since the last. And it was Galen who explained to Winnie that her missing Gwa was an aynga now, Winnie's favorite angel, the one from Canterfields who held in her alabaster hands a pale pink candle with a golden flame.

"See?" Galen asked as she held Winnie close enough to touch, to pat, the Canterfields angel. "Here's Gwa, little Winnie. Here's your Gwa."

We will survive, Julia told herself. Thanks to Galen.

But within two months of Gran's death, Galen, too,

was gone. She *had* to leave for Julia's sake, for *Winnie's*, to protect them from Mark, who was Galen's mother's boyfriend—and a cop—and who'd taken sadistic delight in embarrassing Galen, humiliating her, clandestine encounters which Galen revealed to Julia alone.

Mark had discovered Galen's relationship with Julia and Winnie shortly after Gran's death, and when Galen vanished without a word, Julia knew it was because of him, an encounter which Galen had, perhaps, threatened to reveal—to which Mark had undoubtedly responded with a threat of his own.

If Galen exposed him, Mark would expose *them*, her friends, the truant Julia, whose at-home education had ended when Winnie was born, and Winnie, who in the sadist cop's estimation belonged in an institution, a place where, no matter the compassion of the caretakers, Edwina Anne Hayley would not survive.

Julia dared not confirm her suspicions. She dared not provoke Mark. She merely hoped, prayed, that Galen was gone but safe. *Safe* . . . not dead, slain and unsearched for, because of Julia's own fearful silence.

Gran was gone, and Galen was gone but safe, please, and somehow Julia compelled her trembling fingers to knit a new angel for Winnie's Christmas tree, one with flame-colored hair and turquoise wings, who was Gayla.

We will survive, Julia vowed anew. Winnie and I will survive.

That December, when the world celebrated Christmas and it was time for Christmas for Winnie, too, Julia drove her little sister to Central Avenue to see the twinkling lights and shimmering tree.

Winnie loved that Yuletide adventure so much that Julia drove even farther, to Topeka one day, and another and another, and to Kansas City as well.

The Hayley sisters got out of their car in Topeka, and in Kansas City as well, and they, the Hayley sisters, became part of the holiday throngs that strolled the festive streets and shopped in the brightly decorated stores ...

"*T*hat wasn't wrong, was it?"

It took Jace a moment to realize that the question was directed to him. Julia had been speaking to the blue spruce—and its snowflakes—as she shared the memories that were as rare, and glistening and perishable, as tiny perfect crystals of ice.

Jace had been listening in silence, aching in silence. But now Julia was asking him a question, and turning toward him as she did.

Jace knew the answer to her query. Nothing she did could ever be wrong. Not ever. But what Jace didn't know, did not understand, was the question itself.

"If what was wrong, Julia?"

"Taking Winnie out in public at Christmas. I mean, she had every right, didn't she? Every right to such joy? No matter how ... different she looked?"

"Yes. Of course she did." *You both did.* Jace looked at the faraway ballerina, so delicate, and so strong. "Did you carry her, Julia? Along the brightly lighted streets and into the department stores?"

"In the beginning, yes. But it was better for her, she could see everything more easily and could choose for herself where she wanted to look, if she was in her wheelchair. So that's what we did."

"And?"

"Well, there was never a repeat of what happened in the grocery store in Tierney. Cody's mother was the exception not the rule. And maybe that happened so that Galen and I would meet, and Galen would show Winnie the Christmas tree on Central Avenue, and Winnie would begin to see."

Julia's shrug was a lovely surrender to the mysteries of life that could not be explained. Its cruelty, and its miracles. "In any event, people were uncertain about Winnie. *Uncertain*, not disapproving. And because of that confusion, I suppose, that bewilderment, they always gave us a wide berth. They'd veer off the sidewalk as we approached, sometimes into a busy street, as if Winnie's wheelchair had some invisible aura they had to avoid. No one realized that Winnie was just like every other little girl at Christmas. She would have been skipping down the glittering streets had she been able to. She *was* skipping, frolicking, in her heart. People could have smiled at her, as they would have smiled at any other joyful skipping girl, and Winnie would have smiled back. She had such a bright smile. So *glowing*. And if a stranger had ever said 'Merry Christmas,' Winnie would have exclaimed 'Mirry Kismus!' in reply. But no one ever did, and I pray, I've allowed myself to *believe*, that my sweet little Win never understood the discomfort that others felt."

They weren't touching, these dancers. Jace stood before the window, and Julia stood before the tree.

But Jace reached for her, Jace Colton touched her, with his heart.

"What Winnie knew, Julia, what she understood and all that mattered, was your love."

*T*here was such love. It even seemed for a while that the little girl who wasn't expected to survive would survive forever.

But it wasn't to be. And it was Winnie's survival itself, her growing up, that killed her.

Her heart was small to begin with, little and not quite whole, and it became even more compromised as Winnie grew, nourished by food. And by love.

The bones of her misshapen ribcage grew inward, not out, compressing not expanding and constraining ever more her damaged heart. Eventually, inevitably, Winnie's small brave heart had to fail. And her little lungs, compromised too, compressed too, filled with fluid.

She couldn't breathe.

She gasped and struggled so.

And was so frightened.

Winnie didn't understand what was happening to her. How could she? How could anyone? What sense did it make for a seven-year-old girl to suddenly—it happened *so* suddenly—begin to suffocate, to drown?

There was rescue at first, respite from the near drowning, by medications administered IV-push and misted oxygen that flowed, gushed, through an aquamarine mask.

And once the gasping crisis had passed, her physicians began the process of fashioning the correct regimen of medications for her, a marriage of diuretics and digoxin, and advised Julia that, from then on, Winnie's diet must be virtually salt-free.

Winnie's physicians also told Winnie's loving sister, because Julia asked and it was only fair, that even with the most potent medications and the most severely restricted diet, Winnie would not survive very long. Days. Weeks. Maybe a month. Every day that Winnie lived, that she grew, brought her ever closer to death.

Winnie would die a gasping, drowning death, as even the most potent of drugs and most ascetic of diets inevitably failed. Or, if she was very lucky, she might succumb suddenly, peacefully, to an arrhythmia. V-tach. V-flutter. V-fib.

The bursts of ventricular tachycardia were happening already. Winnie was aware of the sudden flutters, but not alarmed. The ventricular arrhythmias *could* be treated with an additional pharmacy of meds. While the doctors were determining which antiarrhythmics were best, and the optimal dosages for each, Winnie would need to remain closely monitored in the ICU. Her doses of Lasix and digitalis would be adjusted as well during that ICU time, based on EKG tracings—and bloodwork that would need to be drawn at least twice a day.

Julia could learn, during Winnie's ICU stay, how to prepare the salt-free meals that Winnie must eat, the unpalatable food that Julia would need to feed, *force* feed, into Winnie's lopsided and resisting mouth. Winnie wouldn't understand such force, as she *didn't* understand it the one time Julia made such an attempt in the ICU.

It was a gentle attempt accompanied by such gentle words. You need to eat this, Winnie. I know it doesn't taste very good. But it's good for you. It will make you better, my little love. Better and stronger.

It was a lie, Julia knew.

Winnie would never be better, stronger. Better and stronger would kill her, *was* killing her, and Winnie was so confused by what was happening, bewildered and frightened. Except, Julia realized, by the fluttering rhythms that whispered within.

Even the diuretic was making Winnie sick, a necessary nausea she could not possibly comprehend, even though for the moment it had purged the drowning fluid from her lungs.

Two days after Winnie's emergency admission on that gasping, suffocating night, Julia took her little sister home. On no meds and *not* against medical advice. Winnie's doctors, who had cared for her and about her all her life, for those astonishing seven years, understood Julia's decision. And approved. And would be available, they said quietly. At any time.

When the Hayley sisters arrived home on that last day

in August, which would be Winnie's last day, Julia made tapioca pudding for Winnie. And when Winnie was no longer hungry, and was so nourished with sweetness, with love, for the journey that lay ahead, Julia and Winnie had their final Christmas.

Winnie sat in Gran's chair, as she always did for Christmas, watching from that coziness as Julia opened boxes and assembled the tree. Winnie's body was small in the spacious chair, and tilted, a little askew. As always. But she was comfortable in the familiar plushness, and Floppy lay, as always, on Winnie's lap.

Julia put up the Christmas tree, beribboning it with strand upon strand of twinkling lights, until it was time to decide which ornaments, there were so many, beloved treasures all, would adorn its twinkling branches.

The selection of ornaments was part of the renewal, the celebration, the joy. The welcome yet again of dearest friends. And on this August 31, this last Christmas, this final awakening, what friends did Winnie choose? Her angels. Only her angels. And all of them.

Winnie's angels, every aynga she had ever loved, were quite glorious amid the rainbowed lights. And when all were aloft in the twinkling tree, Julia joined Winnie and Floppy in Gran's chair.

Julia held both loved ones on her lap, and together, the sisters and Floppy, beheld the glowing splendor.

Julia believed that as long as they gazed at the luminous angels, her Winnie would not die. And, Julia believed, that they could gaze forever. *Would.* Winnie would, and so would she.

Forever.

But it was Winnie, *Winnie*, who looked away from the angels. Away and up, to her sister. And her hands, small and misshapen and determined, lifted her beloved yellow rabbit from her lap to Julia.

"You," she whispered. "You, Ju-Ju. *You.*"

And Winnie smiled, glowing and knowing and bright, as she gave her sister this final treasure, this most precious gift. And Winnie's small smiling lips, warm still, but not warm for much longer, kissed the sister she loved.

Then Winnie pressed even closer to Julia, as if they were one, and she looked anew at her shimmering angels, and Winnie was smiling still as her heart began to flutter, that merciful arrhythmia, that promise of peace.

Peace, not drowning. *Peace*, not fear.

Julia felt the fluttering angel wings within Winnie's chest, and she felt, Julia did, the soaring moment when Winnie became an angel, when smiling still, glowing still, Edwina Anne Hayley simply flew away.

# CHAPTER NINE

*J*ace wanted to hold her, this faraway angel with the fluttering heart.

But her story was not through. And she needed, he thought, to tell it all.

And Jace needed, wanted, to hear.

"And then what, Julia?" *Lovely Julia.*

She looked so confused by his question. Or maybe it was the gentleness that confused her. The tenderness. The care.

"She died, Jace. Winnie died."

"I know," he said softly. "But what I meant, Julia, was then what about you?"

"Me?"

"Yes, you, Julia." *You, Ju-Ju. You.*

*T*he first few days had been full, filled with the *busy*-ness and the business of death, the events and details that grieving loved ones everywhere managed to survive and looked back upon with amazement that they had.

As she had done for her own death, Gran had arranged in advance what she could for Winnie's. Edwina Anne Hayley would sleep forever in the cemetery behind the white-steepled church. And she would not be alone. The tree-shaded haven where Gran and Edwin slept would be Winnie's as well, and Winnie's name would be engraved with theirs in marble, and the legal aspects were in the kind and capable hands of Gran's attorney in Kansas City.

Julia went through the motions of those first few days, those busy days, with numb and unthinking calm. Then it was over. Winnie was with Edwin and Gran, and the probate documents had been notarized and signed, and Julia Anne Hayley and Floppy Anne Hayley were alone in the house on Willow Road.

Alone and aching and idle. And Julia needed to be busy still, unthinking still. She began to clean, to make sparkling, the silent house. Because she wanted the sparkle for herself? *No.* She was cleaning to glittering brilliance for Winnie and Gran . . . so everything would be so bright for them, so shiny and new, *when they came home.*

Julia battled such anguished thoughts, tried to, by focusing ever more intently on the tasks at hand. Every speck of dirt, every wisp of dust, the shadows of rust that only she could see.

Julia waged a ferocious war, but not a systematic one. There was no method, no order, to her madness. There could not be. For if she began one project, only to move to another before the first was complete, then none would ever truly be finished.

She was afraid, so terribly afraid, of being finished.

Twelve days after Winnie's death, Julia journeyed to the cellar of their home. It was a reconnaissance mission, a search for a reassuringly endless array of projects, a promise of months and months and months of compulsive cleaning to be done.

The cellar offered great comfort, its cobwebs, its mildew, its rust, its dirt. And its cartons. Mementos of Gran's life with Edwin? Julia wondered as she approached the massive cardboard wall. *More* mementos? She had discovered such treasures already, carefully sealed and stored in the attic where it was warm and dry.

The cellar cartons too were sealed. And like the ones in the attic, they were labeled in a manner that disclosed fully the contents within. But unlike the attic cartons, which bore Gran's familiar script, these were emblazoned with the imprint of a French winery renowned for its vinting of the most expensive champagnes.

Julia remembered the day seven years before when the cases had arrived. Her mother, pregnant with Winnie, had only been in Tierney over night. But she'd already placed the champagne order over the phone. It was a precise request and so extravagant—and profitable—that the store's father-and-son owners had made a special predawn trip to Kansas City to collect the cartons themselves.

And that afternoon father and son made the delivery to the Hayley home on Willow Road.

Gran hadn't wanted to disappoint the grateful merchants, even though the mother-to-be would not be drinking. Gran accepted the delivery and generously tipped the proprietors for carting all the cases to the cellar, to which Gran had and hid the only key.

The key returned to its usual place, in the kitchen drawer beside the sink, after Winnie was born and the mother who could not face motherhood—again—was gone.

The champagne was forgotten. Not a part of their lives. But the neatly stacked wall of cardboard remained in the cellar, its subterranean coolness as ideal for the vintage bubbly as the special caves where champagnes were routinely fermented, aged, and stored.

On this day, twelve days after Winnie's death, Julia discovered the long-forgotten wall. It was an appropriate day for such a discovery, for on this very September 12 Julia Anne Hayley turned twenty-one.

Julia had never tasted alcohol before, nor did she truly taste it now. But she felt its astonishing effects, the fluffy cocoon around the pain . . . and the warm bold promise that everything would be all right.

The astonishing effects were renewable, reliable, and immediate as well. Only the most ladylike of sips was required, as unaccustomed to alcohol as Julia was, and as starving, as grieving, as deprived of sleep.

Julia sipped when even the exhaustion of her cleaning could not block her anguished thoughts, and then, when she sipped, it was from a most special flute, shimmering crystal engraved *Edwin* and *Anne,* and their wedding date sixty-one years before.

The treasured flute seemed an appropriate vessel for Julia's new and golden friend. And like the trusted friend it had become, the champagne began offering advice. Such *reasonable* advice, Julia thought when the ebullient warmth heated her veins. And when the bubbles were gone and she was chilled and aching? And contrary thoughts intervened?

It took merely a sip, or sometimes two, to fortify anew her wavering resolve.

Julia held the wedding flute, just filled, filled again, when she placed the call to the local charity.

What sort of donations, she asked the pleasant-voiced volunteer, did the charity accept?

Virtually everything, the voice replied.

Well, that was good, because during the past few weeks, since the champagne had first floated the idea, Julia's list of what could *and should* be donated had become ever longer.

Virtually everything.

She needed very little herself. And, the champagne counseled—and Julia concurred—Gran and Winnie would want her to donate all she could, to help as much as possible others in need.

Gran's clothes, which had hung in her closet since her death, could be donated, and most of Julia's could go as well. She was only wearing cleaning clothes these days. And there were Winnie's clothes, the special garments so lovingly sewn by Galen, and later, as lovingly but far less beautifully, by Julia herself.

Julia couldn't describe Winnie's clothes to the charity volunteer. Even another swallow of champagne, a gulp, would not permit her to do so. But, the champagne promised, it was all right to give Winnie's clothes away. And generous and good. The clothes could be altered, and some other little girl would look *so pretty* in them, as Winnie had looked, and with winter approaching that lucky little girl would be so warm.

Winnie's wheelchair, too, could be put to good use, and there were boxes and boxes of Christmas ornaments, and shiny garlands and twinkling lights. And the Christmas tree. It was artificial, yes, and unusual, true, but lovely and grand.

The kitchen contents could be given away, the dishes, the utensils, the pots, the pans. Julia wasn't eating. Didn't need to. There were calories, surely, in the champagne. But she'd keep the can opener, she decided—an oddly forceful thought—and a fork, and one of these days she'd order a supply of canned goods, and maybe some vitamins, from the grocery store.

The champagne flute would stay, as would the telephone, as would the car that had been a gift from Gran on Julia's sixteenth birthday, when thanks to driving lessons from Galen, Julia had gotten a license of her own.

But the furniture, a household of it, was disposable. Save for her bed, and the chair in which she sat even as she made this call. It had been Edwin's, this chair, then

Gran's, and then Winnie's and hers, and now hers and Floppy's.

And it was, this chair, where Julia had held her Winnie as she'd fluttered away, and where Julia had cradled her sister still, for all those hours after, and kissed her beloved head, and her soft little-girl cheeks, even as the small misshapen body had become ever more, ever more, cold.

Julia's phone call to the charity concluded with firm commitments on both sides. The charity would have a truck and two men at the house on Willow Road at 2:00 P.M. on October 28, ten days hence, and Julia would be ready for them when they arrived.

It was a busy ten days, washing, ironing, folding every item of clothing to be given away, and towels and blankets and sheets, and cleaning the upholstery on the couches and chairs, and polishing every grain of wood furniture, and packing with great care the dishes, vases, glassware, and figurines.

Even after emptying the entire cardboard-carton wall of champagne, and placing the legion of unopened bottles on the cellar floor, Julia needed more boxes. She called the grocery store where she had an account, and where during the years when she and Winnie had been alone, she had shopped by phone.

Julia had paid during those years by credit card or check, and she had tipped in cash whoever made the delivery. Her tip on the October day seven weeks after Winnie's death was lavish and grateful, a thank-you for the abundance of empty boxes, for which there'd been no charge, and for the canned goods and cleaning supplies she'd added to the list.

Julia filled every box, and there were additional items that would need to be carried loose—the TV, the lamps, the landscapes by unknown artists framed in wood.

Julia hoped the volunteers wouldn't mind the unpacked items, and she would know *soon*. The ten days had passed so quickly, and she'd scarcely slept, there'd been so much to do, and whenever she'd wondered *what* she was doing, the champagne had reminded her. She was helping others, as Gran and Winnie would have wanted her to do. And, the champagne vowed, she would be busy still, as she needed to be, long after the charity truck was gone.

Every room in the house needed to be painted. The welcome discovery had come when Julia saw the reverse shadows on the walls, the brightness where—beneath pictures and mirrors—the paint had been shaded from the sun.

The preparation for painting would take weeks in itself. Maybe months. There were cracks to be filled and sanded and filled again, and nail holes, too. The bath and kitchen tiles needed to be regrouted, Julia realized, and the linoleum kitchen floor should really be replaced.

Yes, the champagne assured her, replacing a linoleum floor was definitely something she could do. It might take time. But she had time.

That was all she had.

The charity truck arrived at precisely 2:00 P.M. on October 28. Julia had decided not to have any champagne that day, at least not until after the volunteers were gone. But her decision had been abandoned at noon, earlier in the day than she'd ever sipped the golden liquid before. Of course she'd been up since three, assembling the cartons in neat stacks beside the front door, then dusting the wood furniture a final time, wanting it to shine brightly, beautifully, for whoever would own it next.

By noon, Julia was ready, and it was two hours until the truck arrived, and suddenly she had such misgivings, such terrible doubts, about giving so much away.

Giving *anything* away.

Her confidence was restored by the first few swallows of champagne. But would the men from the charity be able to tell that she'd been drinking? Not by her *behavior,* the bubbly assured her. She was cheery, breezy, *fine.*

But might they detect the scent of alcohol on her breath? Julia greeted them with the smiling confession, the effortless lie, that she'd just returned from a champagne luncheon with friends.

A farewell luncheon? the men politely and logically wondered. They were, after all, emptying her house.

Yes, Julia replied, smiling still. But the moment the men took the first stack of boxes to the truck, Julia rushed to the kitchen and took a gulp, two gulps, directly from the bottle. And there were a few more clandestine swallows as the afternoon wore on.

Finally the men were gone.

Everything was gone.

Farewell. Farewell.

Julia floated for the next hour, more floating than ever

before, and quite receptive to the suggestion that drifted to her brain that she open at last *all* the mail that had arrived since Winnie's death. She had before this day opened only the necessary correspondences, paying promptly the usual bills, and the anguished ones—funeral home, florist, stonecarver, cemetery.

Julia had written thank-you notes, too, in response to the lovely letters of condolence she'd received from Winnie's doctors, Winnie's nurses, and the ward clerks, orderlies, and even answering-service operators that she and Winnie had come to know.

And she'd opened and responded to correspondence from Gran's attorney, *her* attorney, regarding the estate. There were documents for her to sign and checks to write as well—reimbursements to the law firm for the copies of Winnie's death certificate it had obtained, and the letters testamentary, and the required probate filings with the court.

Julia had dealt with the mail that needed her attention, the communiqués that signaled debt not fortune. Death not life. But her bank statements, those trivial accountings of the vast fortune that was hers, remained sealed. As did the statements for Winnie's account, for which Julia had had power of attorney since Gran's death.

She had never touched Winnie's fortune, had paid, easily, Winnie's medical bills from the money she'd inherited from Gran.

But Julia had always reviewed Winnie's bank statements. Which, she told herself, was what she'd do now, on this floating afternoon. It was her responsibility after all as—

*Executor.* The word appeared on Winnie's October bank statement. Julia saw it through the plastic window in the envelope, addressed to her, as "executor for the estate of Edwina Anne Hayley." It was a hated word, piercing and painful. And violent, like executioner. Why hadn't the legal powers-that-be come up with something more apt? Like loving survivor? Loving, grieving, and so very reluctant.

Julia took another sip, another swallow, of champagne, opened the bank statement and made a belated but significant discovery. A large monthly deposit, *the* deposit insisted upon by Gran, had been made on October eighth. And on September eighth as well.

Because her mother, their mother, did not know that Winnie had died.

She needed to know, to be *notified.* And it was her responsibility, Julia decided, as execu—no, as loving, grieving, reluctant survivor—to do so. But precisely where to place the phone call required a little problem-solving, a pop quiz for Julia's floating brain.

Her mother had divorced, Julia knew, and had subsequently remarried someone *other* than her politician lover. But who? How to find out? With a rush of sheer triumph, Julia had the answer. Her mother's new name, and her address and phone, would be imprinted on her checks.

But, save for the statement itself, the envelope was quite empty. And, as Julia finally realized why, her sense of triumph was replaced by concern, just a little, at how faulty her reasoning was. The cancelled checks would be in her *mother's* bank statements *not Winnie's*.

Of *course*.

Julia resisted taking another swallow of champagne to clear her mind. She merely sat in Gran's chair patting Floppy as the autumnal twilight fell around her. Finally, amid the gloaming shadows, Julia placed the obvious, logical call to her attorney in Kansas City.

Yes, he knew how to reach her mother. It was part of the agreement made when Gran had insisted on the monthly checks. He was to be notified of any and all changes in name, address, phone.

The attorney's surprise that Winnie's mother, such as she was, had not been notified of her daughter's death was swiftly eclipsed by his own sense of guilt. He should have thought to ask Julia if her mother knew, and to offer, as he offered now, to make the call.

But Julia declined the offer.

She would make the call. And did.

Much later, when Julia had the perspective to look back on that desperate time of champagne and of grief, she would realize that her mother had undoubtedly been drinking, too, on that night. Their conversation was too effortless, too false, and far too random in its extremes. The mother who had never been a mother was extravagantly distraught at the news of Winnie's death, and she asked with such passion if there was anything Julia needed, anything that *she* could do?

And when Julia, fortified by her mother's champagne,

told her that there was nothing, that she was *fine*, her mother's relieved response had been a mirror image of Julia's own breeziness . . . and when Julia said that she would be reimbursing her mother for the deposits made since Winnie's death, her reply—"Nonsense, Julia!"— rippled over the phone line on a giddy laugh.

Julia said good-bye to her mother on that night. Forever. Then she washed the champagne flute, to remain empty until her return from the errands she would do tomorrow, and spent until midnight crafting a detailed list of things to do while she was out—a list to which, as she drove into town the following morning, she added a mental note.

The necessary addition was prompted by the decorations displayed everywhere. The jack-o'-lanterns were cheerful, smiling and bright, and even the ghosts and witches were the friendly sort. But the Halloween decor sent the ominous reminder that in just a few short days the pumpkins and witches would be replaced by turkeys, by pilgrims, by the bounty of the harvest.

And, after that, Christmas.

The realization made her hand float from the steering wheel, as if reaching for her crystal flute, needing it desperately, at which point she added the mental note, which became an invisible shout line, to her list. *Get enough of everything to last until mid-January.*

Her first stop was the hardware store. She bought gallons and gallons of paint—latex semigloss in the purest of white—and enough brushes, dropcloths, and masking tape to paint a mansion or two. She bought caulking compounds, too, and wood filler and grout, and shiny brass knobs for bath cabinets and kitchen drawers. And cleaning supplies. The prices, she noticed, were better than the grocery's.

She had planned to go to the grocery anyway, even though her stock of canned goods was far from gone. But she could always place an order over the phone, and she was suddenly feeling so tired, so raw, as if she were the most jellylike of creatures suddenly separated from its shell.

She wanted to get home, to that shell, as soon as possible. She needed to. Desperately.

Home to Floppy, to Gran's chair.

To her mother's champagne.

Rows of unopened bottles stood on the cellar floor. Rows and rows. Enough to last until mid-January? Yes. Surely. But as fatigued as she felt, as vulnerable and precarious, Julia drove to the liquor store. Just in case.

And there, at the liquor store, the grieving heiress and reluctant executrix of two fortunes discovered far more frugal ways to get as much alcohol—in fact more—than by drinking champagne. Especially the vintage sparkler that was her mother's choice.

Julia bought hard liquor, the least expensive she could find, then went to the bank to get cash for tips for whatever deliveries she might need in the coming months.

Then Julia Anne Hayley went home, where she remained in busy, empty, blurry silence until May.

Julia liked the silence, wanted it, and shattered it only rarely. She spoke sometimes and mostly to Floppy.

In early February, however, she placed a call to the hardware store. She needed more paint. The whiteness seemed brighter with each layer she applied, so she'd decided to apply several more.

Julia also called the liquor store. Somehow she was running low. She was having a party, she told the clerk, and needed a supply of those large bottles. Yes, she asserted on a giddy laugh that sounded so hauntingly like her mother's, the least expensive brands would do.

Julia controlled the silence in which she lived. The single intrusion came from her attorney. Winnie's attorney. He called on occasion with matters of the estate. And, on occasion, he made personal inquiries, too.

I'm *fine*, Julia would assure him with the breezy cheer of bourbon or vodka or gin. But after a moment and despite the alcohol, or perhaps because of it, she would confess that *fine* was an overstatement and that *okay*, without a zephyr of cheer, was far more apt.

This was all very difficult, she admitted. As she'd known it would be. But she was doing all right, surviving the loss, and slowly but surely getting better, stronger, every day.

Julia believed her solemn words. And for all of that winter the words had been true. Seemed true. Until March. That was when, she realized in retrospect, the downward spiral had begun. And it had picked up speed and fury with each passing day, a whirling vortex toward darkness over which, with each passing day, Julia had less and less control.

Julia had tried to reverse the descent, to become buoyant and lofty and floating anew. The frugal heiress even ordered from the liquor store a case of her mother's champagne, that most expensive friend. But it offered no more euphoria than the cheaper blends, a transient exhilaration which—once gone—left her feeling ever darker, ever lower, than before.

*I have to stop drinking.* The decisive thought, which came in May, was all her own. She hadn't had a drop of faux elation, of whimsical friendship, for more than a day.

She had to stop. And did. Forever. The decision itself made her feel better, less weighted and so relieved, despite the weakness she felt. Food helped the weakness, as did sleep, and two days later Julia left her house for the first time in seven months.

She walked, although it would have been safe to drive, and the springtime sun burned her eyes. But she needed to walk in that glaring sunshine. Just as she needed to visit the cemetery behind the church.

She hadn't visited the grave, *their* grave, since the day Winnie had joined Edwin and Gran. And if, before this too-brilliant spring day, Julia had come? At Christmastime, perhaps?

She would have lain on the snowy ground, wanting so desperately to be with them, and getting her wish, because what—*nothing*—would have compelled her to leave before freezing to death?

But Julia had not visited her loved ones at Christmastime. The alcohol, then her friend, had not permitted her to do so.

And now, without alcohol, she sat on the sun-warmed grass and spoke softly of her love, and her eyes were damp but no longer burning, and when she left she promised to return again and often to this place of peace.

Then Julia walked to the bookstore on Central Avenue. And found so many books she needed to read. On death. On loss. On grief. On grieving. And, she decided, she should read as well about alcohol.

And read she did, curled in Gran's chair with Floppy on her lap. She learned so much. Confirmed so much. An affirmation of what she'd experienced, and what she had done.

The entire world tilted, the books said, when a loved one died. And in her case, Julia realized, she was mourning both Winnie and Gran. And Galen? No. Her girlhood friend was lost from Julia's life. But alive. Julia was sure of it. Alive and happy.

Survivors, the books maintained, tried frantically to right their tilted world. Extreme reactions *and drastic measures* were both typical and expected. How else to counterbalance, to attempt to right anew, a world that had been thrown so devastatingly out of tilt?

Some grieving survivors slept around the clock, and others slept not at all. Some ate compulsively, and others just as compulsively starved. There was gorging on work sometimes, a binge of productivity, whereas others could not concentrate on even the most simple task.

Such was the paralysis of mourning, the books explained—a figurative affliction not a literal one. And the frantic energy that was its diametrically opposite twin? That was denial, vigorously disguised.

The extremes were normal. Every desperate one. Normal. Understandable. And necessary, the experts assured. Even necessary.

Julia was not the first, nor would she be the last, whose desperate response, an extreme that contrasted so starkly with the world she had known and lost, was to drink. Not that alcohol was a method the books—and their credentialed authors—would *ever* recommend. But excessive drinking happened, as did the use, the misuse, of both prescription and illicit drugs.

And did the floating numbness of alcohol help the grief? Yes, Julia knew. It did. It had. The faux confidence, the bubbly assurance that she *would* survive, had enabled her to do just that, to get through that most impossible time when the loss was so fresh, so new, so immense. The false buoyancy had helped, then. It truly had.

And when the alcohol and its depressant effects had made the transition from friend to foe?

Somehow, thankfully, Julia had recognized the spiraling descent. She didn't know why or how—except that all the books insisted that the cliché was true. Time helped. The *passage* of time. Even if that passage was spent in frantic extremes of denial and despair. Even numbing, bubbly, floating ones.

Time helped. Maybe even healed. *Began* the healing.

Avoid impulses, Julia's books unanimously counseled. Especially, they admonished, during the precarious time when the loss was so recent, so raw and so acute, that the

survivor's very survival was in doubt. Do nothing irrevo-
cable, the books warned—such as, for example, giving
things away.

The impulse to do so was quite normal, of course. Expected. As if, in the altered thought processes that domi-
nated that terribly difficult time, it made sense to give
away the tangible mementos of the loved one who was
lost . . . as if, in giving away the inanimate symbols, one
might give away as well some of the pain.

Don't *worry*, however—subsequent paragraphs in
every book reassured—if you have succumbed to such
impulses. Yes, you may feel regret, *remorse*, the fervent
*but futile* wish to have some keepsake to touch, to cherish, to wear. But what matters most, the only true treasures, are the memories. They cannot be lost, will not die,
nor can they be given away.

Be gentle with yourself, every expert urged. Gentle
and careful and caring and kind.

Julia had not, perhaps, taken care of herself. But she
had known somehow when the drinking must stop. And
she had. Easily. Effortlessly.

But was she an alcoholic nonetheless?

She was most definitely at risk—assuming, that is, her
mother's various addictions were the consequence of nature not nurture.

But if it was environment not DNA that mattered, Julia
was quite safe. Her life had been filled, nurtured and
nourished, with love. And until the emptiness that came
when her loved ones were lost, she'd never had the
slightest wish to blur her world in any way.

As Julia had no wish to do so now. Not anymore. Even though she felt great sadness still. The sadness would be there always, the books forewarned. There would be times, even years hence, when the loss would feel acute and she would live those moments of death with exquisite clarity, as if they'd just happened anew.

But those sudden flashes of pain would pass. Quickly. Because time had passed. And, the books promised, remembrance would come with smiles, even laughter, not with tears. And the desperate wish to forget, because it hurt *so much* to remember, would vanish, too. Memories would be wanted, welcomed, celebrated with joy.

Julia would drink no more. She knew that with certainty. That phase of grieving was past.

And the next phase?

She would take care of herself. Be gentle and kind. And patient. She would listen very carefully to the impulses that came to her, but would avoid impulsive action of any sort. Instead, so patiently, she would permit each idea, every thought, time to bud, to blossom, to grow.

Your heart will tell you what you need, the gurus of loss promised. As will your spirit and your soul.

Julia's first need was a surprising one: *sound* where for so long she had wanted only silence. The sound of human voices. The community with other lives.

Which could be found, couldn't it, in Tierney? In the ever-more-plentiful bounty of specialty shops, boutiques, and stores? Yes, and no. The people she met, shopkeepers and shoppers alike, were nice. Always. But no matter how pleasant, how smiling, the encounters felt jarring to

Julia, menacing and harsh, and within moments she was in a rush to get away. To be home.

Did she need then to invite someone into her home? No. The answer was decisive and far transcended the simple truth that there was no one, really, whom she even knew. She needed to *control* the sound, to return to the solace of silence, of solitude, whenever she chose. The moment she chose.

The answer, astonishingly and confidently, was to buy a television set. Julia had given Gran's to the local charity on that monumental October afternoon. It hadn't been used for years, seven to be exact, but Julia had assumed that it still worked.

On occasion and before Winnie, she and Gran had watched selected shows. But after Winnie's birth, when it was clear that the little girl could hear, the television had been silent. The strange voices—and the sudden loudness when commercials were aired—alarmed and confused her.

Julia's new television set was cable-ready, the salesman at the appliance store explained, defining the term for her and suggesting that she order *basic* cable at least. The channels available in Tierney were too limited without it, he said. And the reception was too blurred.

Julia didn't remember blurriness from the time when she and Gran had watched. But blurriness of any kind was no longer part of her life. So she signed up for basic cable and received a signal that was true and clear.

Julia watched the news. And the soaps. Especially the soaps, for here was precisely what she needed—a way to feel involved in other lives *yet safe,* and to make discoveries, too, about relationships she'd never known. Romantic ones, between women and men.

Were the fictional story lines over the top? Sometimes. Yes. And the emotions as well? Perhaps. But Julia cried anyway. And smiled. And spoke.

"Victor is *so* wrong," she told the ever-attentive yellow rabbit. "Nikki needs to know that the reason he didn't come to the ranch that night was because of Cliff's accident. Victor needs to tell Nikki the truth even though he and Nicholas arrived in Las Vegas too late to stop her marriage to Joshua. I can't *believe* he's not going to tell her!"

Julia also spoke to the soap-opera characters themselves. "Don't do it, Jax. Brenda trusts you, she really does. But if you do *this* . . ."

It was all right, Julia decided, to watch the soaps. And to cry and to smile and even to express aloud her exasperation with the choices the characters made. So she watched the daytime dramas, and the noon and evening news, and she took long walks, as she and Gran had done, to the tree-shaded cemetery and for miles and miles beyond.

And, during those long walks beneath the summertime sun, Julia permitted impulses to come to her, and to float, billowy and soft, like the plump white clouds overhead. Julia carefully considered every impulse. Some she discarded, so carefully, and others, and even more carefully, she kept.

Julia kept the impulse that came in mid-July, and when

it had blossomed, confident and sure, she made an appointment for August 31.

She drove on that day—the one-year anniversary of Winnie's death—to the hospital where Winnie had been born, and where she'd been cared for so lovingly, and where she would have died surrounded by compassion had not Julia made the decision to take her home.

There was a new sign at the familiar entrance. RE-GIONAL MEDICAL CENTER had replaced HOSPITAL, and there had been a remarkable amount of construction as well, a growth of mortar and stone that was commensurate, she supposed, with the medical facility's expansive new title.

Julia's appointment was with the woman who managed the answering services for the center . . . and who had written such a lovely note to Julia after Winnie died . . . and who had known Julia, by telephone mostly, when she'd been an answering service operator herself and Julia had called about Winnie and Gran.

Julia explained to the operator-turned-manager that she would very much like to become an operator, too—whenever a position was open and for whatever physician group needed the help. She didn't care, she said, about being paid. And her qualifications, she acknowledged, were meager. Her at-home education had ended at age fourteen, when Winnie was born, and she'd never had a job. But she believed she could answer after-hours phone calls from anxious patients.

*Of course* she could, the manager replied. And she would be paid, like every other employee, and as for qualifications—or lack thereof? The manager remembered well the softness of Julia's voice, its focused calm even when her loved ones were ill.

Julia worked at first at the center itself, in the vast room that was empty on weekdays but full, and alive and ringing, on evenings, weekends, and nights. After a month, having mastered the system, Julia was given the option of working at home. It was an opportunity available to all answering-service operators—but not to the page operators within the hospital itself—and Julia was an ideal candidate, with distraction of neither children nor spouse. The center would equip her home, of course, with the computer, the fax, the supplemental phone lines she would need.

The twenty-mile commute from Tierney was easy three seasons out of four. But at night in winter the roads could be treacherous. And there was that other wintertime hazard: Christmas, with its glitter, its celebration, its pain.

But what of the community with other human beings? The operators in the cubicles adjacent to hers whom she might befriend during the silences between calls?

Julia needed control still. The ability to be alone, to be silent, when she chose. And there was community, communion, even when she worked from home, for in response to her greeting—"Doctors' answering service, this is Julia, how may I help you?"—the anxious voices in the night would reply, "Oh, *Julia,* I'm so glad it's you."

The family-medicine physicians for whom she worked were happy, too, when Julia was "on call." She gathered the necessary information with efficient calm, and although she offered no medical advice, she did on occasion recommend immediate calls to 911—including the time when she insisted on, in fact placed the call herself, such emergent intervention for the elderly woman at the other end of the line.

The woman's only symptom was fatigue, and she hadn't wanted to bother anyone, but she was just so terribly tired.

The woman survived the heart attack she was having, did very well indeed, because Julia had somehow known how potentially serious her nonspecific symptom—fatigue—could be.

*How* had she known? the on-call physician wondered.

She hadn't, not really. Or maybe she had. Maybe her life with Winnie and Gran had taught her to be alert to complaints, however vague and apologetic, from those who never complained.

Julia was alert to the nuances in the voices that called her in the night. And she was alert as well, ever ready, for whatever impulses came. But none did. And maybe her decision to work for the answering service was the only change she would ever make.

It felt right, was right, and although her life was unusual, she felt safe, content, secure.

A year passed, and another and another, until it had been six years since Winnie's death. It was then, out of the blue and with such joy, that Galen appeared alive and well and on TV in Julia's living room.

Julia had never before turned to Channel 39. But the noon news was hyping a story that sounded far too sad to watch, so she had hurriedly and randomly pressed two buttons, 3 and 9, on the remote.

Channel 39 in Tierney was Gavel-to-Gavel TV. Like ratings-rival Court TV, Gavel-to-Gavel provided live coverage of real trials. And who reported for the GTG viewers those authentic daytime dramas? Galen, who was so poised, so articulate, as she recounted that morning's events, the attorneys' opening statements in *North Carolina* v. *Vernon.*

Julia watched every moment of the trial. And, as she did, impulses floated at last. She needed to make a change. She was too isolated, too solitary, too alone. The change need not happen today. Or tomorrow. But she had to start *thinking* about it today.

Julia did think, as she must, bold thoughts that seemed to be encouraged by her friend on TV.

The verdict in *North Carolina* v. *Vernon* came on December 14, and eight days later, when it was announced that Galen would be leaving Gavel-to-Gavel to anchor the news at Manhattan's top-rated KCOR, Julia too had decided on a dramatic Christmastime change.

This would be her last Christmas in Kansas.

And where would she go? Julia didn't know. But she would give herself plenty of time to find out.

Julia already knew some of her future plans, beginning with the money she would give to the medical center where Gran and Winnie had been treated with such kindness, and where she had been treated so kindly, too.

It would be a substantial donation, stunning really, for no one knew that the answering service operator from

Tierney enjoyed such enormous wealth. It would be awkward, Julia thought, to make the contribution while still in the center's employ. She would do it, she decided, when she was on the very verge of leaving Kansas. She would deliver a check, with no fanfare whatsoever, in the names, in loving memory of Winnie, of Edwin, of Gran.

The fortunes were theirs, after all. But Julia would make her own donation as well, from the income she'd earned and saved, and there would be the proceeds from the sale of the house and—

*Wait.* This was why she needed twelve months of careful planning. *And of care.* She could not this time give everything, *even money,* away. She had to keep some for herself, enough—and then a little *more*—that she wouldn't feel pressured to hurriedly, impulsively, find work in her new city the moment she arrived.

She would read again the relevant chapters in her books on grief and loss, the ones that admonished gentleness always with oneself. She'd read those chapters. Memorize that wisdom. And next December, before moving to wherever it was she would live, she'd give the books, among other carefully considered donations—including, she imagined, her car—to charity.

She would even, she knew, leave behind her long hair. *She had to.* The small misshapen hands that had tangled it so, had clung with such determination and such love, were safe, at peace, with Edwin and Gran.

Julia would be starting fresh, beginning anew. She and Floppy and Gran's chair. And the crystal wedding flute, too, that shimmered on the windowsill, filled with sunlight now, not champagne.

Julia created a timetable by which certain monumental decisions needed to be made. It looked reasonable, she thought, crafted as it was on January 1. Vast and unpressured, with ample time for whatever unforeseen impulses floated aloft.

Julia's New Year's Day timetable included the promise to call Galen, to say hello and to *apologize* for failing to pursue Galen's precipitous disappearance from Tierney for fear of antagonizing Mark. And when Julia made that call? Galen was thrilled to hear from her, and apologetic too, for leaving Kansas without a word. But she'd been fearful, like Julia, of retribution from Mark.

Julia was maid of honor at Galen's wedding, in early June, to NYPD homicide lieutenant Lucas Hunter, and they'd kept in touch since by phone. And photo. Galen sent pictures of Lily, their newborn baby girl, and Julia sent photographs of the charming white-brick house where for her first year in Seattle she would live.

The house, in the Emerald City neighborhood called Hawthorne Hills, had been the home for thirty-eight years of Dolores and Charles Wilson. Charles taught anthropology at the University of Washington, and Dolores had been until recently a full-time mom. She did volunteer work now, since their children, all three of them, had for various reasons—love, adventure, a *fabulous* job— moved to the East Coast.

Charles was eligible for a sabbatical, had been for years, and given the current location of all three children, and two grandchildren, spending a year, from January to January, at the University of Virginia seemed ideal.

The only problem was the house. Who would care for it in their absence? The Wilsons had screened and politely declined any number of applicants. In September, in an issue of the Sunday *Seattle Times* delivered to Julia's Tierney home, Charles and Dolores placed an ad in the classifieds under Homes for Rent/Lease.

The lengthy ad never mentioned price—because they'd been planning to pay not charge—and was quite specific, and very particular, about whom they wanted to care for their home. Someone single preferably, and quiet and mature, and who didn't smoke, and who'd owned or leased a home before and understood all the routine upkeep that was required, and who could provide letters of recommendation from an employer of at least three years, and . . .

Julia smiled as she read the breathless ad. Here were people who loved their home, worried about it, treasured it. And from the research she'd done, the Hawthorne Hills location was wonderful, as was the prospect of an already-furnished home.

The white-brick house would be perfect. For her. And even before the Wilsons received the glowing letters of recommendation sent on Julia's behalf, their phone conversations with Julia convinced them that there could not be a more responsible house sitter for their much-loved home.

And for their much-enjoyed hummingbirds.

Julia would be delighted, she assured them, to hang the

hummingbird feeders on their designated hooks at the designated time. Mid-March. And she'd happily make the nectar—one part sugar, four parts water—and keep the sugary sustenance fresh and plentiful through late July, when the migrating flutterers hummed away.

The hummingbirds would come, the Wilsons promised. And they would nest. And the newborn babies would return to Hawthorne Hills the following spring to nest and have their babies, and Julia's willingness to assume this avian responsibility would assuage immensely the Wilsons' worries about abandoning the great-great-great-great-grandchicks of the hummers to whom they'd provided nourishment—and in turn had provided such joy—and Charles and Dolores could enjoy their own grandchildren. At last.

It was perfect all the way around. Including, for all of them, the year-long lease and the commitment it implied.

Julia would be needed in Seattle, *needed*, from the moment she arrived. In late December. After London, after Canterfields, after Christmas . . .

"*So* here I am," Julia said softly. "In London. Facing Christmas."

"Here you are," Jace echoed. *With me of all people.* He marveled at the fate—the flurries of snow and the furies of Alexis—that had brought Julia Anne Hayley here, at Christmas, with him. *Christmas.* She was far too apprehensive, she had confessed, to eat breakfast on this Christmas Eve, and the dark purple smudges beneath her eyes gave eloquent testimony to her sleepless night. Her fear, Jace knew, was quite real. Yet she'd stood before the magnificent Christmas tree, was standing there still, without fear, and she'd made its fragrant teal boughs even more magnificent, and potentially more fearsome, by illuminating the tiny white lights, and she'd touched with wonder the shimmering crystals of snow. "Facing this tree doesn't make you fearful."

"No." Julia frowned, as if suddenly confronted with a new worry, something she hadn't even considered before. But she discarded the concern, needing to, with a lovely smile. "Because, I suppose, it doesn't evoke a single memory of my Christmases with Winnie."

"No?"

"No. Our tree was artificial of course, so that we could celebrate Christmas as often as we liked. As Winnie needed. And there were no snowflakes on Winnie's tree, and no silver bows, and our lights were multicolored and twinkling, not steady and white. But," she said, "I guess the main reason this Christmas tree evokes no memories—and no fear—is because it's teal, not fuchsia."

# CHAPTER TEN

uchsia?"

"Yes." Her smile glowed. "Winnie's Christmas trees were always fuchsia, and her daylight sky was green, and at night the heavens shimmered a bright, bright gold. I assumed in the beginning that those were the colors Winnie truly saw. That she had a color blindness of sorts. But Winnie's ophthalmologist said that switching one bright color for another was not the way color blindness worked. In fact, she said, people with color blindness typically see the world in shades of gray."

"Which," Jace said, "Winnie definitely did not."

"No. And, as I came to realize, she knew the sky was blue, and that Christmas trees were mostly green. But she chose to paint her world with an entirely different palette. I could . . ."

"Yes?"

"Well, I could show you."

"Show me."

As Julia moved away from the teal green tree, its

snowflakes and ribbons and tiny white lights, Jace moved as well, from the window backlit in pewter to the center of the mauve-and-cream parlor.

It was there, moments later, where the distant dancers met at last.

Julia returned from her bedroom with her sketchbook. She opened it to the first page as she handed it to him.

"This is what Winnie saw. What she chose to see."

It was breathtaking, this first portrait of Winnie's world, both in color and in style. Indeed, Jace thought, had the delicately detailed landscape been watercolored solely in color-blind gray, it would have been a work of art.

And this painting that was so very far from gray? He supposed that, had the color scheme been described to him not shown, it might have sounded like a thoughtless clash of whimsical shades and unlikely hues. But there was no whimsy here, no thoughtlessness at all, for the emerald of this sky—was there even a name for this exquisite shade?—caressed the turquoise Kansan cornfields, a rare shade, too, extraordinary too, with the soft splendor of a lover's kiss. And what could be more nurturing, more nourishing, than earth the color of roses?

"You painted this?"

"Yes. But the colors are Winnie's. These precise colors. Her sky wasn't any green, but every green, just as a usual sky can be any and every shade of blue. Winnie's sky changed, its green did, from dawn to dusk and winter to spring."

"How did you know what color she saw . . . chose?"

"I'd ask her, and she'd show me if she could, if the color she envisioned existed in the watercolors I'd bought. And if it didn't, which was most of the time, we'd create it, blending the shades and hues until it was exactly right. At first I'd color an entire scene, like this landscape, and we'd paint in all the colors—well, I'd paint them at Winnie's direction. She didn't have the motor skills to do the painting herself. Eventually I'd just point to a tree or a flower or a bird or a cloud and ask her what color it should be, and we'd mix and match until we found it, at which point I'd use the color to paint a smiling face."

"And then?"

"Then?"

"What would you do with the landscapes—and smiling faces?"

"Do? Nothing. I'd just throw them away. It was the *process* that was such fun. And Winnie wanted me to know *her* colors, of course, and I *wanted* to know them, and once we both knew that I could and would see a given sky precisely as she did, what we'd created on paper no longer mattered."

"So this painting is new?"

"Yes. I decided, as I was planning my future, to paint some memories of the past. If I could. Before Winnie, I'd never painted or sketched or drawn at all. I'd had no reason to, no *passion* to. I'm not even sure, before Winnie, that I *could* have. And since her death, well, it seemed pretty likely that whatever ability I might have possessed had become irrevocably rusted by disuse. And alcohol."

"There's no rust here," Jace observed, even as he marveled at what she'd just told him, and what she apparently believed: that her talent was because of Winnie, a gift from Winnie, and had nothing whatsoever to do with her.

"Well. I can paint *these* images, Winnie's images, still."

She was not, Jace realized, going to acknowledge any talent apart from what Winnie had bestowed. He might have asked her about her own lovely blindness—but there was a far more important question to ask. "And emotionally, Julia? Has it been difficult?"

"No," she confessed. "It hasn't. Just as the books on grief and grieving promised. I've felt celebration as I've painted. *Celebration,* not sadness."

"But?" Jace asked, very softly, sensing more.

Julia answered in a rush. "Once I decided what images I would do, twenty in all, I set a time line, and a time limit, for painting them."

She was being so careful, Jace realized, this woman who had almost drowned in champagne—so very careful not to drown anew, in paint this time, in the intoxicating escape of creating, *re*creating, these portraits of love.

"You're planning to finish all the watercolors while you're here," Jace said. It was a logical assumption, part of Julia's careful plan to journey to the past, its certain memories, its confident joy, before venturing to her own uncertain future.

"Yes. I have two left to do, one for tomorrow and one for the day after."

"May I look at the others you've done?"

"If you like." *If you'd like to see more of my little sister's world.*

Which he did. Jace wanted to see, to know, more about both Hayley sisters, and on the pages that followed he learned so much about the dazzling world in which Winnie and Julia had dwelled. It was a magical domain, an enchantment in which aquamarine moons glowed in bright golden skies, and where stars twinkled purple, and where newly fallen snow was very nearly identical to the mauve of their Eden-Knightsbridge suite—and of the couch to which Julia had retreated as he studied the paintings she had done.

Maybe she needed to sit, this exhausted ballerina, and maybe he needed to stand, distant from her still, and maybe they needed still to dance, only, with words.

"Not all of Winnie's trees were fuchsia," Jace said when he came to a forest of exuberant color beneath a jade green sky . . . and a lavender sun.

Winnie's sun, her daytime star, was the precise lavender of her sister's eyes. Did Julia even realize, Jace wondered, that Winnie had placed that color, that glowing love, at the very center of her universe?

Probably not, he thought. Probably *not.*

"No," Julia replied to the question, the spoken one, he had asked. "Only her Christmas trees were fuchsia. Or any evergreen that might *become* a Christmas tree. But her oaks in spring were lilac, and her maples were magenta and cream, and her birches fluttered both indigo and gold. In fall, however, all the autumnal leaves became the same color, her favorite color."

"Turquoise."

"Yes."

Turquoise, in every imaginable shade and hue, was Winnie's favorite color. And as Jace journeyed through the enchantment of Winnie's world, he discovered her favorite Christmas ornaments, too. Angels. And reindeer. In every imaginable shade and hue.

Jace had known about the angels, the only adornment chosen by the dying angel for her final fuchsia tree. And now he was seeing them, the entire flock, singing, soaring, floating on this snowy-white page. They were all beloved, Winnie's angels, and painted that way. But the two in the center, he knew, were the most treasured of all.

Jace knew, too, and at once, who these most special angels were. The Canterfields angel, cream and pink and gold, was Gwa, and the one in the flowing turquoise robe, with the flame red hair, was Gayla.

Jace didn't speak as he viewed the angels. Could not.

But Julia, who knew so well the page that had silenced him, could—eventually—and did.

"Winnie loved her angels. And her reindeer. You'll find a herd of them on the next page."

It was a single herd, just Santa's soaring nine, each flying creature unique in color and in style, and labeled in Julia's elegant script beneath.

"Rudolph's nose is red."

Julia smiled. "Red worked well, nose-wise, for Winnie."

"But otherwise he's quite . . . what color is he?"

"Hyacinth, I think, with a few dashes of silver."

"And Dasher is?"

"Apricot, with just a soupçon of lime."

And Cupid was marigold and rose, and Blitzen was carnation and plum, and Jace compelled Julia to name for him every shade, every hue, in this rainbow of reindeer. It was a soft request, and answered so willingly and with such an enchantment of colors—from bluebell to jasmine to marmalade to wine—that Jace wanted the magical recitation never to end.

But it did. And with it came to an end the eighteen portraits of happiness and joy.

"What are the final two watercolors going to be?"

"The church nativity, which I thought I'd do tomorrow, on Christmas day, and on the day after I'll paint Floppy."

"And what color will Floppy be?"

"Floppy color. The daffodil yellow she was when she was new. Winnie saw Floppy just as she was, and Galen, and Gran, and our home. And the figures, too, in the crèche."

"And you?"

"Yes. And me. Winnie never made any changes in the people, the places, the rabbit she loved. She never would. She was so gracious, so lovely."

Gracious, Jace mused. And so lovely. Of course. Winnie was Julia's sister. And beyond Winnie's innate graciousness was what the extraordinary little girl artist undoubtedly knew—that even her artistic eye, her magnificent gift, could not conjure a color scheme more magical than her sister's blend of lavender, of raven, of roses, of snow.

"Floppy's had many baths in her lifetime," Julia was saying, with such fondness. "She's always been the cleanest little rabbit there is. But she's quite a bit less yellow these days, and less fluffy."

"She's been loved."

"Oh yes, she has."

As Julia's loving voice recalled images of misshapen little fingers curling tight, and small lips curved into their lovely and lopsided smile, Jace saw images, too: Floppy on Julia's lap during the flight from O'Hare, and in the cab from Heathrow, and Floppy, on her cottony belly, atop the downy mauve comforter on Julia's bed.

Floppy had been loved by Winnie, and was loved by Julia still, and . . .

"As she will be loved, Julia, by your own daughter."

Julia's eyes, the lavender of Winnie's sun, met his. But it was a winter sun, a wintry one, cool and pale.

"I'm never going to have a daughter, Jace. I can't."

Her quiet words were punctuated by sound, soft and low and faraway. A Christmas Eve explosion, perhaps? A signal of death and loss? Disguised for a moment of sheer wonder as the delicate pluck of a celestial harp?

No. This sound, albeit from the heavens, was real. Familiar. And quite expected, given what had become of the pewter sky and drizzling mist. The sky was pewter no more, but charcoal. And sobbing.

"Thunder," Julia murmured with a slight shrug, a wry acknowledgment of the timing of the sound, as if on cue, a dramatic punctuation to the pronouncement she had made, like the crash of cymbals—and symbols—in a Gothic opera. "And lightning."

"And," Jace said, "an impressive amount of rain."

"A torrent."

"A torrent." Jace waited until her winter-sunlight eyes looked from the storm to him. And when they did, he said very softly, "Can't, Julia? Or won't?"

"Both," she confessed. "Emotionally I can't, wouldn't, *won't* imagine it. Even if I could. But since I can't physically, the point is moot."

Can't physically. Dr. Jace Colton considered Julia's definitive assertion, and the diagnoses it implied. Did pregnancy pose a danger to Julia? A risk *beyond* the ravages to her heart should she love, only to lose, another little girl? If so, what physical danger could it be? True, Julia was delicate. Small. In centuries past a woman of her delicacy might well have died during childbirth, her pelvis shattering as her baby, far more robust than she, made its determined way into the world.

Such peripartum deaths occurred still, in places where maternal-infant care did not exist and where nutrition was marginal at best. But such tragedies need not, should not, occur in Kansas. Or the Emerald City. And as for other threats to a mother's health? Certain underlying illnesses conferred substantial risk, and Julia Anne Hayley was thin, yes. And delicate and small. But she was healthy, this ballerina. And strong.

"Why not?"

Jace's question, as soft and low as the distant thunder, evoked a reaction that surprised them both: a sudden blush, snow upon snow, Winnie's rose pink enchantment on Julia's snowy white cheeks.

"I'm sorry, Julia. I didn't mean to embarrass you."

"No, Jace. It's *fine*," she insisted even as her cheeks flushed warm and bright.

She *was* embarrassed. But why? She had confessed so much to him, such emotional intimacies, every raw and naked truth. Jace knew about her desperate sadness, and the drinking she'd done, and the solitary—and unusual—life she'd lived thereafter.

She'd confessed so much to Jace, as if they were soaring still miles above earth, in that enchanted place where he had touched her damp and ravaged lips, and gazed at her as no man ever had . . . as he was gazing now, searching, wanting, demanding—so gently—that she share with him this other intimacy.

This womanly one.

Julia gave herself a mental shake. Beginning with Gran's stroke, she'd become accustomed to, in fact expert at, discussing medical conditions of all kinds, including, and with unembarrassed candor, with the women *and men* who called her at night. They sometimes shared, those women and men, explicit symptoms, intimate concerns . . . which she faithfully and factually transmitted to the physician on call.

And now? To this man, this *doctor,* Julia gave a forthright reply.

"I don't ovulate. I probably did before Winnie's death. My periods then were quite regular. I stopped menstruating, though, after Winnie died. It didn't matter. I scarcely noticed. Then came my answering service job, and the required preemployment medical questionnaire. The history of my amenorrhea prompted a referral to one of the center's gynecologists. My absent periods made perfect sense, she and I decided, given Winnie's death, and the drinking I did, and the eating I didn't do. My periods would return, we agreed, with nutrition and time. But they didn't. Not for a year. Then two. Not ever. Eventually the gynecologist insisted on investigating a little further. We didn't do all the tests she wanted. I really didn't care what the answer was. But based on the data we had, she concluded that I'd stopped ovulating."

"Anovulatory cycles can be treated."

"Yes. I know. But that's where the *can't* becomes the *won't*." Did she need to explain the *won't*? No. Of course not. For here was the man who'd identified Alexis's pregnancy as pure fraud because the faux mother-to-be had forgotten the most essential ingredient of all: fear, terror, amid the joy. The fear, the terror, of loving so much, too much. And losing everything. "I am, after all, afraid of even facing Christmas."

Thunder sounded anew, closer now, an ominous rumbling, a ferocious growl, which they greeted, both of them, with gentle smiles.

Jace spoke without smiling, but with such gentleness still, as lightning illuminated the night gray sky.

"I think, Julia, that you are absolutely fearless."

"No, Jace. I'm *not*. On paper maybe I might *seem* that way. On plans conjured months in advance and oceans away. But now that I'm here . . ."

"I'd be very happy to prove my point. By accompanying you to Canterfields."

"Really?"

"Of course."

"I . . . yes. Thank you. That makes me feel safe."

*Oh, Julia Anne Hayley, you are not safe with me.*

# CHAPTER ELEVEN

*T*here was no longer any need to stroll the festive streets of Mayfair and Knightsbridge. Julia's memories of wandering such streets with Winnie had already been amply evoked. Besides, this sobbing London day would have recalled few memories. Christmastime trips to Topeka and Kansas City had happened only when the weather was fair enough for strolling, when even though the ground might have been blanketed in the soft mauve of freshly fallen snow, the sky sparkled bright emerald with a glowing lavender sun.

No one strolled on this soggy London day. What souls braved the elements did so rushingly, runningly, their umbrellas engaged in valiant if futile battles with the wind.

Jace and Julia saw the breezy battles below as they crossed the skybridge from the hotel to Canterfields.

Canterfields.

The department store's exterior was architecturally subdued, a sedate edifice of mortar and stone. Traditional. British. Stiff upper lip. One expected, given the austere shell, a darkness within, and the dankness of an ancient palace.

But Canterfields within was warm and bright, and shimmering with glass. It felt, in fact, like being inside a prism eight stories high. Crystalline elevators, like bubble lights on a Christmas tree, carried shoppers aloft, and twin escalators crisscrossed the central atrium with garlands of gold, and twinkling icicles of light spilled from mammoth chandeliers and draped the glassy balconies that were everywhere.

A pianist played Christmas carols, and there was a harpist, too, and carolers like minstrels of yore wandered from floor to floor. The store's most welcome guests, the shoppers who flocked to the warmth on this storm-tossed day, sang as well. Their Yuletide purchases long since made, and their holiday feasts already prepared, many came expressly to sing, to celebrate, to enjoy.

Christmas twinkled and glowed throughout the prism. But it was the eighth floor, the top floor, which became from November until January home to the Christmas Shoppe. The world-renowned ornaments remained bountiful throughout the holiday season. Each purchased item was promptly replaced. And nothing, either before Christmas or after, ever went on sale.

Which meant, as Jace and Julia ascended by escalator, their journey became ever more private . . . even as for Julia there was ever-crescendoing dread.

Jace saw her steel herself for what lay ahead. Her muscles grew taut, and her hands curled into bloodless knots of fear, and when they reached the virtually empty boutique, there began the merciless ravaging of her lips.

Clenching his own fists to prevent the touches that pleaded within him to be made, to gentle the devouring—at least—of her lips, Jace commanded himself to do nothing to distract her, and to walk behind not beside, so that she might roam, as he knew she must, wherever her heart led.

Julia led, and Jace followed, a constant, gentle, watchful shadow.

A shepherd.

His one-woman flock was sightless at first, as Winnie had been sightless until her first Christmas. But Julia had to see. Must. She'd made that fearsome and so fearless vow.

Jace, her shadow and her shepherd, sensed the moment when she compelled her eyes to focus. To see. A crystal crèche, a prism within the prism that was Canterfields, glittered before her, catching light, spinning color, shimmering clear and bright and pure.

And Julia's reaction to the pristine image she beheld? Her fists uncurled, her muscles relaxed, and as Jace moved slightly, to see her face, he discovered sunbeams, faint but true, aglow amid the lavender clouds.

And her lips, devoured no more, smiled softly, and so lovingly. At Winnie, he realized. For Winnie.

Winnie was here, in her sister's embrace, cradled by the fists that had unfurled from fearful knots to delicate grace. And now Julia's smiling lips began to move faintly, tremblingly, as in silence she whispered to her sweet little Win of the crystalline splendor of Madonna, of lamb.

And of child.

They stood for a long while before the glittering crèche. They. Julia and Winnie. And the shadow-shepherd who was Jace. And when at last they moved, it was to wander, with such wonder, to another nativity, and another and another, and then to a place that was home to angels, only angels, a glorious confluence of cloth, of crystal, of porcelain, of shell.

These were such busy angels. They floated. They flew. They sang. And played lutes. And flutes. And harps of gold. Some held doves in their angel hands, or roses or candles or ribbons or bells. They cherished those treasures, in their angel hands, as Julia cherished hers.

Julia held her Winnie. And Winnie was holding Julia, too. Her small fingers tangled Julia's hair, which was long again, flowing and bountiful, and Winnie's determined grasp freed one of Julia's hands to point as she whispered, in silence, Look, Winnie, look and see.

They saw so much. Every Canterfields ornament that Winnie had ever loved, and new ones too, wonderful ones, including—a discovery of pure joy—a spun-glass meadow of reindeer. The grazing reindeer were crafted, as the angels had been, of porcelain, of crystal, of cloth. But in lieu of shell, the mother-of-pearl glossiness of angels' wings, some of Santa's magical herd were carved of wood, and of stone.

There were changes to be made of course to these creatures that flew. The Rudolphs that *could* be painted *would* be, in hyacinth with a dash of silver, or *re*painted, all save the bright red nose. Julia would paint Rudolph, and all his magical comrades in flight. Her faintly moving lips made that happy vow.

There were more treasures beyond the meadow of reindeer, and more and more, until they came to the alcove of snowflakes, the flurry of crystal that fell on gossamer threads from a ceiling that was as golden and glowing as Edwina Anne Hayley's nighttime sky.

No purple stars sparkled in this golden heaven. No aquamarine moon. Just snowflakes, shimmering as they'd shimmered in the mauve-and-cream suite, and evoking neither remembrance nor fear—for on Winnie's fuchsia Christmas tree there had been no snowflakes at all.

And now, as in their Eden-Knightsbridge suite, Julia's ballerina hands, *both* of her hands, drifted from snowflake to snowflake, with wonder, with grace, and her eyes shone luminous and bright, and—

Suddenly her hands flew from the crystal snowfall, as if from a Christmas Eve inferno, her delicate fingers ravaged and seared. And her eyes, so luminous, glowed no more. The lavender sunlight clouded. Became gray. And wild. Anguished. Fearful.

And darting, as Winnie's eyes had darted with nystagmus, the rhythmic metronome that had pulsed without surcease until it had been balmed, been calmed, by Christmas.

Julia's wild eyes were cloudy, and darting. But seeing,

Jace realized. *Seeing so clearly.* There was no confusion. None at all.

Only truth.

Only pain.

"Tell me," he urged softly, seeing too, so clearly, the truth. "Tell me what you fear."

As Julia heard his gentle command, she recalled her possible replies when Jace had asked her before to define her fear—that she might scream forever, drink forever, go crazy . . . forever.

In her wildness, Julia almost laughed at the worries that had so recently swirled. Such *trivial* whirlwinds, which she would welcome now, please, with sheer relief.

But it was too late. The true fear, that fearsome reality, was known. And it was far, far worse.

"Julia?"

He was telling her, with his voice and with his eyes, that she could confess anything to him, anything at all, as if they were defying gravity still, flying amid angels and reindeer. And snowflakes. And they were soaring so high in that enchanted stratosphere that even crystals of snow could float forever, fly forever, never melting, never shattering, never falling—to their certain death—on the earth below.

For an extraordinary moment Julia believed it was true. She could confess. She could. She whispered two words before faltering, "I still . . ."

Still, Jace mused. That all important word. Do you love him still? he had asked of her, demanded of her, when she had told him the fiction of her faithless fiancé.

"You see the beauty still, don't you, Julia? The wonder, the purity, the joy?"

Yes. *Yes.* There it was. The unspeakable fear, yet spoken by him, the betrayal so great and so shameful that she had been unable, or perhaps unwilling, to imagine it.

"I do," she whispered. *I see the wonder, the beauty, the joy without Winnie. I see life, my life, without my Winnie.*

"It's okay, Julia."

"No, it's *not*! It *can't* be."

"But it can, Julia. And it is. You loved her," Jace Colton said gently, proudly. "Winnie was so loved. And she's with you. Always."

He seemed so certain, and so very unashamed of her. And she wanted to believe. But she couldn't. Jace was—she knew—soaring with reindeer and angels and snowflakes *still*. In that magnificent illusion. But she was here. Shattered. On earth.

"Winnie *was* here, Jace. Here, in this Christmas Shoppe, with me. She was, and then she . . . wasn't."

Her fists clenched tightly again, even more tightly, so that her nails might dig deeply, punishingly, into the flesh that had dropped Winnie, discarded Winnie, *forgotten* her.

"Winnie was here, Julia, even when you were touching the snowflakes. She was with you, still with you, when you began to see Christmas through your own eyes." Those lovely eyes stopped beating as he spoke, as Winnie's nystagmus had vanished forever with that first Christmas, that first awakening. Was Julia awakening, too? Perhaps. For her lavender eyes were searching now, wanting to believe, wondering if she dared—as Jace himself had wondered, on that midnight clear, if he could hear sleigh bells in the sky. Jace hadn't dared. Had been unable to believe. But she was Julia. "Winnie was with you, Julia. She *is* with you. She's a wondrous and wonderful part of who you are and will always be. It's all right to go on with your life. *All right.* I think you know that. In fact, I think that's why you came here today, fearful but so fearless . . . because you knew it was time at last to face that truth."

Had she known, subconsciously, what she would find, would face, at Canterfields on Christmas Eve? Maybe. For there had been chapters in her books on grief that had forecast precisely this devastating realization, that there would come a time when she could go on without Winnie. When she could make new memories, happy memories, without her little Win.

The chapters had made no sense, seemed impossible, *were* impossible.

Until now.

"Oh, Jace."

It was a whisper of despair, bewildered still, yet believing. *Daring* to. And, as Jace gazed at her, bewildered yet so brave, the image came to him again of the snow globe he once had seen: the solitary ballerina, encased in glass, dancing in moonlight, twirling in snow.

Moonlight glowed here, soft and gold, and crystal snowflakes sparkled overhead. She wasn't dancing, this ballerina. Not yet. But she was solitary no more, in glass no longer, and now they were touching—these dancers—

touching at last. And they were dancing, at last, as they touched.

Julia's tears spilled as Jace held her, as they swayed so slowly beneath moonglow and snow. He whispered too, reassurances that caressed her weeping soul even as his lips caressed very softly her silken black hair.

Julia trembled in his embrace, trembled, fluttered. And finally fluttered away. It was a short but monumental flight. And a purposeful one. To look at him. To *see* him. To face him as courageously as she had faced Christmas.

She was searching again, but with wonder, with awakening, a *new* awakening, for there was new magic now, a different splendor in which she might dare, this fearless ballerina, to believe.

She looked from the dark green magic of his eyes to the lips that had whispered such gentle reassurances, and to the glittering green splendor again.

"Jace?"

Jace forced himself to see the scant distance between them for what it truly was—a vast abyss of fire, its searing flames lashing his eyes and scorching his throat.

"Bed," he whispered hoarsely, harshly.

Julia didn't hear the harshness, at least not its burning edge. She heard only, this awakening woman, the desire that smoldered beneath. And wonder shimmered anew. "Bed?"

"You're exhausted. And, I think, you can sleep now. And should. And when you awaken, we'll play a little gin rummy if you like. A lot of gin rummy."

And we'll eat, Jace amended silently. *You'll* eat.

He would order, while she slept, thermoses of piping hot chocolate, and macadamia nuts—surely the luxury hotel had a luxuriant supply—and platters of whatever else would safely keep until she awakened.

And while Julia slept, Jace Colton would remind himself of the truth. Julia had come to London to face angels. And she had. She had.

Angels. And snowflakes.

And he had come to London why? To face demons, as he did each and every Christmas—and as he was destined, each and every Christmas, to do.

Demons. And fire.

Jace would remind himself, as Julia slept, what demons did to angels . . . and what fire, a vast and ravenous abyss of flames, would do to the delicate perfection of snow.

# CHAPTER TWELVE

$\mathcal{J}$ace watched the rain as she slept, and as daylight surrendered to darkness, he saw the gentle caress of sunlight through the clouds and the rainbow, her Christmas rainbow, after all.

Julia didn't see the pastel arch. She slept. Perhaps she dreamed.

But Jace saw the shimmering twilight promise sent by the heavens for her. And he saw, too, what that same sky had in store for him. Torment. For as he watched and blackness fell, the storm clouds floated away, like vanishing ghosts, creating for him—and his demons—a midnight clear.

*The* midnight clear. As bright as that long-ago night. As glittering. As aglow.

The rain-washed streets below became a mirror as perfect as the icy Loganville lake, and in the glistening reflection, now as then, Jace saw a golden moon and silver stars.

Very soon he would hear the soft thud that had shattered the peace, and the golden mirror would shine ever brighter, and the crimson that was neither shooting star nor Santa's sleigh would slice its blood-red slash.

Jace had been so helpless on that distant night. But he was in absolute control on this. The ancient images came only when he permitted them to, and with a pace and fury that he alone prescribed, and it was solely in his power to decide how long they would remain to haunt, to taunt, to sear.

He kept at bay for the moment the remembered sound of the devastating thud. And he challenged himself, who had dared not believe in chiming sleigh bells, to even more magic.

Could he see, on this midnight clear, Winnie's sky? A heaven so golden and so pure that even the most blazing earthly inferno would be lost, vanquished, in its glow? And might there be in that pristine gold an aquamarine moon amid twinkling purple stars?

Could he see such enchantment? Would he dare? And if so, what then?

"Hi."

The voice was a mirage, as silvery as phantom sleigh bells, as delicate as gossamer whispers of a celestial harp. It was an angel's voice, magical, impossible.

And quite real.

She wore mauve, this angel, a luxuriant robe provided by the hotel for its guests. The Eden-Knightsbridge bathrobe was large on her, a billowy cocoon, and even more modesty, pale blue and flannel, ruffled at her wrists and throat.

"Hi," Jace greeted. And as moonlight illuminated her lovely face, he said, "You slept."

"I did." She had slept, and she had dreamed. It was her dreams that awakened her, and made such urgent commands. Go to him, they instructed. Yes, with your hair sleep-tousled and dressed only in nightgown and slippers and robe. Find him *now*. And what Julia found on their private balcony beneath the midnight sky was this man, taut with torment, yet smiling so gently for her. "Jace? Will you tell me?"

"Tell you what?"

"Whatever it is that makes you face Christmas alone. Makes you believe that you *must*. It has something to do with bells, doesn't it? And a little girl? I've seen, I think, that much."

That much, Jace thought. *So* much. Julia had seen far more than anyone else ever had, ever cared to, ever dared. True, he permitted only the most fleeting glimpses of the ice and fire within—calculated glimpses designed to send fair warning to anyone who ventured near. Proceed at your own peril.

Which no one did. No one *wanted* to. Not even, especially, the women who wanted his passion, and the pleasure he could give. Jace Colton's lovers stayed very far away from his heart, from his soul. Precisely where he wanted them to be.

He had never told anyone about Loganville. Had never wanted to. And did he want to now? Yes, and no. Jace wanted Julia to know of Mary Beth, a mother as fiercely loving as Julia had been, and of Grace, a precious little girl, like Winnie.

But Jace's angels, the fierce one and the golden one, had perished too young in a terror of flames. And Julia's angel? Her beloved Winnie? She had survived against all odds because of Julia, and she had fluttered away, loved and at peace, in her sister's arms.

"I know something terrible happened," Julia said in the sudden silence. "Something for which you feel responsible, I think, as if there was something you could have done, should have. Even though, I believe, that isn't true."

She was imagining, Jace supposed, a Christmastime tragedy at the trauma center—the emergent arrival of a little girl, like Sophie or Winnie or Grace, clutching a much-loved cotton animal that chimed, and dying, dying. And who *had* died, but might have survived, had Dr. Jace Colton acted more quickly, more decisively, to save her.

Julie was prepared to hear such a story. And to forgive it. *To forgive him.*

And? Jace had to tell her. Everything. She needed to know about the searing fire, the bitter cold, the brooding darkness that dwelled between . . . so that she might understand, and surely she would, that not every crystal of ice was destined to the delicate perfection of snow.

"I was thirteen and on my way from Savannah to Seattle."

"Seattle?"

"Yes. The Emerald City. The one place on the planet where I was quite certain my father would not be."

"You and your father didn't get along?"

"I never knew him, Julia. No one did, including my mother . . ."

$\mathcal{H}$is name, he claimed, was Jace Colton. Which was a lie. The first of so many. He was the sole heir to a Seattle shipping fortune, he said, the black sheep of an eminently respectable family, its proverbial prodigal son.

He'd spent the past decade, since being expelled from his father's Ivy League alma mater, racing cars in Europe. He was precariously low on funds, he confessed with the charm that disarmed even the most savvy of skeptics. He'd managed to lose most of his trust-fund allotment for the year at the gaming tables in Monte Carlo.

It *wasn't* a big deal, he insisted. Well, he amended with his devastating smile, assuming he didn't starve to death in the next ten months—at which point, the day he turned thirty-one, the entire trust, not just the miserly allowance he received, would be his. His inheritance was iron-clad. No attorney on earth—not even an army of same—could prevent, or even delay, the transfer of wealth.

Jace Colton told his con, his lie, to Sheila Shay. And was the Savannah beauty an easy mark, the most susceptible, most gullible, of Southern belles? No. For two reasons. First, the con artist's art was so perfect, so perfected, that he needed no longer to be excessively careful about the victims he chose. And second, he wanted Sheila, wanted *her,* even though she was a risky target, the riskiest ever, as worldly, as manipulative, as greedy as he.

Sheila was an exotic dancer. A stripper. And a hooker, too? No. Never. Her body was for sale only as a work of art, a treasure to be admired but not touched. Sheila disdained the men who paid to watch her strip, especially the kind who frequented the sleazy bars in which she'd worked when she was underage. But Sheila had fled from poverty, and she had vowed never to be poor, not starving poor, ever again, and the money—even at the low-rent bars—was good, and so unbelievably easy.

Eventually both money and clientele improved. Sheila was dancing at a private club in Savannah, upscale and posh, when the man claiming to be Jace Colton entered her life.

Sheila wasn't the only citizen of Savannah who was fooled by him. The wealthy men for whom she danced, and who embraced her without touching, embraced Jace Colton as well. He was one of them, the elite gentlemen of Savannah believed. Born rich and destined to become even richer. And the Seattle shipping heir was beyond them, too, for he was permitted into the bed of Sheila Shay. For free. And they had not been, none of them, no matter how much they'd been willing to pay.

The Savannah gentry invited the impostor to sail with them, and golf and gamble and carouse, and they believed, as did Sheila, that Jace Colton was thrilled about her pregnancy.

The timing was perfect. His thirty-first birthday and Sheila's due date were virtually one. As soon as the new mother felt like traveling, he promised, all three would go to Seattle, claim his millions, and marry in the family mansion on Magnolia Bluff.

In the weeks before his son's birth, the charming con convinced an array of bedazzled bank clerks at Sheila's several banks to provide him with the documents necessary to add his name to Sheila's accounts. The balances on the accounts were impressive, substantial. The girl who'd fled from poverty had worked hard and saved fervently.

He and Sheila were about to wed, he told the clerks. Even though, he added charmingly, disarmingly, his bride-to-be was already quite pregnant. And on bed rest. Doctor's orders. Would it be possible for him to take the requisite papers home to her to sign? And return them the following day?

Jace Colton was an accomplished forger. This particular forgery, the one that would steal everything that Sheila had, took place while Sheila was at work. At the club. She was in her eighth month, and no longer dancing, although there were club members who wished she would, who surprised themselves with such a wish.

Sheila was hostessing instead. And sometimes the woman who had disdained from clients even the slightest touch permitted these wealthy men who were her friends, and Jace's friends, to feel her unborn baby dance and kick.

Jace Colton—liar, impostor, thief—left Savannah

while Sheila was in labor with his son. And he left her with? Anger. Rage. His baby. And nothing else.

In the beginning, and for a while, Sheila regarded the baby boy as valuable collateral, the flesh-and-blood heir of the man who she still believed *was* an heir. It was with that baby, that son, that she would compel the deadbeat father to pay and pay.

And pay.

But her baby's father could not be found, not even when Sheila hired one of Savannah's premier private investigators, whom she paid with her lush and luscious body. She had no choice. The man she'd loved, and now loathed, had left her with no choice.

That man, however, that Jace Colton, did not exist and never had. There was not even in the upper echelons of Seattle society a black-sheep heir to millions, shipping or otherwise, who fit the impostor's description but bore a different name.

There was just that other Jace Colton, Sheila Shay's illegitimate son, the bastard child she did not want. So when at age thirteen Sheila's unwanted son announced that he was leaving Savannah, she offered neither protest nor concern.

Jace Colton, the son, chose as his destination the Emerald City, the one place, he was quite certain, where his con-artist father would not be. But Jace never made it to Seattle. His hitchhiked journey took him to Loganville. To eleven months of joy—and worry—and that midnight clear, the flying sleigh bells he could not hear, did not dare, and the sound, soft and low, that might have been a celestial harp, but was instead an earthbound signal of destruction and death.

Jace had raced toward the inferno, a desperate dash of fear, and he had found, upon reaching the searing fireball on Bluebird Lane, Loganville's emergency response units—fire engines and police—and Loganville's worried citizenry as well.

Save two.

Grace and Mary Beth were inside, *within* the blaze that raged despite waterfall upon waterfall arching overhead. The flames puffed with disdain where the falls of water dampened but failed to douse the fire, and sent defiant plumes of smoke into the midnight sky.

Jace ran toward that smoke, those flames, not breaking his frantic stride even for an instant of sheer hope to search the crowd for Mary Beth and Grace. He knew where they were.

He *knew*.

The house had become a skeleton, its front-porch entrance, so recently wreathed and welcoming, now a massive skull.

No one could stop him. Or so he believed.

But just before his leap into the gaping jaw of death, he was captured, imprisoned, by the fierce might of two grown and anguished men.

Rawley and Troy. Their faces glistened, these men who had loved Mary Beth, damp with flaming heat and spraying water.

Their eyes glistened too.

And their voices, when they spoke, were clogged,

choked with emotion and with ash, the dark black snowflakes that filled the air.

Troy spoke first, addressing him as Sam, not knowing, as Jace already knew, that he would never be Sam again. "There's nothing you can do, Sam. *Nothing.*"

"But they're *inside.*"

"Yes. But they aren't alive."

"You don't *know* that!"

"We do know," Rawley's tear-and-cinder voice asserted. "We do. I went in as far as I could and—"

"I can go *farther.*"

"No, Sam. You can't. They're dead, son. Grace and Mary Beth are dead."

Rawley's strangled voice was as certain, as stark, as death.

Jace replied with quiet calm. "Let go of me. Please."

The two men believed they heard acceptance in the calm voice, and comprehension, too. The bereaved teen would remain where he was, with them, and when it was possible to go inside, they would go together, a trio of love, to recover the charred bodies.

Troy and Rawley released in unison their imprisoning grasp.

But Jace Colton, son of the con artist—and liar, impostor, thief—deceived the men who held him, the ancient rivals who'd been bonded by the summertime fire in which Mary Beth's mother had died and who were bonded still, fiercely bonded, on this Christmas Eve night.

The instant he was free, Jace charged anew the blazing skull.

It was Rawley, the star football player whose career had been shattered by his prom-night fight with Troy, who stopped him, tackled him, at the very edge of the flames. Jace fell to the snow, feeling its coolness on his cheeks even as the fire scorched nearby, and Rawley fell on top of him.

Struggle for Jace was futile. Rawley was bigger, heavier, and Loganville's chief of police was empowered by decades of emotion. Decades of loving Mary Beth.

Rawley's whispered words, hoarse and harsh, were identical to what Troy's had been. "There's nothing you can do, Sam. *Nothing*."

Yes there is, Jace thought. *I can die.*

"*What* happened?" Julia asked so softly on this London midnight clear.

*I didn't die. Not all of me. Just my heart and my soul.*

Jace's silent answer came even as he realized that Julia's question, the first words she had spoken since his story began, made no sense.

He hadn't told her, of course, of his desperate rush toward smoke and flames. Julia might interpret, might so generously *mis*interpret, such a frantic dash as heroic on his part. But he'd told her that Troy and Rawley were at the burning house by the time he arrived, and that the two men had told him that it was already too late.

Too late. Jace had spoken those anguished words

aloud. Hadn't he? Here, on this private balcony, where no one could hear him but she?

He had been speaking to her. To Julia. But he'd been staring at the sky. The moon. The velvet. The stars.

Now he turned to her, to the eyes that had been so wild at Canterfields, until she'd faced without fear both angels and snow. The lavender was steady, and clear and true, as she looked into the darkness of his soul—and brightened, this gifted artist, the savage blackness to shimmering gold.

Gold, *where there was none.*

"They died, Julia. Grace and Mary Beth died."

"I know," she whispered. "But why? I mean . . . you said the sound you heard might have been an explosion. Was it?"

"I don't know. I left Loganville that night."

The grown men who loved Mary Beth and Grace would not permit the unworthy shepherd to die with his abandoned flock in the seething flames. So he would die, he decided, in ice. As soon as possible. He wanted to be dead, needed to be dead, long before it was safe to remove from the house their beloved remains.

Voices had spoken to Jace Colton as he walked away. Sympathetic voices. Familiar ones.

Stay with us, Sam, Dinah's family urged. As did the parents of the Loganville High School cheerleader he had saved. And so too Loganville's librarian Mrs. Bearce. And Troy and Carolyn, who were to be wed in just two days, a Christmastime wedding that was to have been celebrated by the entire town and at which Grace Alysia Quinn would have been the flower girl.

And did Rawley Ramsey offer shelter, too? Sanctuary to the boy he'd just deprived of a fiery death?

No. Rawley knew perhaps, as Jace knew, that there was no sanctuary, no shelter, anywhere.

Except here. Now. On this moonlit balcony. With her.

"You left?" Julia echoed at last. "That night?"

"Yes. That night."

"So you don't know what happened?"

"I do know what happened, Julia. I broke the promise I'd made to Grace, and while I was gone Grace and Mary Beth died."

"But it wasn't your *fault*. You can't possibly believe that it was. The ashes in the fireplace were cold, you said, before you left the house, and you *know* that was true, Jace, because you'd so carefully checked. And the Christmas tree lights were off, *had* been for two hours, and the batteries for the *many* smoke detectors were new, you said, replaced at Thanksgiving, as Mary Beth always so compulsively did, because of the way her mother had died. And it's really unlikely isn't it, *inconceivable,* that fumes from whatever small amount of gas you *might* have spilled as you filled the generator could have sparked an explosion? Especially since you probably didn't spill any gas at all, and the cans, like the generator itself, were in the garage? *If* gas fumes caused the explosion, and that's likely, I suppose, it must have been from a massive leak within the house. A *rupture* that happened *after* you left and which was so sudden, so catastrophic, that even Mary Beth, who was being Santa, couldn't detect it in time."

She was ferocious, this angel in pale blue ruffles and billowing mauve. Ferocious, impassioned, for him.

Jace told the angel the truth.

"In the beginning, during that first desperate year of grieving that you know so well, I believed it was my fault, that there was something I should have detected before leaving and had somehow missed. Eventually, though, I realized that what you've suggested was undoubtedly true. Whatever happened was sudden, catastrophic, and occurred after I was gone. I'm not to blame for the explosion. I know that. But if I'd been in my first-floor bedroom, as I'd promised Grace that I would be, I might have been able to save them."

"Or," Julia said quietly, "you might have died."

"I might have," Jace conceded. "We might have died together."

As she might have died with Winnie and Edwin and Gran, *would* have had she visited the cemetery during those winter months of such despair. But Julia hadn't visited.

Her mother's champagne had not permitted her to do so.

Did she truly owe her very survival to the golden bubbles? Or was there something deep within—enabled by the alcohol perhaps, encouraged by its floating intoxication—but basically, essentially, her?

Yes, Julia thought. And that essence, a gift from Gran

since the moment of her birth, was one of hope, of love, of joy.

Did such hopefulness bubble deep within Jace? A fountain of joy that compelled him to survive even those most perilous months?

No. What had compelled Jace to survive, his essence, was stark not hopeful, and disciplined and fierce. And its mandate was harsh and clear. He could not die. He had promises to keep. To patients, to soldiers, the most gravely wounded, the sickest of the sick—even as his broken promise to Grace would haunt him always.

Julia had no such haunting memories. But . . . "If I'd gone shopping one day, and promised Gran and Winnie that I'd be back in an hour but didn't return for two—because the clouds were so golden in the forest-green sky that I simply lost track of time—and during that second hour a gas line ruptured and they died, I would have realized, I suppose, *eventually,* that it wasn't truly my fault. But I would have felt *so* responsible. And you know what, Jace Colton?"

He knew nothing at this moment except her loveliness. And all he saw, at this moment, was enchantment.

The moonlight on her face was the softest gold, and her own star glowed in her lavender eyes, and her cheeks flushed roses on snow, and her dream-tousled hair was the black velvet of the midnight sky.

But as he gazed at her, Jace saw other colors, too, a treasure trove of gemstones that sparkled, glittered, on her glossy black hair. Emeralds glowed from an aquamarine moon. And sapphires, too. And amethysts from twinkling purple stars. Rubies shimmered, so many rubies, gleaming reflections of a flying crimson sleigh.

If he turned to the heavens would he see the magic of Winnie's sky? Yes. *Yes.*

But Jace did not turn. For the true magic stood before him, lovely and fierce.

For him.

"What?" he whispered at last, his voice touched with wonder.

"You would have told me that I'd suffered enough, *punished* myself enough, and that it was time for me to forgive myself, *past* time ... especially since, you would have told me, Gran and Winnie would have forgiven me, would have never blamed me in the first place ... just as Grace and Mary Beth would never *ever* have blamed you." As Julia's head tilted, the precious gemstones spilled away. But the lavender, the roses, the snow remained. The magic remained. "Wouldn't you have told me that?"

"Yes. But ..."

"And then you would have held me." *And danced with me.*

It was she, lovely and fierce, who reached for him, who offered to him her mauve-and-ruffled embrace.

And they danced, swaying slowly in moonlight on this midnight clear. And eventually, in moonlight, Julia fluttered away, just a little, as she had in Canterfields, that she might see his face.

And when she saw that moonlit face, she spoke the

word he had spoken so harshly in the gold-and-crystal alcove of snow.

"Bed," she whispered to his dark green eyes. There was wonder in the glittering fire. And desire, *such desire*. And such worry. "Unless you don't want . . ."

"I want, Julia." *I want, I need—you—desperately.*

But Jace needed, desperately too, more desperately, to see again the fiery abyss, to be lashed by its searing flames as he told her again and again, until she truly understood, what such a raging blaze would do to snowflakes.

And angels.

But Jace couldn't see the inferno between them.

He could not even see the abyss.

He saw only lavender, only roses, only snow.

Only her.

And what did Julia see? The dark fire. The ice green torment.

"I can't get pregnant," she reminded him softly.

"I know." *I know, and I wish*—the selfish, impossible wish should have ignited the inferno he could not see, should have filled with fury the hidden abyss. But Jace saw, still, only her. Generous and lovely . . . and pure.

"Jace?"

"I want you, Julia. More than you can possibly know. But I wonder if you should permit this impulse to float for a while?"

"No."

"No?"

"No," she repeated quietly, decisively. "And it isn't an impulse."

*All the journeys of my heart, you see, from love to loss, and sorrow to joy, have been made so that on this night, Jace Colton, I may journey at last to you.*

# CHAPTER THIRTEEN

*I*t was new for both of them. But especially for the man with such vast experience. And no experience at all. Jace had never known a wanting like this, a desire so powerful. Nor had he felt, ever, the need to cherish, this need to cherish . . . her.

And Julia, who had never been touched, not in this way, knew without experience about love, about loving, and she welcomed his passion with wonder and no fear.

Never fear.

The fear belonged to Jace, that he might crush her with his desire. Frighten her with his need. But Julia was neither crushed nor frightened—she was fearless— and Jace was gentle, far more gentle than she needed him to be.

But Jace needed to be so very gentle with her.

They loved, and loved, and loved. And when they slept, it was entwined as one.

Jace Colton, for whom sleep when it came was dreamless—if he was lucky—or afire with nightmares when he was not, slept peacefully with Julia. One with Julia.

And with Julia he dreamed wondrous dreams.

They loved and slept and dreamed and talked. And touched. Always.

Always touched.

Julia asked him, as they touched, to tell her about Loganville before that Christmas Eve. The eleven months of joy before the blaze.

It had been hidden for so long, the Loganville happiness. But with her, for her, Jace painted a portrait as vivid, and extraordinary and rare, as Julia's brilliant tableaux of Winnie and Gran.

In words, in emotion, and in the glorious colors of love, Jace painted Grace. And Mary Beth. And Grace's best friend Dinah, and all the other children in his care.

Jace painted Sam the kitten, too. In shades of gray. For Sam the kitten had been gray—but shimmering, then and now. Troy appeared in Jace's vibrant portrait, and Rawley, and Mrs. Bearce, the town librarian with whom he and his little charges had spent so many safe and happy afternoons.

Jace took Julia, in emotion and in words, to Loganville's sapphire blue lake, and he confessed to the terror he'd felt amid the gleeful splashes of summer and the wintry twirl of skates. He told her of carving pumpkins, too, and of the accident on Sycamore, and . . .

"*You are so beautiful.*" The whisper, his, was low and soft, and it came as he traced a map of Loganville—Julia wanted to see such a map—on her snow-white palm.

Julia looked from an invisible intersection to him.

"In case," Jace clarified gently, "you didn't know. I'm not talking about your heart, Julia, or your soul. You know the beauty there, and that it's all that counts. But just for the record, the shell that houses that lovely heart, that beautiful soul, is exquisitely breathtaking, too."

Julia frowned briefly, consideringly. Then she smiled. Glowed. "I'm very lucky," she said. "I have Winnie's hair and Gran's eyes."

Julia had frowned, but not blushed, at Jace's compliment. But as he gazed at her now, with such intimacy and such pride, pinkness bloomed, and with a soft shrug she looked anew at her palm.

"Okay," she murmured, pointing to the place still warm from his touch. "Loganville General is here, on Crystal Mountain Road, and the library is where?"

They journeyed on her palm to Loganville Library, and to the ice-and-sapphire lake, and finally, and it was such a terribly difficult journey for him to make, even on her snowy palm, to Bluebird Lane.

"*You are so beautiful,*" Julia whispered as that journey neared its fiery end. "In case you didn't know."

Jace did know, of course. He was, after all, the bastard son of seducer and seductress, of the lush and sultry Sheila and the sexy and sensual liar-impostor-thief. Indeed the love child, the hated child, possessed the most stunning features of each.

"You're very lucky," Julia told the man with the gorgeous shell. "You have Grace's goodness, and Mary Beth's grace."

*J*ulia's London itinerary wasn't forgotten, merely dismissed, save for her return visit to Canterfields.

She wanted to return, needed to, for Winnie. *Bye-bye Kismus.*

And for Jace. *Hello, Christmas. Hello, hello.*

Jace, too, wanted to return to Canterfields. For Winnie. And for her.

Each knew in advance the gift for the other, and each confessed in advance that there was such a gift. So when they reached the Christmas Shoppe, they didn't separate, did not unclasp for a moment the hands entwined as one.

Julia's gift for Jace was a Canterfields angel, porcelain, winged, and strumming with delicacy the silver strings of a harp of gold.

It would have been from anyone else a cruel reminder of that midnight clear. But from Julia the ornament was a promise, the luminous certainty that there would be for Jace another midnight clear . . . when he, even he, would hear the glorious chime of a celestial harp.

Jace knew the meaning of Julia's gift, just as she knew why he chose the Canterfields snowflake for her, the very crystal she had touched, first, on Christmas Eve, when she'd seen the wonder, caressed the splendor without her little Win.

Jace and Julia returned after Canterfields to their Eden-

Knightsbridge suite. And there they stayed, in their private world, and touched, and talked, and loved.

And, in their private world, Jace Colton laughed. It was very soft, Jace's laugh, and deep and low. And new. Never heard before. It sounded like desire with a smile. And it felt, inside him, like lavender starlight aglow in his veins.

Another sound, so far from laughter, intruded, too. Once. It was a trilling telephone, and it brought to their private world a message, and a plea, about war.

Jace's team would be going to the Balkans as planned. The precise destination had changed, however, to a place which until Christmas Eve had been a haven of relative calm within the region of such turmoil.

Yes, ancient enmities had smoldered in that Balkan locale. The entrenched rage of generations past. But for a while, decades, neither side of the centuries-old dispute had been significantly armed or meticulously organized, and children whose ancestors had slain each other played as friends. And there had been marriages even. Even marriages.

Any illusion of a lasting peace had vanished with the Christmas Eve massacre, a slaughter executed with state-of-the-art weaponry and strategy that bespoke funding as well as guidance from an outside source.

Multinational organizations had responded to the urgent pleas of the citizens who had survived, dispatching neutral observers to analyze, to assess, and to recommend—eventually—the appropriate superpower response. It would take some time to determine which side to choose. Was the newly armed faction the brutal aggressor? Or had the perennial victim finally found a way to fight back?

The politics were uncertain. But there was no doubt that the victims were in desperate need of medical help. The organization for which Jace volunteered would be sending in a team, Jace's team, as soon as it was safe enough to do so, as early perhaps as the twenty-ninth, which was three days sooner than they'd originally been scheduled to leave.

Would Jace be willing to be on call as of that date?

Yes. He would. Of course. And why not? Julia was, after all, leaving at dawn on that very day.

Jace was going to war, and Julia was going to the Emerald City, and the only intrusion after that phone call was time, the invisible clock that was moving—oh, it was racing—toward that December dawn.

Too soon it was the evening of departure—of hers, at least. She needed to pack, a fast and easy task for the most part, her clothes, and a more deliberate one when it came to her treasures, the gifts from him, the Canterfields snowflake and the glossy white card.

It was his business card, elegant and engraved, and quite impersonal on its shiny front. *Dr. Jace Colton,* it read, and *Grace Memorial Trauma Center* and address and phone and fax.

But there was intimacy on the back, and gentleness and care. His home address, handwritten by him, and his unlisted phone, and *Garek McIntyre* with another Windy City phone number as well.

There was intimacy in Jace's voice, too, and gentleness and care, when he'd given her the card. "If there's anything you need, Julia, anything *ever,* I want you to call. And if you can't reach me, call Garek."

"Who is?"

"My attorney."

"Whom you trust."

"Whom I trust," Jace said. "Absolutely."

Julia put both treasures in her purse. The snowflake, snuggled safely in a side pocket within its Canterfields case, and the business card in her wallet within its own plastic sheath.

There. She was done. It was time, these few minutes that had seemed so long, to return to Jace. For the rest of the night. But Julia didn't immediately return. She took a few precious moments to write, in her artist's script, on a sheet of stationery provided by the hotel.

Jace stood near the teal blue tree, its white lights aglow and casting rainbows through snowflakes onto its silvery bows. But he wasn't looking at the Yuletide décor. He was watching for her, waiting for her.

His gentle smile when she appeared said that it had been so long, too long. He had missed her.

"All packed?" he asked.

"All packed." Julia handed him the mauve notepaper. "I wanted you to have my address in Seattle, and my phone number, too."

Jace took the sheet of mauve, but his smile vanished as he looked, perhaps without seeing, at the written words.

Julia looked too, and seeing so clearly, at his hands, the

gentleness with which he held the paper even as, it seemed, the gifted surgeon wanted to crumble, to crush.

As she watched, Jace let the paper fall, let it drift delicately, like snowfall, onto the nearby mauve couch. Mauve on mauve. Snow on snow.

Then, his hands free, he reached for hers, holding them with the same gentleness with which he'd held the paper, despite the power—and the torment—that churned within.

And his eyes, when he looked at her, were gentle. And tormented, too.

"I'll never be in Seattle," he said. Nor, his solemn gaze told her, would he ever write. Or call.

His voice and his gaze were soft, tender.

But his words were devastating nonetheless. To her heart, to her soul. Even though she'd known, hadn't she, from the very start that this time in London was all that she and Jace would ever have?

Yes, she admonished herself. *Of course* she had known.

True, Jace hadn't told her in words. Or so explicitly until now. But he'd been telling her in every other way, eloquently and intimately, *from the start.*

The gentle good-bye had been there always. In his eyes, in his passion, in his touch. It was a reluctant farewell, a marriage of longing and regret. But it was fierce, even as it was tender. Ferocious in its resolve.

Even the Canterfields snowflake he'd given her had been a forecast of farewell. But, the crystal promised, the memories of this Christmas would shimmer always, catching light and spinning rainbows.

And even now, with his fierce and tender gaze, Jace was making that shimmering promise to her.

"Julia," he whispered. *Lovely Julia.* "This time we've had has been . . . wonderful. Extraordinary." *Magical,* thought the man who did not believe, had dared not believe, in magic. "But not real." *It can't have been real.* "Not in any real-world way. It's been a time out of time. Without time."

Yes, she thought. We've been soaring in the stratosphere, you and I, in a magical place where angels sing and reindeer fly and snowflakes never melt.

"I know, Jace. I understand."

"Do you?"

"Yes. I do." *I do.* "You wanted this time, Jace. Our time together. I know you did. But you didn't, you don't, want more. And that's *fine.* It doesn't diminish what we've had, or what you've given me."

"I haven't given you anything, Julia, that wasn't already yours."

"But you helped me find the hopeful girl I once was, the one who'd been raised with such love. I thought she'd died. Or maybe I just believed she *should* have. But she's alive again, living and so very hopeful, thanks to you."

"You would have found her without me. You came to London to find her."

His voice was cold, harsh, for himself. Toward himself. Even as it remained warm and tender for her.

And when she took a steadying breath, his heat, his

fire, warmed her still, and glittered deep within her as she spoke. "But I wouldn't have found, without you, the woman she's become . . . a woman in love."

*Oh, Julia, do not love me. Not me. Even though, my Julia, I love you, too.*

Jace had planned on this final night together to tell her of his love. *I love you, Julia. I love you.* After which, he had planned, he would explain why their love, why *his* love, could not be. Why this magic—yes, this *magic*—could not last.

Because of him. Who he was. A man who needed often, and often desperately, to be alone and silent for hours on end. And who worked beyond exhaustion in the hope that when sleep came he would not dream. And who even when not awakened drenched and gasping by his nightmares knew so well the demons within.

They were quite ravenous, his demons. Relentless. And they lived quite happily, in fact flourished, in the uninhabitable extremes of fire and ice that were his soul.

Yes, for these days and nights of magic, of love, Julia had kept his demons at bay. And he'd wanted, needed desperately, to have her with him. Always. He had not wished, even for an instant, for solitude.

Julia had illuminated every darkness within him, flooded it with pure gold. Her gold. And she'd at once banked the fire and melted the ice, until all that remained was a glorious warmth.

But it couldn't last. This magic. Which is what Jace had planned to tell her on this night. Gently, patiently, until she understood. And agreed.

*I love you, my Julia. But I'm damaged, my precious love, far too damaged for you, for us, for this fragile wondrous joy.*

Jace had believed he could convince her. But that was folly, he realized now. She wouldn't be convinced, would *never* agree, once she knew of his love.

She wouldn't leave their love. Not Julia. And she would fight *so hard* for him. She would not see, his lovely Julia, that loving a damaged angel, her Winnie, was quite different from the danger of loving a man like him.

So she would fight. But she would not win, couldn't possibly, and it would destroy her. His demons would. His nightmares would. *He* would.

And now Julia had told him that she understood. Even though she didn't understand at all. But it was *fine,* she'd told him; this lie she believed, the fiction that he'd wanted this time with her . . . but no more.

Julia believed the lie, accepted it, *embraced* it, for she was Julia, who treasured every moment of love she was given no matter the loss, the death, that inevitably came.

She was accepting his good-bye without anger, without hurt, cherishing what they'd had and not fighting for more.

So Jace Colton permitted the lie to survive.

And he told her, as he cupped in his hands her lovely face, the truth. "I wanted this time together, Julia. Very much. I will never forget it . . . or you."

# CHAPTER FOURTEEN

*J*ulia slept during the flight from London to O'Hare. Slept without dreams. But with decisions, made during sleep, certain and confident and clear.

She wouldn't be connecting on to Seattle, the decisions told her. Not today. She'd be flying to Denver instead, where she'd spend the night, in an airport motel, painting in pastel watercolors the Tierney crèche and the just-born Floppy. And in the morning, she'd drive a rental car to Loganville to learn the truth of what had happened on that Christmas Eve.

It would be easy to do. There would be articles in the *Loganville Star*. Written, she imagined, by Troy. Loving eulogies for Grace and Mary Beth. But with salient facts as well: the gas line rupture that was so sudden, and so mercifully massive, that Grace had never awakened from her sugarplum dreams, and Mary Beth, who'd been filling the stockings that hung by the chimney with care, had been smiling even as she died.

There was nothing you could have done, she would write in the note that would accompany the articles to Jace's Windy City home. Nothing except die. And they wouldn't have wanted that, Jace. You *know* they wouldn't have.

Or maybe she would send no note. Jace would know, he already knew, every gentle reassurance she could give. But maybe, when he saw the truth in black and white, it would set him free, and he could go on, with remembrance, with celebration . . . and to love.

Julia wished love for him, the wonderful man who'd given her such gifts. Love, and peace.

If she could give him the peace, she would.

And if she discovered in Loganville that an ember had smoldered in the fireplace despite Jace's compulsive search? Or that despite his careful watering a parched pine needle had sparked to flame?

Then she alone would know.

*B*ut that wasn't what she'd find, she told herself as she drove the following morning beneath a sparkling Colorado sky. It was the pale blue shade of winter, she realized, that Winnie'd always colored seafoam green.

The Rocky Mountain air was pure and clear. And cold despite the sun. Just as it had been, she thought, on that long-ago day when a starving and exhausted hitchhiker walked from the interstate into town and found warmth and welcome and love and pain.

Loganville felt so familiar to Julia, was familiar because of the portrait painted for her by Jace. Here, on Crystal Mountain Road, was Loganville General, where the wild unwanted Sams, both kitten and kid, had found loving homes.

Julia was so tempted to go inside, to stand in the foyer where Grace had spotted her Sam and had tugged him by his rough and ruffian hands to Mary Beth, whose heartstrings had been tugged by the proud and starving boy.

I *will* stand there, Julia promised herself. As soon as I've found what I've come to find.

Then, after making copies of the words that would set Jace Colton free, she would visit—with celebration— every place he had painted for her. The lake. Grace's school. Dinah's house. Sycamore Street.

And Bluebird Lane? Where the Quinn home had been?

Yes. She would journey even there. And she would see the new house, the new home, that had risen from embers of joy and Christmas Eve ash.

But first, now, she needed to visit the place where his tromping young parade had marched, with such relief for Jace, for afternoons of safety, of sanctuary, of fairy tales.

Jace had drawn on her palm the safest route to the library, the one that required crossing the fewest number of streets, down Crystal Mountain Road to Ponderosa, then west to the end of the road.

Jace had painted what lay within Loganville Library, the welcome and the warmth, but he'd failed to mention, for he did not know, that the sprightly woman who would greet her, who was in her seventies but still so young, would be so very much like Gran.

She was Mrs. Bearce, the lovely woman who greeted Julia with a smile that was so grandmotherly, so Gran, and with an offer of help. Mrs. Bearce, about whom Jace had spoken with such fondness, and with such gratitude for her welcome *always* of his precious flock . . . and who'd offered Jace haven in her home on that Christmas Eve night.

Would Loganville's librarian remember the boy she'd known as Sam? Of course she would. And fondly, too.

He liked you so much, Mrs. Bearce. Julia wanted *so much* to say the words. But they were Jace's to speak. And maybe he would speak them.

Someday.

Julia envisioned Mrs. Bearce's happiness at seeing again the man she'd known as a boy, the shepherd turned physician who was a shepherd still.

"Yes," Julia replied to Mrs. Bearce's smiling offer of help. "Thank you. I was wondering if you carry back issues of the local newspaper?"

"The *Star.* We most certainly do. The November and December issues are in the reading room, and the rest of this year is at the reference desk. If you need information from previous years, the back issues are available on disc."

"That's what I'm interested in, Mrs. Bearce. The back issues."

"Well then, come with me." Mrs. Bearce talked as she walked. "Are you familiar with computers? With mice and the like?"

Julia smiled at the notion of many mouses being mice.

"Yes. I am. Somewhat. We used computers at the answering service where I worked."

"Which means you won't have the slightest problem with our setup here."

It was a state-of-the-art setup, Julia discovered when they reached the glass-walled room. State-of-the-art. And cozy.

Only four cubicles filled the glassy walls. Two on the left, two on the right. Just one, the first on the right, was in use on this bright blue December day. A young mother sat at the terminal, her arms at once reaching for the keyboard and corralling the curly-haired girl in her lap. She was a bit wiggly, that daughter, although mostly she was chattering to the purple dinosaur she held, and, between chatters, she hummed.

Her brother, who was older, stood beside his mother's chair. Stood and moved, twisted and twirled, as he queried, plaintively, "How much *longer*, Mom? *Mom,* how much longer?"

"A minute," the mom replied with loving sympathy. "Maybe two. I'm *almost* finished, and you guys are being *so good*. Oh, Mrs. Bearce, hello!"

Mrs. Bearce greeted the mother and her children with her warm smile, and as she and Julia passed, Loganville's librarian patted with obvious affection the little boy's head.

When they reached the second cubicle on the left, Mrs. Bearce said, "Have a seat, Julia, and I'll show you the basics."

Julia felt uncomfortable sitting while Mrs. Bearce

stood. But it was precisely what the lively librarian wanted her to do. And again, and so achingly, it was very Gran. They would be playing gin rummy, and Gran would remember another trick that Julia really should know, and she'd leave her spot at the card table to stand behind Julia, and together they would study Julia's hand—and plot, together, how best to outfox Julia's opponent . . . who, of course, was Gran herself.

Mrs. Bearce was to computers what Gran had been to cards. A veritable whiz. She'd been forced to learn, she cheerfully explained to Julia, *at her age,* because, well, she simply had to. Just as in her mid-seventies Gran had learned every subject taught at Tierney Junior High. The genetics of blood type for example, which Gran had never known before.

Like Gran, Mrs. Bearce had had a young accomplice. Her grandson Robbie. "He's only fourteen, Julia, but he can program *anything*!"

Mrs. Bearce explained the hot links between given articles, or designated keywords within, and showed Julia how with merely a single mousey click all related articles, even ones not yet previewed, would be printed out.

Even as she was describing the print feature, Mrs. Bearce was checking the nearby printer's paper tray. It was almost full, but Mrs. Bearce topped it off anyway, with the tidiness and efficiency that symbolized the library that had been for decades in her care.

And even before Julia asked how she should pay for whatever copies she might want to make, Mrs. Bearce said, "Thanks to a grant from Troy Logan, as in *Lo-*

*gan*ville, you can print anything you like free of charge. Troy owns the *Star* among other things, *many* other things, and since he and his family believe strongly in literacy of all kinds, including computer literacy, he's provided the grant."

"I won't print anything I don't need."

"I know you won't, dear. Now if you'll just tell me what issues you are interested in, the approximate month and year, I'll go find the correct disc for you."

"Well. The month would be December, this week in fact, and twenty-two years ago."

Julia had believed that Mrs. Bearce's smile was a feature as constant as her bright eyes and gracious warmth. But Julia saw now an expression that was reminiscent, hauntingly so, of Gran's when Winnie's doctors had explained within hours of Winnie's birth that the newborn little girl was not destined to survive.

"You want articles about the fire?"

"Yes," Julia said quietly. "I do."

"Are you a reporter?"

A reporter? *Why?* "No, Mrs. Bearce. I'm not." *I'm Jace's—Sam's—friend, as were you . . . are you . . . aren't you?*

# CHAPTER FIFTEEN

*S*omehow Julia's fingers worked, enough at least to command the computer to print all the articles. There were so many. And every letter to the editor. There were so many, too, of those. And the photograph, there was only one, of the impostor named Sam.

As the printer whooshed, Julia stared at the computer screen, and the devastating words that just kept scrolling by.

Mary Beth Quinn's skull had been fractured, "fatally shattered"—those words asserted—before the fire had begun. *Had been set.*

The Christmas Eve inferno had been arson, not accident, although Mary Beth had perhaps died, been killed, accidentally. A rush of rage. A burst of violence.

But Mary Beth's killer, confronted with what he'd done, had decided to conceal his brutal deed. Using gas to create the conflagration, the many gallons beside the generator in the garage, he'd poured a lethal trail upstairs and down.

It was while he was upstairs that he became a cold-blooded murderer. Had Grace, the five-year-old innocent, witnessed her mother's inadvertent death? Probably not. For Grace had died, *been murdered,* in her upstairs bedroom, not in the living room with Mary Beth.

But she'd most certainly overheard the argument that preceded the violence, and gotten out of bed to investigate, and recognized the killer's voice, and maybe even seen him, as from the top of the stairs she'd asked her mommy what was wrong.

Nothing, Mary Beth would have assured her. Everything's fine, Gracie. Go back to bed, sweetheart.

Grace's imprisonment in her own bedroom was traditional and monstrous—a chair propped against the door from outside—and it had doomed her to die alone. In flames. In terror.

Mary Beth had been killed, and Grace had been murdered, and it took very little deduction to determine who the monster was. Sam Quinn. Who, by the December 27 edition of the *Star,* had been exposed for the impostor he was.

Dr. Samuel Quinn, Mary Beth's adored husband, had been like Mary Beth herself an only child. A Samuel Quinn nephew and namesake could not possibly exist. Yet from the very start Mary Beth had perpetuated the fraud.

Why?

Letters from the citizens of Loganville, faithfully

reprinted without editing of any kind, offered possible replies.

Mary Beth was so *nice,* Dinah's parents asserted, and so *trusting* that she would have believed without question whatever compelling fiction, convincing lie, the renegade teen had told her. His frantic flight, perhaps, from a lifetime of abuse. After which Mary Beth herself had crafted a story so that he would be accepted, welcomed, with neither pity nor alarm.

And he had been accepted. Welcomed.

But *not* by everyone, various other letter writers, parents too, felt constrained to remind. *We* knew it was odd, *pathologic,* for a teenage boy to baby-sit our children, to *want* to. Which is why *we* would not permit it.

But he was quite wonderful with the children, Mrs. Bearce—*Mrs. Bearce*—dared to write. The Sam she had known could not possibly have committed this horrific crime. But, she supposed, if her Sam had been having a psychotic break . . .

She'd done quite a bit of reading on psychosis, she wrote, since the tragedy of Christmas Eve. The library had several relevant books on the subject, should anyone else care to learn. A psychotic break, Mrs. Bearce insisted, was a way—the *only* way she could think of—to explain the inexplicable. And if such an affliction had suddenly stricken Sam, he would have been powerless to control, much less defy, the evil voices that thundered within.

Nonsense! countered a fire fighter who'd been, from inferno to ash, at the Christmas Eve murder scene. Sam was a *psychopath,* not some pathetic victim of psychosis. And Mary Beth and Sam, whoever the hell he really was, were lovers. Obviously. How else to explain Mary Beth's breakup with Troy? But, on Christmas Eve, Mary Beth had finally come to her senses, refusing to let Sam touch her ever again.

And the sicko, the psycho, couldn't stand the rejection. So he killed her. By accident? Maybe. Or maybe by design. The fire fighter, for one, wouldn't rest until the demon was found *and punished.* Although, he conceded, it was difficult to imagine an appropriate punishment for what he had done.

The single photograph of the impostor named Sam had been taken by an admiring teenage girl.

Whatever photographs might have existed in the house on Bluebird Lane had burned to ash in the Christmas Eve flames. And Sam hadn't sat for the high-school yearbook, a decision undoubtedly due, in retrospect, to a reluctance on his part for graven images of any sort. His reason at the time had of course seemed quite innocent. And responsible. His after-school commitments to Grace and her friends.

The photo that did exist had been taken the previous summer at the lake. And was it a reliable blueprint of the face of the man? A forecast of the way Jace Colton would look, looked now, to the world?

Hardly. Because it was an image of the shepherd before he failed to protect his flock—before the loss, the death, in which so much of him, too, had died.

Jace Colton was not recognizable as the shepherd

named Sam. Nor was Sam recognizable as the shepherd named Jace.

He's safe. *Jace is safe.* The thought was a rare reassurance amid the chaos Julia felt——although it faltered precipitously as she became aware of the two men who towered overhead.

Julia knew at once the identity of the men. Rawley and Troy. The men who had loved Mary Beth.

They were handsome. Mary Beth's men. Very handsome. In very different ways.

Rawley was rugged, rough. And Troy? Elegantly urbane. But they were the same, these men, identical when it came to the piercing interest with which they gazed at Julia.

Politely, elegantly, Troy Logan made introductions for them both, their names and their jobs, his as editor of the *Star* and Rawley's as chief of police.

"I've been reading your names," Julia murmured. *And I know so much about both of you.*

"Yes," Troy Logan said. "We know you have. A concerned citizen gave us a call."

The young mother, Julia thought, who had certainly overheard, in the cozy glass room, her conversation with Mrs. Bearce—and who'd left with her children soon after Mrs. Bearce had gone to retrieve the discs. Julia looked toward the cubicle where the woman had been, and where Mrs. Bearce, not smiling, stood now.

"No," Troy said as he followed Julia's gaze. "It wasn't Mrs. Bearce who called us. It was someone else."

"But the point," Rawley spoke for the first time, "is that we're here."

"Because the case is still open?" Julia asked, as she realized she must. "Because he hasn't been caught?"

"That's right," Rawley affirmed. "He hasn't been. We don't even know who he is." Loganville's chief of police stared at her. "Do you?"

Somehow Julia stared back. And did not blink. And looked surprised, she hoped, authentically stunned.

"No! Of *course* not."

"May we ask your name?" Troy asked.

"Oh, *yes.* Sorry. I'm Julia Hayley."

"And why," Rawley queried, "are you here?"

Julia had lied before for Jace. To help Jace. Then, high above earth, the lies had flowed. As they flowed now. Lies and truth. As much truth as she could possibly, could safely, provide.

"For the past six years I've worked for a physicians' answering service in Tierney, Kansas. Last year, on Christmas Eve, I received a call from a woman who was terrified, she said, of that very night. She was new to the area and didn't have a physician—or anyone for that matter to whom she felt comfortable confiding her innermost fears. A physicians' answering service was not a crisis line, she knew. But she wasn't *really* in crisis, and maybe if she shared her fears with me, I'd be able to recommend a physician to whom she could be most appropriately referred."

"You agreed." Mrs. Bearce's quiet observation was a lovely vote of confidence.

"Yes, Mrs. Bearce. I did. When she was six, she told me, her family spent Christmas in Colorado. With relatives, I imagine, or maybe with close friends. I don't recall which, and maybe she didn't even say. In any event, on that Christmas Eve, she was awakened by the scream of sirens. Everyone was. And she, like everyone else, rushed to the site of the tragedy, the late-night fire where a mother and daughter had died. She'd actually blocked for years all memories of that night. But since becoming a mother herself, a single parent with a little girl of her own, the memories had returned. She was terrified that such a Christmas Eve blaze would consume them, too. She knew her fear was irrational. But it felt *so real.*"

What was real at the moment was the image of Sam, before he became Jace again, on the computer screen. Julia spoke to that image.

"We talked past midnight, which was the time, apparently, when the distant tragedy had occurred. She felt safe once that time had passed. Calm. Still, I gave her the names of several physicians who I knew would take seriously her fears. And that was that. I assumed I'd never hear from her again."

"But you did," Troy prompted.

Julia looked from the screen to him. "Yes. Three weeks ago. She hadn't seen any of the physicians I'd recommended, and felt fairly certain she'd be all right this year. But, just in case, she wanted to know if I'd be working on Christmas Eve. I told her I wouldn't be, that I was leaving Kansas, moving away, a few days before that night. That concerned her a little, and she wondered if we could just pretend, right then, that it was Christmas Eve, and talk as we'd talked the year before. She told me the name of the town this time. Loganville. And the year the fire had occurred. Since she had no idea what had caused the blaze, we discussed the possibility that it might help her if she did."

"Help her, dear?" Mrs. Bearce asked. "How?"

"Well, she could focus her fear if she knew, *channel* it in a preventive way. If, for example, she learned that faulty tree-light wiring was to blame, she could make very certain that her lights were safe. Or if the Loganville mother had left a cigarette burning—"

"Mary Beth didn't smoke." The harsh interjection was a duet from the men who had buried their own enmity to comfort Mary Beth after her beloved mother had died smoking in bed.

"Oh!" Julia exclaimed, as she must, at the startling intrusion. But . . . I know, she thought. I *know*. But I am crafting a tale of partial truths and plausible lies. For Jace. "The woman who called me didn't know that of course, and she *is* a smoker, although she's trying very hard to quit. Anyway, it made sense, at least to me, that learning what caused the fire might help. I have no idea if she followed through. But maybe you do?"

The question was rhetorical. Obviously. But even had it not been, Julia realized, neither man would have answered it. They, not she, were the inquisitioners. The gentleman journalist. The quarterback cop.

The two men alternated questions, and politeness and harshness, in the interview/interrogation that ensued.

"What's the woman's name?" Rawley began.

"I know her first name only. Anne. It was my great-aunt's name and spelled the same way, with an *e* at the end."

"And she lives in Tierney?" Troy asked.

"Not necessarily. In fact, my guess would be not. I'm not sure why I think that. Maybe simply because the medical center for which I worked is twenty miles from Tierney and draws its patients from a wide radius. All the small towns, basically, in that part of Kansas."

"Did she know your name?"

"My first name. I always answered with 'This is Julia, how may I help you?' "

"Why are you here today, Julia?"

"It was an *impulse*. I was in Denver, and noticed Loganville on a map in my motel room, and it was such a beautiful day for a drive. I suspected that Anne hadn't followed up on learning the cause of the fire any more than she'd called any of the physicians I advised. If *I* could discover the cause, I thought, maybe I could let her know."

"You don't know her name."

"No. But I could ask the answering-service manager to see if any of the operators had heard from her during the holidays, and, if they had, if they'd happened to get her last name or phone number. Then I could let her know what I'd found, and she could be reassured. But now . . ."

"It's not very reassuring, is it?"

"No. It's not."

"But you've printed the articles," Loganville's chief of police observed without sympathy.

"Well, yes. I have." It was a task, Julia noticed, that had finally ended. The whooshing had stopped and what remained atop the silent printer was a mountain of snow. "I'd like to take them with me, if that's all right, and although I know there's a grant, I'd be happy to pay."

"That's what the grant is for," Troy said. "Don't let her pay, Mrs. Bearce."

"No. I won't."

"Why do you want the articles, Ms. Hayley?" Rawley Ramsey wanted to know.

"I'd like to read them carefully, to see if there's a way to reassure her after all. And, I suppose, to reassure myself. Her fear touched me, and now . . . it's really awful, isn't it? Horrible. You must be so desperate to find him." *As Jace will be so desperate to find whoever killed his precious flock.* "I'm sorry I'm not the lead you've been waiting for."

"We're sorry, too, for startling you," Troy said. "And for interrogating you."

The apology came from Troy alone. Although, Julia realized, it was offered for both of them. And it was the only apology from Rawley Ramsey she would get.

Indeed, the police chief said nothing else, nothing more, and moments later Mary Beth's men were gone, and she and Mrs. Bearce were alone. At which point Loganville's librarian apologized, too.

"But *you* didn't call them," Julia insisted to the woman who was so like Gran. "And, even if you had, I would have *definitely* understood." And then, she couldn't help it, she had to ask, "Did you know him, Mrs. Bearce? Did you know Sam?"

"Yes, Julia. I did. He was so gentle." Mrs. Bearce sighed. "Even the most gentle of creatures could, I imagine, succumb to a sudden blinding rage. Although to have *hurt* Mary Beth, to have shoved her so violently that her skull simply shattered . . . that seems far beyond what any gentle creature ever would do. Could do. And the cold-blooded murder of our sweet little Grace. I still can't believe it."

*Don't believe it, Mrs. Bearce. Believe in Jace. Please.*

*J*ulia did not, after leaving the library, drive the streets of Loganville. She left as Jace had left on that midnight clear.

Jace had gone on that night of fire into the emerald forest to die.

And her destination on this cold December day?

The place where she would live, begin to live, again.

The Emerald City. Where Jace Colton had never been, and would never be.

# CHAPTER SIXTEEN

*J*ulia had known, before leaving the Loganville Library, that she was going to let Jace know what she'd found. She'd even wondered during the drive back to Denver if she should try to reach him in London, on the chance that the team hadn't left on the twenty-ninth after all . . . that it hadn't been safe enough, yet, for them to go.

But they *would* be going. Jace would be. And if he learned just hours before leaving for war the truth of that night? Would he break the promise he'd made to those fighting and dying on foreign soil?

No. Jace Colton did not break promises. Had not for twenty-two years.

The shepherd would go to war as promised. But even as he worried about the wounded flock before him, he would be churning with torment, with rage, about the loved ones who had perished, had been murdered, in the Loganville blaze. He would feel helpless, as he'd felt so helpless on that Christmas Eve, because there was nothing he could do for Mary Beth and Grace *again*. At least nothing, this time, until his February 14 return.

Julia didn't place a call to the Azalea Suite. She would send the tormenting articles, as she'd planned to send the reassuring ones, to his penthouse on Lake Shore Drive. With a note, too, words she would write, the right words, sometime during the six weeks before February 12—the date, she decided, when she would put the articles in the mail.

The right words. Julia wrote to Jace, in her mind, as she explored her new Emerald City home. Seattle was beautiful, as promised, if drizzly—as promised too—and the Hawthorne Hills house was lovely, charming, and so ideally located that Julia abandoned her plan to buy a car. There were several grocery stores within easy walking distance, and for more elaborate shopping, the University Village with its potpourri of shops and boutiques was walkable, too. And she could always take the bus.

Julia walked for those first six weeks, and wandered, and marveled, and explored. There were favorite places on her wanderings that she visited again and again—Miller-Pollard in the Village, and Sami's Cards and Gifts, and Barnes & Noble, Williams-Sonoma, and Fiorini Sports.

And Starbucks. Of course Starbucks.

Could she be a *barista*? she wondered. Could she memorize the regulars' favorite drinks as she had come to recognize within a syllable the faceless voices that called her in the night? She believed she could. And this always vibrant hub of humanity would be such a happy place, such a *good* place for her to work.

Maybe after February 12 she would inquire about a job. And until then? Julia made copies of the Loganville articles. For herself. And she wrote and rewrote the letter to Jace in her mind. And she walked and wandered and marveled and explored. Julia spoke to the Wilsons, too, to report that everything was fine, *wonderful,* and to Galen as well with similar raves.

In the end, despite the myriad words she had imagined, and the pages and pages that might have been, Julia's letter to Jace was quite short. She didn't speculate about the identity of the killer, even though there was that *so obvious* possibility, nor did she include anything else that was self-evident in the least.

Julia did not say, for example, to the man she loved that she knew he was innocent. Or that she believed he would want to know what she'd discovered. Or that he needn't let her know such a belief was correct. Because this was *not* an attempt to resume their relationship in any way.

Julia's letter, in the end, was simply a recitation of facts. Her visit to Loganville, but not the reason why. Jace would know why. And the fiction she'd told Rawley and Troy, but not the reason for same—to permit Jace to fight this war when and how he chose. When. How. Not *if.* Jace would avenge the slaughter of his beloved flock. That went without saying.

So Julia didn't say it.

Julia transferred custody of her concise letter and the

snowy mountain of articles to the United States Postal Service on February 12. As planned. After which she walked in the drizzle, for it was drizzling again, at last, after an entire week of sun.

She had missed the drizzle. The overcast skies. And the London gray.

The whispers in bed while it rained gray.

Now the drizzle had returned, and it was a usual February Emerald City day. Except that this day was far from usual. Jace would be returning to Chicago soon. He was already en route perhaps, and safe.

It felt so bright, this soggy day. The shimmering sky spilled silver raindrops. And diamonds. And emeralds. Too.

Emeralds *too,* for Julia was seeing this misting gemstone heaven through her own eyes *and* Winnie's.

Had Edwina Anne Hayley colored even her cloudiest skies the brightest emerald because she had known—oh, could she possibly have known?—that there would come a time, after she herself became an angel, when her sister would need a magical place to live, and that Julia would be beckoned, as she *had* been, by a place named the Emerald City?

When the bleeding started, it felt like raindrops, and warmth and hope and love.

Her period had returned. After all these years. And why not? She'd begun gaining weight on the flight from O'Hare and had been eating well, nutritionally, ever since. And festively, too, a nourishment, a nurturing, of its own.

Julia always ordered, at the Village Starbucks, a two-percent no-whip venti hot chocolate, and she carried, in her rain gray purse, a small stash of macadamia nuts.

She'd taken such good care of herself during these first six Emerald City weeks, had *cared* for herself as her books on grieving, and on living, had so persuasively advised.

She'd been *especially* careful during these first six weeks, when she alone guarded the secret of Loganville. She hadn't even been running. Walking, yes, and walking and walking; but so careful each and every time she crossed a street.

Now the secret was in the mail, and Jace was on his way home, and the sky was spilling diamonds and emeralds and warmth and love. There was such warmth, too, in the womb that spilled again and at last its crimson raindrops. And although, even beneath this gemstone sky, Julia couldn't imagine becoming pregnant, that joy and that terror, maybe there would come a time after all. Someday.

*Oh, Julia, I'm so glad it's you.* The memory of the late-night phone call in Tierney came with a piercing jolt. And the raindrops turned to ice. And the remembered words from the faceless voice named Millie whirled and flooded and flowed, as Julia herself was whirling, and her womb, flooding too, flowed. And flowed. *I'm two months pregnant, Julia. And we've wanted this baby so much. But now I'm bleeding. Bleeding. Help me, Julia. Please. Call the doctor right away.*

# CHAPTER SEVENTEEN

*I*t was a threatened miscarriage. Which meant, the OB-GYN physician at University Hospital explained, Julia might miscarry. Or she might not. But if she did, the doctor counseled, it would be because the pregnancy had not been viable, *not* because of anything Julia had or had not done.

First-trimester miscarriage, especially during a first pregnancy, was not unusual. Nor, however, was first-trimester bleeding without fetal loss. Julia needed to rest, but to return immediately if any of a variety of things—including the passage of tissue—occurred. The doctor provided Julia with a list of phone numbers, emergency ones and one wonderful one, the number of the prenatal clinic at the university where she could be followed, if she so chose, in the event that the threat of miscarriage passed.

And it did pass, it *did*, after two days of rest, of sleep, of dreams. Some of the dreams were memories. Of London, and the gentleness in which their baby had been conceived. But other dreams were new—new gentleness, new caring—as Jace comforted and encouraged her.

His tender whispers were so clear in her dreams. But they floated just beyond clarity, muted and blurred, when she awakened to joy on Valentine's Day.

She bled no more. And her baby, their precious little girl—Julia was so certain she was a daughter—danced with life, with love, deep within.

Julia prepared a nutritious breakfast for both of them, and as they sat in the kitchen's cheery breakfast nook, she touched the snowflake Jace had given her, the perfect crystal that fell on a gossamer thread from a small chandelier.

The snowflake caught light, even on this cloud-dark day, and when Julia touched it, spun it, a bouquet of rainbows adorned the alcove walls.

This is where, Julia told her baby, the hummingbird feeders will be. And where, she promised, we'll watch the fluttering families nest while *we* nest.

Her promise, Julia realized, had been made aloud. With a soft shrug, she chattered more happy words.

"It's raining. But that's cozy, don't you think? We'll stay right here today, my little love, warm and cozy, and we'll celebrate, my sweet one, your daddy's safe return."

Julia made a habit, morning and evening, of watching the news. So she turned on the kitchen TV, out of habit in part, but in part as well because on this day, and for the two days she had dreamed, the news had surely been magnificent for everyone.

*Including* Alexis Allen, whose calculated cruelty had

so unwittingly given Julia such gifts and who on this Valentine's Day was apparently sharing with the *Good Morning America* audience her personal prescription for love.

Except that *Windy City's* romantic heroine wasn't smiling.

"Jace Colton was—no, *is*—a wonderful man, a true hero, as the entire world knows now, but which *I* have known since Jace and I met last fall. I made mistakes, though, with this wonderful man. This *heroic* man. And because of those mistakes, Jace and I parted with anger, such *awful* anger, two days before Christmas. I *permitted* us to part that way. Let him suffer! I decided. Even though, as furious as I was, I *knew* we'd get back together. *Today.* Valentine's Day. When he was supposed to return. It would be such a romantic reunion, I told myself. So *passionate.* But now, well, Jace was *distracted,* the other brave members of his team have said. Distracted amid the danger, the war, even as he fought to save all those other lives. Jace took care of others. But not of himself. And I'm afraid, so *terribly* afraid, that Jace didn't *care* enough to *care* for himself because of what had happened between us."

Alexis drew a dramatic breath, a signal it seemed for the camera to zoom even closer to her distraught and beautiful face. And when it did, to *GMA's* rapt and enraptured television audience, she implored, "*Please* don't make the mistakes I've made. Don't *ever* allow a loved one to storm away in anger, even if he's simply running an errand down the block. Not if you *love* him, and no matter *how angry* with him you are."

As the tear-glistening image of Alexis faded into a commercial, Julia's trembling fingers commanded the remote to switch to Channel 53, FOX News, where the top story, the plight of Dr. Jace Colton, was being recounted for viewers just tuning in.

The dedicated team of doctors and nurses, Jace's team, had flown to the site of the latest Balkan carnage on December 30. At dawn. Long before, Julia realized vaguely, her discoveries in Loganville. And they'd been scheduled to return to London yesterday, February 13, even as a new group of volunteers flew in.

And it had happened. As scheduled. Jace's team had returned to London, and from there, home.

Home. Safe. All save Jace. He'd remained behind. He'd had no choice. Because of what had happened at twilight on the twelfth.

A new mother, carrying her just-born son, had made a frantic dash through the center of town. The road on which she ran was blanketed with snow—old snowflakes, trampled and dirty, and stained, those dead snowflakes, with layer upon layer of blood.

The woman's own blood, from her weeping womb, left fresh splatters on the snow. But all that mattered was the baby she carried, the product of love not rape, and fatherless since Christmas Eve when her husband had been slain.

Sanctuary was in sight, but still so far away, the hospital at road's end with its medical professionals inside and its guards, trained peacekeepers, stationed without.

There were rules in many hospitals in the United States which prohibited on-duty emergency-room personnel from leaving the premises to bring patients in. The rationale was medically sound. It was unconscionable, everyone agreed, to abandon a patient who'd arrived in good faith in favor of one who might refuse care even if offered. What if the known patient, the good-faith one, died during the abandonment?

There were legal considerations, too. Patients consented to be seen. Chose to be. But if a patient was retrieved away from the hospital grounds, especially if that patient was so grievously wounded—or so soaringly high—that true consent was impossible, the very act of retrieval was in the view of certain attorneys tantamount to kidnapping.

Jace Colton, who'd never cared very much about rules, much less frivolous lawsuits, had been known to orchestrate such rescues.

No such rules, of course, applied in war. There were different rules, however. Such as wariness. And caution.

Dr. Jace Colton knew the rules of war. But he ran on bloodied snow to mother and child. The grateful mother implored in a language Jace had not yet mastered—but with emotion that was eloquent and clear—that the doctor take her baby *now*.

Her baby, not her.

Jace complied, and didn't comply, with the maternal command. He scooped both refugees in his arms, taking the infant as the mother had consented . . . and kidnapping her.

The gunshot wound, witnesses would report, was to the doctor's leg. His thigh. And, the witnesses would say, although the bullet startled him, it in no way impeded his fleet journey with his bleeding bundle toward safety.

The journey was substantial, even for Jace's long limbs, a gauntlet of leaden bullets in the gloaming shadows as tiny missiles flew at him from both sides.

The snipers were not expert marksmen. They were civilians turned soldiers only since Christmas Eve. What killings they'd managed had been, barring sheer luck, accomplished at close range.

Jace was a moving target, and the snipers weren't expert, and the shepherd who had once led a tromping parade of lively children in Loganville attracted a parade of sorts now.

Townspeople, armed with chunks of ice and frozen rocks, became human shields, and other doctors and nurses rushed out to relieve Jace of his weighty bundle, and by their very presence the professional peacekeepers—experts in war—subdued the amateur ones.

Mother and child were whisked to safety inside, and cheers filled the twilight air, and the gunfire ceased.

The episode, this skirmish, was over.

But Jace Colton was gone. Kidnapped.

How?

No one knew, really, how it happened. Only that it had. He was there, and then he wasn't, like a shell game, a sleight of hand, amid the chaos and celebration.

And now, FOX News was reporting, Dr. Jace Colton was being held for ransom. His captors wanted so much. Everything. Including the release of "political prisoners" held in various countries around the globe. The latter demand confirmed the speculation that the ragtag army with its state-of-the-art weaponry was being funded by a well-organized terrorist cabal.

The demands were not going to be met. Of course. Or even seriously considered.

FOX News promised to keep its viewers fully, fairly, and promptly informed, as for the twenty-eight hours since the story first broke they had faithfully done. In the meantime there were other, albeit less dramatic, Valentine's Day news items to report.

Julia switched to Channel 99, CNBC, where a biography of the captured physician had just begun.

Jace Colton had been born in Savannah, a reporter said, and had lived in the City of Festivals until his teens. He'd moved to Nevada then, where he'd graduated with honors from Reno High. His teachers remembered him as a serious student, focused and intense, as did his professors at UNR, and Stanford Med, and so, too, the doctors at Mass General with whom he trained.

The man who'd lived on both coasts decided to settle, the reporter noted, in the heartland, Chicago, where he worked in the celebrated trauma center he'd founded.

Like FOX, CNBC concluded its coverage with a promise to keep viewers apprised of breaking news. Then, like FOX, CNBC shifted to other news of the day.

As had, Julia discovered, all other news channels. It

was twelve past the hour. The top story, the Jace Colton story, was—barring breaking developments—through for the moment.

Julia returned to FOX, muted the volume, and reflected in trembling silence on what she had learned. On February 12, when her own pregnancy had been in such jeopardy, Jace had risked his life to save another mother and child.

And Jace had saved them. Both of them. All of them. Both mothers, both babies, the son, his daughter.

*Oh Jace.* Julia stared unseeing at a heart-shaped chocolate cake on the television screen. Her mind's eye saw another image, the photograph of Jace that had been aired by both FOX and CNBC.

It was a recent photo, and it definitely looked like the man she loved, so handsome, so solemn, so intense.

But it did not, Julia knew without checking, look like the photograph of the teen shepherd that had been printed twenty-two years ago in the *Loganville Star*. No one, not Troy Logan, not Rawley Ramsey, not even Mrs. Bearce would see the photo of Dr. Jace Colton and think *Sam.* Nor did the biography, at least as presented by CNBC, provide beyond his Savannah boyhood even the slightest clue. Colorado had not been mentioned, much less Loganville, and as for the two years between his departure from the Savannah school system and his enrollment at Reno High? The gap hadn't been discovered, apparently, or if found, dismissed.

And there weren't, either, any links between Jace and her. Alexis hadn't revealed the truth of her relationship with Jace, never would, nor had she mentioned, never would, the woman named Julia to whom she'd given the first-class ticket she had bought. And in Loganville Julia herself had spoken of Tierney and Kansas, not London and love.

Jace's secret was safe. As he would be. Please.

*Yes.* Unless . . . what if some eager reporter decided to investigate Jace's Valentine's Day mail? To document the number of romantic missives the gorgeous trauma surgeon received?

The investigation would be innocent at its outset. To chronicle, not to pry. But there would be that intriguingly bulky package postmarked in Seattle on the twelfth—no. The doorman of the Lake Shore Drive building where Jace lived, and who might have innocently abetted the initial look, *count,* could not be bribed to relinquish the package itself. Surely. Because he respected Jace so.

It was beyond paranoid, Julia told herself, to presume a fateful confluence of unethical journalist and unscrupulous doorman. And yet *what if?*

The State Department wasn't going to negotiate with terrorists, not even for the heroic doctor. But there would certainly be aggressive efforts to convince his captors to set him free. Enthusiasm would vanish, however, if it was believed that whatever diplomatic currency existed was being squandered on a murderer. And Jace's value to his captors would vanish as well. They might even harm him, *execute him,* as a gift to the US, to save the taxpayers the cost of incarceration and trial.

Jace's business card was in her wallet. Julia removed it

from its protective plastic sheath, stared for a blurry moment at the beloved writing on the back, then dialed the Chicago phone number of the man, the attorney, Jace trusted. Absolutely.

"Garek McIntyre."

"*Oh*, Mr. McIntyre. I . . . this must be your direct line."

It was more than a direct line, it was a private one. Garek recognized at once the few voices that had this number. This soft voice wasn't one of them.

"May I help you Ms . . . ?"

"Hayley. Julia Hayley. I—"

"Julia," Garek interjected quietly. "I'm Garek, Julia, and I'd been thinking about calling you." *Thinking about you, wondering about you, worrying about you—for Jace.*

"You know who I am?"

"Yes." *The woman to whom, just hours before going to war, Jace Colton left his entire fortune.* Jace had never cared about a will, except for that brief time when he'd believed he'd fathered a child. There had been urgency then, to make certain that his baby was protected, cared for, always. And there'd been softness, too. Gentleness. As there'd been for Julia. Because of Julia. "Jace called me from London before he left. He said that he'd given you my name, and he gave me yours, and your phone number in Seattle as well. I was going to call you today, within the hour in fact, to share with you what I know."

"You know more than what's being reported on the news?"

"I do. A bit more, anyway."

The information came from an impromptu underground of grateful citizenry, the ravaged townspeople whom Jace had so tirelessly helped. The trauma surgeon was alive, they reported. And well. The gunshot wound was superficial and would heal.

Jace was being held in the newly formed army's principal encampment, a fortress of advanced weaponry, albeit in mostly novice hands, which was located in dense forest and rugged hills. Garek didn't explain to Julia the significance of such a locale. He didn't need to. The watching world knew well the treachery of the Balkan terrain. Rescue missions, even under cover of darkness and by the elite of the elite, were guaranteed to have casualties for some, if not all, involved.

Still, Julia said, "Jace wouldn't want anyone to risk their lives"—*lose their lives*—"to save him."

"There are men who are trained to take such risks, Julia. Who choose to." Garek McIntyre knew such men. Well. He'd been one of them. Once. One of the best.

"But Jace wouldn't want it, Garek. He would *hate* it."

"No rescue attempts are being planned," Garek said. *Yet.* "And Jace is all right. He's working, caring for the wounded on the other side."

"Is that why they kidnapped him? Because they needed surgical care?"

"I . . . yes. Sure. And it means, Julia, that they will treat him well."

Garek cursed himself for his hesitation, as fleeting as it

had been. He was better than that. *Used to be.* And he'd recovered quickly, he thought.

But not quickly enough.

"Why else?" Julia asked. "Please tell me. Jace said that if there was ever anything I needed and couldn't reach him, I should turn to you. I need this, Garek. Please. I need to know everything. No matter what."

She's remarkable, Jace had told him. Fearless and strong. "All right. But this is speculation only, Julia. We don't know. There's concern, however, that whatever group is behind the newly energized civil war may have done a little research on the various persons who've been sent in to help. Even a little research would reveal not only Jace's medical expertise, but his personal wealth as well—which coupled with his missions to such places as Afghanistan, Nairobi, and Kosovo might raise questions about an agenda beyond altruism."

"Oh *no*," Julia whispered. "They might think he was working for the government?"

"It's a possibility."

Julia closed her eyes, which was a mistake. An image came to her in the darkness, an American hostage executed by his captors for his presumed crime—espionage—against them. Her eyes opened, found the snowflake and its rainbows, and she asked, "Is he, Garek?"

"No. He's not."

"Are you?"

The question surprised him. But, surprising himself, Garek answered with the truth. "I did at one time."

"I'm *so frightened* for him."

*She's remarkable, Garek. Fearless and strong.* "I know, Julia. So am I. But the concern I've just shared with you is speculation not fact, and the facts we have are basically good. Jace is alive, well, and of great value to his captors just that way."

"And," Julia murmured, "caring for the wounded will give him something useful to do." Her shepherd would be caged, and so restless, but helping . . . as he needed to do.

"Yes, it will. I'll call you immediately, Julia, whenever there's news."

"Of any kind."

"Of any kind."

"Thank you."

"You're welcome."

"I . . ."

"Yes?"

"Well, I've done something which I'm afraid could be very harmful to Jace."

"Okay," Garek replied calmly, unable to imagine her harming anyone, least of all Jace. "Tell me."

"Two days ago I mailed a package to his home. If it fell into the wrong hands, *media* hands . . ."

"It won't. Besides being a federal crime to tamper with the mail—which, I suppose, wouldn't be a deterrent for some—all of Jace's mail is being forwarded to my office. That's usual, whenever he's scheduled to be away for any length of time. We hold his mail unopened unless he's gone longer than planned, in which case we pay whatever bills he hadn't prepaid before he left. Your package hasn't yet arrived, but neither has today's mail.

But it will arrive, Julia. I'll call you, if you like, the moment it does."

"Yes. Thank you."

"And shall I keep it here, sealed and safe, until I can hand it personally to Jace?"

"Yes. Please."

Before the conversation ended, Garek asked Julia to confirm for him that the home phone number he had for her was correct. It was. And in response to her worried request that he leave a message if she wasn't there, or that he call back if the line was busy, he promised, "I will persevere."

Was there a work phone, too? he wondered.

To which Julia replied, without a heartbeat's hesitation, that she would be working at home.

*Painting,* she realized after the conversation ended with Garek's solemn promise *again* that he would keep her informed no matter what.

Painting, not making lattes. Creating watercolor images of Seattle in her own palette. Through her own eyes.

The plan was confident. Certain and sure. And loving. And it had come from? Jace. In her dreams. For this was what he'd whispered to her as she slept, the suggestion that had made such sense to her while she dreamed, but which had floated, billowy and blurred, when she'd awakened.

Jace's words were bright now, and shimmering. And there was more, remembrance with celebration of Winnie. For Jace had told her, in her dreams, that she should send copies of her Winnie watercolors to Hallmark. Yes,

*Hallmark.* The company would *want* her images, Winnie's images, for their famous greeting cards. They would appreciate the imagination, the enchantment, the joy. And, Jace had asked her in her dreams, Hallmark's Kansas City headquarters seemed right, didn't it? So close to where she and Winnie had lived?

Yes. *Yes.*

"I'm going to paint," Julia told her daughter. "At home. *We*'re going to. And it will be such fun."

Julia stared for many moments at the tiny rainbows that danced in the perfect crystal of snow. Then finally, softly, she spoke again. To her daughter.

"I think we should call your aunt Galen. To wish her Happy Valentine's Day." And would she and Galen talk about the hostage-surgeon who'd been kidnapped on foreign soil? Perhaps. Or perhaps not. But Galen would never know, Julia would not tell her, that he was the man she'd met in London, and who'd helped her so much, given her so much, and who had wanted the time they had together, wanted it *very much,* but no more. Julia had told Galen all that. Already. But not Jace's name. She *almost* had, even though there'd really been no point. And she *would* have, had Galen pushed. But Galen hadn't. Never would. And now . . . "I'm so glad I never told Galen your daddy's name. She'd be terribly worried, and would want us to come to Manhattan to stay with her. But we're supposed to be here, my little one, where your daddy believes we are and wants us to be. Here, in the Emerald City, this magical place, painting pastel watercolors and watching hummingbirds fly.

And talking to Galen. About happy things. I won't tell her about you, though. *Even* though you're the greatest happiness of all. But you're a secret, my sweet girl, just like your daddy."

*Your daddy.*

# CHAPTER EIGHTEEN

*T*he reply from Hallmark came in mid-March, twenty-two minutes after Julia finished filling the hummingbird feeders with sugary nectar and hanging them outside the kitchen alcove.

As always her heart raced with fear and hope at the telephone's trill. In the month since Valentine's Day, Garek had called as promised. And the news remained good. Jace was caring for wounded soldiers and being well-treated by his captors. For now.

Galen had called, too, with happy news about everyday things. As had the Wilsons, not wanting to intrude yet concerned that all was going smoothly for their house sitter-guest.

And now Hallmark was calling.

The greeting-card company wanted her artwork. Every image she'd sent. And, they wondered, was there more? No, Julia told them. Nothing, that is, in the palette that had been Winnie's. She'd been doing some watercolors of her own however.

Her Emerald City images, the Hallmark people feared, would be quite ordinary, her muse long since spent, especially when she described the paintings she'd done so far: the cherry trees in her yard—yes, the blooms were cherry blossom pink—and the view from her living room of Lake Washington and Mount Rainier.

Well, it didn't really matter. The "Winnie" collection would be magnificent. And abundant. Indeed, three distinct collections were already being planned. There would be nine cards in the Winnie's Reindeer collection, one for each pastel creature that flew, and twelve in Winnie's Angels, and eighteen *at least* in Winnie's World: the turquoise cornfields, the lilac oaks, the magenta-and-cream maples, the birch trees fluttering indigo and gold. And Winnie's dawns, Winnie's sunsets, Winnie's twilight clouds. And Floppy. Of course Floppy.

Then there was Winnie's fuchsia Christmas tree . . . and the crèche alight on mauve-colored snow, beneath a golden sky, an aquamarine moon, a single purple star.

It hadn't yet been decided how those two Christmas-tide watercolors would be packaged. And sold. But they would sell, as all of Winnie's images would, and sell and sell and sell.

No more watercolors were needed from Julia Hayley. It was simply usual, when a new artist was discovered, to inquire if she had anything else. But when Julia mailed to Kansas City the Emerald City paintings she had done . . .

She'd neglected to mention, over the phone, that the cherry blossoms were blooming through a crystal-snowflake prism, or that the majestic white mountain and sapphire blue lake were viewed from a chair, flowered and quaint, that beckoned one, welcomed one, to sit. Forever.

*Gran's Chair,* Julia named the painting when she was asked for its title. And the enchantment of cherry blossoms through a crystal of snow? *Love.*

Hallmark wanted whatever she could give them. Yes, flowers would be fine. Rhododendrons, azaleas, daffodils, tulips. And hummingbirds? Certainly. And à la Toulouse-Lautrec—their description not hers—the gaiety of a Starbucks café.

Whatever. Whenever. Not that they wanted to push.

Julia didn't feel pushed. She was where she wanted to be, needed to be. Painting during the day, at the kitchen table beneath the snowflake, and journeying at night in her dreams to Jace. To the forested encampment where he was being held.

Julia was so aware, in her dreams, of the Yuletide scent. It reminds me of London, Jace told her. Of London, of our Christmas.

Of you.

Julia watched as he cared for the wounded, the overnight soldiers who were, so many of them, mere boys. And she offered to help, to cradle a bloodied torso, to hold a severed limb. But Jace told her no . . . thank you. It was far safer, he said, if she remained unseen.

But if she would float overhead, visible only to him, he would very much like to talk.

I'm not entirely happy, he would confess with a wry and gentle smile. I truly don't enjoy being held against my will. But I'm not the only captive here, Julia. These children, these boy-soldiers, are prisoners, too.

Julia told him, because he wanted *so much* to know, about the Emerald City. Its rainy splendor. Its lush and luxuriant green.

And did she tell him as well of the murderous truth of Loganville? Of course not. Nor did Julia tell the man who would have married a pregnant Alexis, whom he did not love, about his baby girl. Jace had enough torment, enough imprisonment already, in his faraway forest of pines.

Julia was so careful in her dreams to keep secret their little girl . . . even though, in her dreams, it was Jace who gave their baby her name.

Julia was floating one night in early April, visible only to him, and Jace was speaking, in words that only she could hear, about Sophie, the little girl on the flight from O'Hare who'd galloped, giggling, into first class.

Was she really Sophi*a*? Jace wondered. Or Josephine?

No, he mused as he answered his query himself. Josephine as a little girl would be Josie, not Sophie.

Josie, he whispered softly. Isn't that a pretty name?

We're such an *alliterative* family, Julia told their un-born daughter thé following day. *J*osie and *J*ulia and *J*ace. And we're a family of three, my precious one, just like the hummingbird families that flutter outside.

\*          \*          \*

*I*n May, Alexis Allen won the Emmy for Outstanding Lead Actress in a daytime drama. Her acceptance speech was breathless, breathtaking, and failed to mention even in passing hero-hostage Jace Colton. Such glaring omissions had happened to other actors of course. Lost in the emotional chaos of the moment. Tom had forgotten to mention Nicole once, hadn't he? Or was it Dustin?

Admittedly such oversights were typically realized, and effusively rectified, right away. And had anyone reminded her about Jace, Alexis would have doubtless gasped, and tearfully effused.

But no such questions were posed. The media had forgotten about Dr. Jace Colton. Too. There'd been no reports, or even reminders, for months. Nothing new. No news.

Nothing new. No news. Except that Jace was alive, well, working. Garek called Julia at least once a week to reaffirm that reassuring truth.

On June 28, and long before Garek called to tell her that everything had changed—before he, or anyone, even knew that the news was *no longer good*—Julia learned, in her dreams, what had happened.

The dreams began with happiness, and surprise. Jace was asleep, and she'd never found him sleeping before. But she was so glad that he was. He'd been working so hard. And was exhausted.

His slumber felt hopeful to her, too. If Jace was sleeping not working, then maybe the fighting had ceased, and there would be a negotiated truce—which would include as a provision Jace's immediate release. For unlike Alexis and the press, the United States government had *not* forgotten its captive hero.

Julia's hope shattered as Jace awakened, *was* awakened. She hadn't seen them coming, had had no time to warn Jace of the impending assault. It was an assault. They were *hurting* him. And there was no need. He'd been rendered instantly helpless, blindfolded and bound.

But they hurt him still. Beat him.

Stop! Julia cried to the brutal assailants. Please stop! But she was invisible, as Jace insisted that she be, to everyone but him. Her pleas went unheard—except by him.

His blindfolded face lifted to the place where she floated, unseen on this night even by him, and smiling, he spoke just to her.

I'm okay, Julia. This is a nuisance. I admit it. I was enjoying my sleep. But it's trivial. Couldn't matter less. What matters, Julia, is that you remain calm and happy for our Josie.

But you don't *know* about our Josie! You mustn't, Jace. You *can't*.

And Jace's reply? There was none, for Julia awakened, fearful and gasping . . . and then calm, as he'd smiled at her to be. Julia calmed herself with stern reminders of the truth.

It was only a dream. Her dream. Her dream*s*. She wasn't truly a floating gossamer in a pine forest far away. It just felt that way. That real.

What was *really* real was the internal conflict she'd

been choosing to ignore. Her subconscious, however, was clearly on the case, conjuring metaphorical perils in her dreams that would be an analyst's delight.

So, let's see . . .

The *true* peril for Jace was that he might learn about his baby. Julia needed to *blindfold* him from that truth, lest he feel obliged to become bound, *imprisoned* in a loveless marriage, the moment he was free.

But, her subconscious wondered, did she have the right to hide the joy of Josie, whom he had named *and would love,* from Jace forever? And did she have the right, what gave her the right, to deprive their Josie of his love?

Julia's subconscious had quite obviously been addressing such issues in her dreams. And, she promised herself in the darkness, she would do some confronting of her own in the light of day.

She would maintain a very firm grasp on what was real. And what was not.

The grasp faltered—how could it not?—when Garek called to tell her what she already knew. Jace had been kidnapped again. And taken where? Garek didn't know. The CIA didn't know. Yet.

"But out of the region, Garek?"

"I think so, Julia. That's a guess, but yes."

Garek didn't elaborate, even in a general way, what that might mean. He didn't need to elaborate for both of them knew. Jace's days of tending to wounded soldiers, and of being treated well himself, were over.

No one knew precisely which terrorist training camp Jace Colton was in. Except Julia. And she didn't know, precisely. But it was terribly hot where he'd been taken. And sandy and dry. There were no pine trees, no fragrance of Christmas, and neither the hope nor the promise of snow.

Jace was bound, always, in the tent that was his prison cell. And he was blindfolded. Always. And they hurt him, beat him, starved him, and refused him water even though his parched lips bled. And bled.

Jace didn't want her there. He even pretended, it *had* to be pretense, that she was not . . . that he couldn't sense behind his blindfold when she floated nearby . . . and couldn't hear, even when she cried to him to hear her, her loving words.

The hummingbird families left, as Dolores Wilson had told her they would, in late July.

As Julia's mind's eye saw a small misshapen hand waving *adieu* to the fluttering birds, as she had to her reindeer, her angels, her tree, she felt an excruciating sadness, an irretrievable loss, as if it was Winnie, her precious Winnie, who'd just fluttered away.

The sadness softened, gentled, as Julia whispered to Josie, and to Winnie, too, about the fun the hummingbird families would have as, together, they journeyed on.

The sadness floated gently from Julia's heart. But there remained the mysterious pain in her hands. Her fingers. They'd been hurting since mid-July, an ache deep within the bone, in every bone. There was nothing, no findings at all, on physical exam, nor on the special battery of blood studies her obstetrician ran.

Julia's fingers ached for some unknown reason. But

her pregnancy was progressing nicely, perfectly, and in another seven weeks her healthy, dancing Josie would be born.

Seven weeks, or so. Her due date, calculated from the night they first had loved, was September 17.

On August 4, in her dreams, Julia told Jace about their Josie. She *had* to, for he was dying in her dreams, *dying*.

You have a daughter, Jace. You *do*. She's Josie, the name you gave her, and you *knew* about her, and you even knew her *name,* on that night in June when you were so brutally awakened from sleep. But it's as if you've *forgotten* her now, forgotten your Josie, because you've stopped fighting to survive. And you must fight, *you must,* for Josie.

She needs her daddy. She'll *always* need you. We won't marry, Jace. It's not necessary. I'll move to Chicago, Josie and I will move, and you'll see her *all the time,* and when you do marry, the woman you choose, *the woman you love*, will be a loving mother, too, for our Josie. I *know* she will be.

In her dreams, on that August night, Julia revealed the truth she'd vowed to hide—at least—until Jace was free. And which, she realized too late, she should have kept hidden *always*.

Jace hated her confession. *Hated* it. His dark black head, already bent, fell even more, and his body, hunched and starved, crumpled further, and Julia knew what she would have seen in the dark green eyes beneath the blindfold. Anguish. Torment. Pain.

She had tortured him more than his captors had, and

had promised him forever imprisonment should he ever be free, and as Julia awakened, drowning, aching, whirling, she realized—even before the bleeding began—that it was Josie, her Josie, who'd been punished *for her impulse* most of all.

# CHAPTER NINETEEN

*J*ulia was with him. She had never left. Even as she'd flown on that December day into the silvery London sky, she'd been inside him still, filling him with lavender warmth and shimmering light, making golden and glowing the desolate darkness deep within.

Julia was with him, in his thoughts not his dreams, for his first six weeks in the Balkans, in the blood-splattered town where the slaughter had begun on Christmas Eve. And, as he cared for the wounded, the boys who'd become soldiers overnight, he imagined that Julia was there, helping him—she was so happy to help, and so fearless—and helping them. The boy-soldiers.

In his imagination, Julia showed the wounded warriors her turquoise cornfields, her soaring angels, her rainbows of reindeer that flew. And the injured boys were comforted by that magic, Julia's and Win's. And, Jace thought, if only Julia could show her watercolors to both sides in this sudden war, and whisper to them of gentleness and of love, there would be peace.

The thought was, Jace knew, hopelessly naive. And hopefully, fearlessly, hopeful. As she was. And as, with her aglow inside him, was he. Jace Colton. Hopeful. Even in war.

Jace didn't dream during those first six weeks. At least not when he slept. But he dreamed wide-awake, and constantly, of her. And when he slept? No nightmares came in the darkness. For there was no darkness, even in sleep. Julia glowed within him still.

She was with him at twilight on February 12, when he rescued the hemorrhaging mother and her just-born child. Indeed it was the lithe ballerina who led the way on the bloodied snow.

Jace was kidnapped in those twilight shadows, and later that night, in the pine-fragrant forest, Julia was there, for the first time, in his dreams.

And did she leave when he awakened? No. She was with him still, helping the wounded soldiers, the boys armed with advanced weaponry, not merely frozen rocks, and with centuries of hatred which would vanish—he was so hopefully hopeful still—if only Julia could intervene.

Which she would, she told him. Happily.

And could. It was simply a matter of his permitting her to become visible.

No, he told her in dreams. And even, silently and urgently, when he was awake and she felt so close, so real . . . right there, his gossamer angel, floating gracefully, courageously, nearby.

Jace saw her clearly. And he heard her, too, her soft,

soft voice as she spoke of flowers and raindrops and hummingbirds. Jace's voice too was soft. He heard it, and felt it, that night in his dreams when he spoke of Sophie . . . who became Josie . . . and who was no longer the little girl on the flight from O'Hare.

She was new, this Josie, and fluttering. An angel. His angel, Jace decided. Not his gossamer one—she was floating here and smiling—but the porcelain gift Julia had given him.

Jace had brought the Canterfields ornament to war, wrapped carefully in the duffel bag which had returned to London, safely and carefully, please, with the rest of his team. His porcelain angel was in London, strumming her harp of gold as she waited for him, and she had a name now, such a pretty name.

Josie.

Jace was dreaming of Julia and of Josie on that night in June, a sleep so wondrous he hadn't sensed the danger until far too late. Not that a premonition would have done any good. The midnight intruders were determined, and they were men not boys, and their hatred was entrenched, carved into their hearts and their souls.

They believed in murder, these men. And torture and terror. And they enjoyed, very much, inflicting pain.

Jace didn't want Julia to see what boys without magic could become. But Julia did see. She traveled with him from the pine-fragrant forest to his dark and desolate desert cell.

Jace knew she was there. But he pretended neither to sense her golden light in his blinded darkness nor to hear her voice, so loving for him—and so fierce, and lovely, when she implored his captors to hurt him no more.

The brutal men didn't hear her pleas. Or perhaps they did.

In mid-July they began to break his bones. Each and every bone in the surgeon's hands. One at a time. And slowly.

Tell us, they commanded of the man they believed to be a spy. Tell us everything you know.

But Jace had nothing to tell, and he would not have told even if he had. There was just that one secret, his alone. I love Julia. *I love Julia.*

They broke his bones, bone after bone, finger after finger, day after day, and when every bone had been broken once they began breaking again the bones that were beginning to heal, trying to heal, despite the starvation that was part of his torture, too.

He was dying. His body was. It had become such a meager shell, fragile, frail, and curling as July became August, too weak to resist even the gravitational pull.

Jace curled, what was left of him did. Hunched and caved. But he was curling around her, sheltering her, creating a sanctuary of love for her.

With her.

It was a lovely place to die.

Julia was touching him now, kissing his parched lips with the sweet taste of raindrops, of love, of her, and as the world beneath his blindfold began to glow pure gold, Jace saw in the shimmering light her beloved face.

She was so worried for him, imploring him to fight, to

keep fighting, and now, oh now, she was whispering such wondrous words about Josie.

*Josie.*

There was sound then, a symphony of joy, as in the desert at last Jace Colton heard the chime of sleigh bells and the celestial melody, fluttering and pure, of harps. A heavenful of gold.

Jace curled his meager shell ever tighter around his Julia and their Josie. His family. Loving them, protecting them, and then frowning beneath his blindfold, for Julia was frowning, and now she was speaking words he couldn't hear amid the glory of harps and the singing of bells.

Jace couldn't hear Julia's words. But he saw her anguish clearly. He curled tighter in reply, deeper, as his lips, sweet with the taste of her, whispered the truth that was secret no more.

*I love you, Julia.* Hear me, please. *Please.*

But Julia didn't hear, and in moments and so anguished still, she and Josie flew away.

Jace's world became dark again. Black. And silent. The harps and sleigh bells chimed no more.

He was dying, almost dead, when the blackness became a glaring light. The blindfold was ripped away, torn from the living skull his face had become.

A skull, like the charred and blazing house on Bluebird Lane.

The inferno—hidden for so long, doused by Julia— had returned at last. And the demons, too. But they were real, both demons and flames. The inferno was the searing desert sun. And the demons? The men who had so methodically broken his bones, had rendered useless and misshapen the agile fingers that once had been.

"You have to perform surgery."

The command came from the voice that Jace recognized as the bully who had enjoyed the torture most of all. And who, Jace felt certain, was a minor player, a foot soldier under orders to torture what could be tortured from the prisoner-spy.

The precise form of torture, Jace imagined, had been left to the discretion of the bully and his comrades. And when it was discovered that they'd chosen to systematically cripple the hands of the prisoner who was not a spy? And whose value as a surgeon had become paramount once again?

Their punishment would perhaps be the swift forfeit of their lives. And they weren't eager to die. Jace saw their fear. Not eager at all to become martyrs to the cause.

The bully repeated his impossible demand.

"You must operate."

Jace replied by looking at his damaged hands, seeing them for the first time as the desert sun blazed inferno bright.

Discounting the pain—as, long ago, he had—could these woefully bent fingers even *hold* a scalpel? Was it possible to grasp with these hands in any meaningful way? Or would his cracked bones, malnourished and wobbly, shatter further as he tried to clutch unyielding steel? And what of suturing, and . . .

"We'll kill you," the henchman asserted, "if you don't."

Jace shrugged. "You'll kill me anyway. So why should I bother to help?"

The bully had no answer.

Nor did Jace.

But the sun did. The inferno did. Its burning amber fury softened, gentled, until it glowed with the pastel brilliance of Winnie's daylight star. The luminous lavender of Winnie's sister's eyes.

"Take me to the patient," Jace commanded. "And to whoever is requesting my expertise." Jace's lips, the parched flesh which so recently had broken and bled with the slightest of movement—with no movement at all— smiled broadly, without breaking, at the stunned demon limned in lavender overhead. And Jace's voice, hoarse no longer, as if balmed like his lips by raindrops and by love, said softly, powerfully, "Now."

They were father and son, the patient and his desperate loved one, who was, not surprisingly, the leader of this particular enclave of terror.

Leader. Terrorist. Son.

Liar. Impostor. Thief.

Jace Colton knew well the bonds, of loathing or of love, between father and son, and how such potent bonds defined the contours of one's life.

The son's life.

Jace spoke son to son to the man whose bond with his father was love not hate . . . and who, beneath the pastel sun, was a patient's frantic relative, no more, no less.

"Your father has what's called an acute abdomen. I don't know the cause. I won't know until I operate."

"But you *will* operate."

The son was a frantic relative. And more. But the lavender star shimmered still. "I will, and I will try my best to save him. It's my oath as a physician, and I make you that promise, too, as a man, and as a son. But you must make an oath as well to me."

"What oath?"

"That no matter the outcome you will let me go."

"If my father survives, only."

"No. Not only. You must promise, no matter the outcome, to permit me to go home."

Home. To the Emerald City. To my Julia. My Josie.

# CHAPTER TWENTY

*J*osie was delivered by emergency Caesarean section. The doctors had no choice. Julia's bleeding from placenta previa was profuse, a gushing that placed the lives of both mother and baby in peril.

Besides, although they had no choice, the prospect of delivering the infant seven weeks premature wasn't daunting for Josie's doctors. Not in this modern era of neonatal care. A thirty-three week premie could be expected to do very well, and for all her life, especially when the prenatal care had been as loving as Josie's had been. And despite Julia's precipitous hemorrhage, there'd been not the slightest indication of in utero compromise.

But all was not fine with Josie.

Yes, she was perfectly formed, and not even particularly small. But her breathing was distressed, rapid and gasping, as if her lungs were disproportionately premature, and as if far more immature than her gestational weeks, she was unable to maintain an adequate body temperature on her own. And mysteriously, and startlingly, her serum electrolytes were markedly awry.

Had she been conceived in late January, perhaps, rather that the Christmastide conception of which her mother had been so sure?

No. *No.*

Perhaps she was septic, then. Maybe Julia's membranes had ruptured undetected before she'd begun to bleed.

Josie's physicians treated her possible sepsis expectantly, with broad-spectrum antibiotics pending culture results, an adjunct to Josie's already-aggressive care: the incubator, the ventilator, the continuous monitoring, both human and electronic, in University Hospital's Neonatal ICU.

Josie's doctors didn't know why their newborn patient was so critically ill. But Julia did. It was she, after all, who'd caused her baby's distress. *She* who'd failed to protect the precious little life from the worry—amid the wonder—of her dreams.

Josie had journeyed with her to Jace. Julia had permitted her to do so. Even though it had been bitterly cold in the forest of pines. Josie was cold still, dangerously chilled without the incubator, although she'd journeyed with Julia to the desert, too. And she'd been damaged, too, in the desert, deprived of water as Jace had been, until her serum electrolytes were dramatically and perilously disturbed.

And what of Josie's respiratory distress? That damage, Julia knew, had come not during her dreams of Jace but while she, Julia, was wide-awake. And it was the most shameful negligence of all. *Even though she'd been so careful.*

She'd used watercolors only, as always. Nontoxic. Safe. Without noxious fumes of any kind. She'd bought palettes designed especially for children, and had read and re-read the labels anyway. Her kitchen studio beneath the snowflake was open and airy, and since late May it had been possible on so many days to open the doors and windows to a balmy breeze.

But there must have been fumes after all, invisible and scentless, like the phantom fumes of gasoline, those fatal fumes, that Jace had tormented himself with for failing to detect. But there had been no such lethal fumes in the house on Bluebird Lane. No threat whatsoever until the murderous monster arrived.

Jace was not to blame for what happened in Loganville. Had never been. But she *was* to blame for the damaged little lungs that gasped so desperately, so frantically, for breath.

Julia Anne Hayley was postop, postpartum, with significant anemia—and bacteremic, possibly, too. Any one of which was an excellent reason for her to remain in her four-bed room. But Julia needed to be with her baby girl, insisted on it, and was.

And when the NICU nurses became gently but firmly insistent as well? And even wheeled the desperately worried, and desperately exhausted, new mother to the maternity ward and tucked her into bed?

Julia closed her eyes to rest not to sleep, *not to dream.*

She was only vaguely aware of the other sounds in the room, until from the television overhead . . .

"This just in. Reuters News is reporting that Dr. Jace Colton, who has been held hostage since February 12, has been released. No further details are available at this time. But, repeating the headline, physician-hostage Jace Colton has been released."

Julia's pale and aching hands moved with trembling grace to her bedside phone. She pressed "O," and in response to her anxious query was informed by a pleasant hospital operator that she could dial directly both local and long-distance calls. Her account would be automatically billed.

Her fingers stalled for a moment before dialing anew, halted by a memory forty-eight hours old, the early-evening call she'd received from Garek just hours before she'd awakened, bleeding, from her dreams.

He would be away from his office, he told her. Beginning the next day. Out of the country with a client whose overseas business interests were of such magnitude that he wanted his attorney with him every step of the way.

There wouldn't be, Garek told her, an easy way for her to reach him directly. But he'd be checking often with his office, and he'd let her know, as always, if there was news.

Julia dialed then, to her—the Wilsons'—answering machine, and there it was, the message faraway but glorious from Garek.

Jace was alive, safe, free. And *fine*, Garek said. Would be. True, he'd apparently lost a lot of weight, and his blood studies, when obtained, would undoubtedly be abnormal. And there were injuries to his hands as well.

But mentally, emotionally, Jace Colton was strong, and so focused that he'd insisted on being flown to London, he was en route there now, in lieu of the various American military bases that were the usual choice.

Garek provided the name and phone number of the London hospital where, soon, Jace would be. Soon, and for a while. Garek himself would be out of the country for at least another week. But Julia should call his office, as they'd previously discussed, if she needed to reach him for any reason at all.

And if not . . .

Garek McIntyre's voice, which Julia had come to know so well, changed as he left the final part of his message to her. For months, the deep voice had been solemn, lawyerly, cordial. But not personal.

It was personal now.

"I want to thank you, Julia. Yes, *I* want to thank *you*." A smile seemed to touch the solemn voice. "You've always thanked me, even though there was no need. I did nothing. Not even, by the way, sending in the rescue team which, you believed so strongly, Jace would not want. There was a team, Julia, and they were ready and willing to go. But they never had a chance. Jace rescued himself. And I know you were right. He would have hated any risk of life, any loss of life, taken by others, however willing they were, to save him. I did nothing, in the end, for Jace. But you did a great deal, Julia, for me. It mattered to me, all these months, to have someone to talk to—*you*—who cared, as I did, about Jace's safe return. So thank you. Very much."

"Thank you, Garek," she whispered. "Thank *you*."

Julia returned the receiver to its cradle, then lay down, eyes closed, and for a soaring moment felt a rush of sheer joy.

Jace was alive, safe, free.

And desperately ill, she knew, despite the lawyerly calm with which Garek had reported his status.

Desperately ill. Like his Josie.

Including injuries, Garek had said, to his hands.

Joy shattered into an infinity of splinters, sharp and piercing and mercilessly bright.

Did Josie's tiny perfect hands hurt like Jace's? Like Julia's own? Would her baby be screaming from pain if only she *could* scream? If her breathing wasn't already so precarious that a plastic tube filled her little throat?

# CHAPTER
# TWENTY-ONE

*J*ulia was discharged from University Hospital on her fourth postpartum day. She'd been given iron but no transfusions, despite an anemia that was profound. Her bone marrow was normal and with the iron was mounting a brisk response to her loss of blood.

Julia's doctors might have transfused her, probably would have, had her newborn baby girl been being discharged, too. But Julia's daughter wasn't going home, might never go home, and whatever weakness Julia's anemia imposed might compel her to do what she needed most and had resisted so far—rest. Sleep.

Yes, maternal-infant bonding was important. And there was no doubt that Josie responded to her mother's presence. Even when Julia wasn't whispering through the pores in the translucent cocoon in which her baby lay, and struggled so, or reaching through the incubator's protective sleeve to touch, Josie knew her mother was there.

The recognition was remarkable, a wondrous bond. But it had a downside.

Josie was wakeful when her mother was near, and her pulse raced, an excited fluttering that stressed ever more her galloping heart, and her breathing became more rapid—excited too—which caused her distressed lungs to battle more fiercely, more exhaustingly, the ventilator's carefully regulated puffs.

It would be best for Josie to sleep as much as she possibly could. So, when Julia was discharged home, it was for the entire night. Yes, she could return in the morning. *Of course* she could. And she could visit her daughter throughout the day. And they would call her right away if there was any change, and she should feel free to call them *any* time.

Julia went home by cab, a ten-minute journey even at five-thirty on a weekday, workday, afternoon. And did she curl into bed, as she was supposed to, the moment she walked into the Hawthorne Hills house?

No. She dressed for cleaning, not for sleep. For there was cleaning to do. She wore the jeans that hadn't fit for months, but hung loosely now, and the sweatshirt that had become ever more tight, gloriously stretched, as her breasts had filled, had blossomed, for her Josie.

There was milk, still, in Julia's breasts. For her Josie. Julia was doing everything the doctors prescribed to encourage that nourishment, that nurturing, to stay.

But her breasts were wilting nonetheless, withering, just as the hormones that rendered a womb fertile had disappeared so swiftly after Winnie's death.

Julia looked pregnant no more.

Pregnant *never*.

She cleaned furiously as she had after Winnie's death for Winnie and Gran, so that everything would be sparkling and bright when they returned.

But this was *different*, Julia told herself when the realization hit. Josie *was* coming home. Besides, there was legitimate cleaning to do. Her own blood, for example, on the bathroom floor. It wiped away quite easily, she discovered. But the towels were ruined. Julia folded them neatly in a plastic sack, and the sheets and mattress pad, too. And the bed itself? Purchased new by the Wilsons for their house sitter–guest? It was fine. Pristine. Still.

Julia made the bed, but didn't crawl in.

There was more cleaning to do. In the kitchen. While she listened to the evening news? No. The only news that mattered she'd heard already during her hospital stay. The physician-hostage was "truly remarkable," his London doctors proclaimed. "Amazingly resilient considering his horrific ordeal."

Alexis Allen, too, had things to say. She did so on *Larry King Live*. No, she wouldn't be flying to London. She couldn't abandon the cast and crew of *Windy City*, not given the predicament her character was in, nor would, *did*, Jace want her to.

Besides, she confessed, both she and Jace needed time. His months of captivity had been difficult for them both. And maybe they wouldn't get back together. But she was relieved, and so very grateful, that the man she would love *always* was safe at last.

Julia cleaned the kitchen in silence, removing from the tabletop the recent watercolors she had done and the many trays of paint. And did she throw everything away? She was so tempted.

But these were Josie's images, Josie's art. Her baby girl had been Julia's Emerald City muse, as Winnie had been her Kansas one, and, it seemed, the watercolor paints were not to blame for Josie's respiratory distress after all.

Julia had not shared with Josie's doctors her belief that Josie was so cold, and her blood chemistries were so awry, because she'd permitted her daughter to journey to Jace in her dreams. There was no medical antidote, was there, for dreams? A miracle potion that would reverse the damage to Josie her dreams had wrought?

No, Julia knew. The only cure for dreams was the harsh bright light of day.

But there might be, mightn't there, an antidote to the noxious fumes to which her baby had been exposed? A recipe so potent it would extinguish all vestiges of poison?

Julia told Josie's doctors within hours of Josie's birth about the watercolors she had used. And they took seriously Julia's worry. But after careful research they had assured her, more than once and categorically, that the paints were not to blame. And gently, and categorically, that neither was she.

Julia put both paintings and paints in a cupboard nearby, then cleaned to mirror shininess the table, the counters, the stove. And the windows. This was where she and Josie would sit, as they had all these months when Josie fluttered inside. Here, and in the living room in Gran's chair, as they had, too, marveling at the trees, the clouds, the mountains, the lake.

Which meant the living-room windows needed to be cleaned. Too.

Now. Tonight.

The glass cleaner streamed at first like teardrops. Weeping. Sobbing. A torrent of despair that matched the deluge Julia felt inside.

Until, as if by magic, the twilight sky beyond the weeping window began to shimmer a rare and exquisite pink. A *baby-girl* pink. The teardrops became raindrops then, a nourishing mist.

Julia's world was rosy, suddenly, and as cozy as the Emerald City rain, and warm. She felt rosy, too, cozy and warm, and fatigued in that lovely cozy way that she and Josie had felt so often, when they would surrender at day's end and with smiling welcome to sleep.

To dreams.

Julia curled into the familiar comfort of Gran's chair, and gazed at the glistening pink, and even when her eyes drifted shut, there was pinkness still.

She fell to sleep, to dreams, in that rosy glow.

She slept. Deeply. And dreamed. In all the colors of the rainbow. In watercolors, billowing and soft, and floating and fluffy, like summer clouds filled with joy.

No images appeared in her watercolor tableau. Only hope, only happiness, only love.

No sound, either, accompanied her watercolor dream.

Until, that is, its very end. And the chime in her dream chimed still, as she awakened. To pinkness.

Pinkness still. Pinkness again. For it was dawn.

She'd slept all night in Gran's chair, had dreamed in pastel clouds of happiness throughout the darkness.

And she must have been sleeping still. Dreaming. Because the chiming, her doorbell, didn't frighten her. And it would have, surely, had she truly been awake.

For who, she would have asked herself, would ring her doorbell at daybreak but Josie's doctors and nurses—having come to tell her in person, and as gently as it could possibly be done, the shattering news?

But Julia wasn't frightened. Pastel hopefulness shimmered still. As she floated, as if on a watercolor cloud, toward the door.

And she thought, as she floated on rainbows, how silvery was the sound. Magical and pure.

Like sleigh bells, she thought.

*Like sleigh bells.*

# CHAPTER
# TWENTY-TWO

*S*leigh bells, Jace thought as he, too, heard the delicate chime.

The *illusion* of sleigh bells, he amended swiftly.

Fiercely.

Dr. Jace Colton knew very well why his brain floated with such enchanting defiance to illusions, to dreams. It was the same reason that his muscles quivered, *quaked,* even when he was lying down.

His electrolytes were seriously disturbed. Gravely awry. And his renal insufficiency, although presumably prerenal and hence reversible, had yet to be definitively diagnosed. And the abnormalities in his liver function indicated that his systematically starved body had, for some time, been cannibalizing itself.

Yes, he'd conceded to his physicians when he'd informed them of his plan to leave, then and there, the prestigious hospital in Londontown. His medical condition *was* far from perfect. Precarious at best. But there was really nothing, he'd asserted, that a little hot chocolate—

and a mountain of macadamia nuts—couldn't instantly cure.

The glib comment from the trauma maven had alarmed further the white-coated academicians who surrounded his bed. Perhaps their patient wasn't as mentally intact as he'd seemed.

But Jace had been intact enough. Then. Had pretended to be. He'd managed to tether his floating brain just close enough to reality that he'd been able to answer, with apparent but illusive ease, the mental-status questions his physicians posed.

Dr. Jace Colton was rational, they'd decided. Sane. He'd even agreed that his diet, as unpalatable as it was, should consist only of the liquid nutrients they'd been giving him, the simple sugars and basic amino acids that placed the most minimal demands possible on the ravaged organs within.

He would drink the liquid potions, he'd promised. At least, he'd amended silently, until he was *with her.* Then, with her, he would drink hot chocolate. But, the physician within him insisted, he would defer the magic of macadamias, a calorie-dense challenge to even the most robust of metabolisms, for a while.

The hot chocolate would be magic enough.

*She would be.*

He would, Jace Colton told his doctors, take with him a supply of the powder from which the liquid potion came, and would feed himself, as they were, at frequent intervals around the clock.

But he *was* leaving, despite his chaotic bloodwork, his quaking frame, and the horrific plight of his hands.

The surgeon would need extensive surgery. In Chicago, by a hand surgeon colleague there, once his overall medical condition improved to the point where transfer *to another hospital* was deemed to be safe.

His bones would need to be broken again, every one, and the freshly shattered shafts would be impaled with steel, an intrusion which would straighten as much as possible the badly mangled bones.

With painstaking surgery, followed by months of painful rehab, the trauma surgeon would be able to operate again.

But he already could operate. Had. In the desert. And successfully, too.

Jace declined from the hand surgeons in London even the most minimal care. No casts, no splints, no massive mittens of snowy white gauze. Nothing that would impede in any way his naked fingers from touching her beloved cheeks.

Julia wouldn't be repulsed by his misshapen hands. She had loved once, always, a little sister with such hands.

But the world was repulsed by him, the same strangers who not so long ago would have stared without apology at his staggering good looks.

Jace Colton was a skeleton now, a most ghastly ghoul, and the world veered away from him as he neared, scurried away . . . as holiday shoppers once had stepped from

Yuletide sidewalks into snowy Kansas streets when Edwina Anne Hayley came into view.

Jace had been reunited at the hospital with his duffel bag. Such a reunion had been in fact the ravaged patient's first and most urgent request. His duffel bag—the Canterfields angel safe inside—had arrived from the organization headquarters on Charing Cross Road. His garment bag, with his London and Chicago clothes, was delivered, too, as were his wallet, its credit cards and its cash, and the mauve notepaper that had been neatly folded, caressingly folded, within.

British Airways was happy, sort of, to sell the skeleton on a mission two first-class seats, 2A and 2B, for its nonstop to Seattle. But they needed to know, they really did, if he had any communicable disease. And when he assured them he did not, and that yes he was *that* Jace Colton, his passport photo provided such proof, the ticket agent wanted to know, to be reassured, that his nurse or doctor would be accompanying him on the flight.

Jace lied, sort of. His traveling companion, the one for whom he was purchasing seat 2B, would take the best care of him imaginable. As she had, he clarified silently, for all these months, and visible only to him.

It wasn't until Jace Colton was miles aloft that he realized just how disturbed, how distorted, his floating brain truly was. He had been envisioning so clearly what lay at the end of this Emerald City flight. He could see it, feel it, hear it. *So clearly.*

It would be nearly nightfall when he reached Julia's

Hawthorne Hills home. She wouldn't yet have gone to bed. But she might have been napping in Gran's chair.

Her hair would be tousled, her cheeks flushed pink, and her lavender eyes would glow, luminous and bright, when she opened the door to him.

Joy would shimmer. And welcome and love. But not shock. Not horror. For Julia knew well the skeleton he'd become. She had seen him, after all, just four days before, and for all the forest-and-desert nights before that.

She would touch without the slightest hesitation the ravaged skull that was his face. And he would touch her, too.

There might be shock then, would be, when she saw his hands. She hadn't seen them before, the mangled mass they'd become, because he'd hidden that trauma, and its torture, from her.

Just as Julia had hidden her pregnancy from him. He should have known of that splendor though, should have guessed, because with each passing month her hair had grown ever longer, she'd permitted it to grow, and there were even times, when she visited him in his dreams, that her head tilted, she would tilt it, as if in offering to the tiniest of hands, still within her womb, but which one day would tangle and curl in the glossy black silk.

Tonight, in the Emerald City, Julia's pregnancy would be hidden no more, just as his hands would not, and he would touch with those hands—she would want him to, *would guide him to*—her abdomen, where their precious Josie danced and grew. And then—

Then, in midair, in midflight, Jace realized the folly, the fantasy, of his imaginings of joy.

Julia might or might not be happy to see him. She would be glad, certainly, that he was alive. But such gladness would have come days ago, with the news of his release.

It had been eight months since Julia had seen him. Eight months. *Not four days.* And what she knew, all she'd known since December, was the lie he'd permitted her to believe, that he'd wanted no more life with her, no more love with her, than what they'd already had.

The rest was fantasy. Dreams. His.

Yet here he was hurtling through space, and planning on this very night to walk out of his dreams and into her arms. Even the notion of *walking* was fanciful. He was a wobbly skeleton, a trembling ghoul, and the quaking had become ever more pronounced in the hours since he'd left the hospital against medical advice.

Julia would invite him in, of course. She was that generous. And she would listen carefully, and so thoughtfully, as he tried to explain. There would be hot chocolate, too. She would make for the quivering vision of death a steaming mug.

And, because it was so obvious he needed to lie down, she might even invite him into her bed.

Jace knew, in midair, that his journey to her could not happen tonight. He needed to lie down alone, and sleep if he possibly could, and make it very clear to his floating mind what were dreams and what was real. In the morning, when he was coherent, *more* coherent, and could stand for a while without swirling, and sit even longer without needing to crumple to the floor, he would go to her.

In the morning. Not tonight.

Jace spoke by airphone to the concierge at Seattle's downtown Hilton on Sixth. The hotel wasn't *that* close, the concierge admitted, to the Hawthorne Hills address. She knew, she explained, because she'd been raised in nearby View Ridge. There were hotels that were quite close, however, including in the Village a Silver Cloud Inn.

Jace made, from midair, a reservation at the Emerald City hotel that sounded like dreams, and when he spoke to the pleasant receptionist at the Silver Cloud, he asked about getting from the airport to the hotel.

It was *easy*, the pleasant voice assured him. Especially at twilight, when he was due to arrive. And although there could definitely be traffic long after the evening rush, tonight there shouldn't be. It was a weeknight, which helped, and the Mariners were playing away.

Jace hadn't planned, in the dream in which he'd arrive at her doorstep on this night, to rent a car. But now he'd want a car, would need one, so that he could drive to her in the morning, and without delay, the moment he felt strong enough, coherent enough, to do so.

And the drive to the Silver Cloud Inn, even with his crippled hands and drifting brain, did sound easy, straightforward. And safe. He would drive carefully, cautiously, in the far right-hand lane.

He rented the car by phone from the stratosphere. And

since he was a preferred customer, and his signature was on file, the car would be ready without paperwork.

And was.

He drove carefully, cautiously, on the Emerald City interstate, which in the summer twilight was, blessedly, traffic free. And, far sooner than he'd expected, his Montlake exit beckoned just ahead.

Once off I-5, he needed merely to turn left at the light toward the Montlake bridge. Once across the bridge, the Silver Cloud receptionist had cheerfully explained, University Hospital would be on one side and Husky Stadium on the other. All he had to do was keep driving straight. He'd come to the Village in a mile or so, and in a few more blocks to the Inn.

Jace was making the left turn now, onto Montlake, and he was going to reach his destination safely. Barely. But he would.

And in the morning he'd be so much better, so much stronger. For her. He would have it no other way. And now he was crossing the Montlake bridge, and there was the stadium, and the hospital, and—

Jace Colton couldn't breathe. Could not. He could only gasp for oxygen that was not there.

And his heart raced. Fluttered. Flew.

And his brain, floating already, clouded, darkened, swirled.

He was in the far-right lane, the safest and most cautious, and University Hospital, and its Emergency Room, could only be accessed from the left. But it didn't matter. He would have been unable to make the drive.

He managed, barely, to pull to the side of the road. And stop. And clutch the steering wheel with his shattered hands even as his lungs drowned and his heart galloped and his entire being lurched and twirled.

He would die in a minute. Or two. Or five. Without seeing Julia. Or Josie.

No. *No.*

Jace didn't imagine, even with his dreaming brain, that his protest, which was a prayer, would be heard. But somehow it was, in a minute or two or five. Heard and answered, for suddenly there was such glorious calm, such shimmering peace, and the sky had become—in those minutes of death, of dying, of prayer—a brilliant rosy pink.

It enveloped him, that pink, as his journey continued to the Silver Cloud, and it blanketed him still, so rosy, so warm, as he fell to sleep, to dreams . . . to pastel watercolors of love.

And now he was here, on her porch, and the sky shimmered still that astonishing pink, and Jace had believed he was better *for her,* stronger and clearer. Until he touched her doorbell and heard sleigh bells.

The illusion of sleigh bells.

And now the door was opening, and he was dreaming still, for her lavender eyes glowed with wonder, and neither shock nor horror, at the skeleton on her doorstep.

"Oh," she whispered as she welcomed him, wanted him, in her home. "You're here."

Then she touched his face, the ravaged skull within the gossamer flesh, and her fingers drifted thoughtfully, caressingly, to where his blindfold had been so tight it left deep scars in his fragile flesh.

Jace touched her too, the beloved face that was so pale, too pale, but abloom with roses for him.

"Your *hands*," she murmured with shock, such shock at last.

"Are fine," he said so softly. "My hands are fine."

But Julia wasn't reassured by his words. She seemed desperate, in fact, in her worry.

*Desperate.*

"They must *hurt*, Jace. They must hurt you *so much*." *You must want to scream with the pain . . . if only you could scream.*

"Julia. My hands are fine."

But *she* wasn't fine, he realized. And now she was backing away, and now turning away. Jace saw in the moment before she turned from him the anguish on her lovely face. The shame *and the guilt*, as if there was something terrible that she'd done.

Something unspeakable.

But she was going to speak it, Jace realized, too. She was going to confess to him whatever it was that she perceived to be her unforgivable crime. And yet was not. Could *never* be.

Julia confessed. To him. But she looked far away, through the living-room window that sparkled in the brilliant pink light as if streaked by an infinity of recent tears.

"You have a daughter," she whispered. Confessed. "Her name is Josie, and she was born four nights ago, and she's sick, *so very sick*. I didn't take care of her, our little girl, as I should have. She wasn't safe, *as she should have been,* inside me."

"Oh, Julia." *My Julia.* "It's not your fault. How could it possibly be?"

She didn't answer his loving query. Wasn't listening. Did not hear.

"Her tiny heart is fluttering, and her lungs . . . oh, Jace, *she can't breathe.* But I left her last night. *I left her.* They wanted me to, told me to, and I *did.* They said they'd call if there was any change, and that I could call to check on her *any* time. I was going to call before I went to bed, and again and again throughout the night, as if I was in the hospital still, visiting her at all hours, as I was permitted to do. But . . ."

"But?" *My love?*

"*I fell asleep.* I was cleaning, and suddenly the sky became so pink." Julia faltered then, because he was there, standing between her and the window of tears, and he was gazing at her with a gentleness, a tenderness, she did not deserve.

"It's not your fault, Julia, that Josie is sick. It could never be your fault. And you needed to sleep, didn't you? For Josie. To be strong for her. And the sky last night . . . I saw it, too. It shimmered over me, Julia, and over you, and over Josie."

And it saved me, Jace thought. That sky. When I was so close to our Josie and could not breathe. It saved me, and it will have saved . . .

"Why don't you call the hospital now?" he asked. *While the shimmering grace envelops us still?*

She agreed softly, quietly. And so fearfully, Jace realized. He saw her fear clearly, and more: what these past four days and nights had been for her. The frantic anguish. The desperate guilt.

Oh, there should *never* have been guilt.

Jace saw, too, her strength. And her courage. This woman, his Julia, who'd been facing this sadness, this despair, all alone.

She was alone no more.

His mangled hands took, very gently, the telephone receiver from her trembling ones. Although it was her quivering fingers that dialed.

And then he was telling the NICU ward clerk who he was.

Josie's father.

*Josie's father.* Julia heard the emotion as he spoke the words, the love amid the worry, the joy amid the terror, and she saw his tears as Jace listened in silence to what Josie's doctor had to say.

The tears spilled freely from Jace Colton's sunken green eyes, and made the tortuous journey over the ridges of his bones and the valleys of his cheeks.

And when Jace spoke again, the tears flooded his throat.

"We'll come now." Then, the conversation ended, and with tears flooding but not drowning, he whispered to Julia the glorious truth. "She's all right, Julia. Our Josie is all right."

"Jace?"

"It's true. She turned the corner last night, when the

sky was its brightest pink. It happened suddenly. Miraculously."

"But they didn't *call*."

"No. They wanted to be very certain that the miracle was real. And it was, Julia. It is. Very real." *Like my dreams, my Julia, of you.* "She's fine. Our little Josie is fine. And the three of us are going to have the most happy—"

"No."

*No?* The single syllable, spoken softly but with such resolve, froze his heart, his soul.

He was in the desert again, but ice-cold despite the heat, and he was dying, as he'd been dying on that day . . . until in his dreams, *which were real,* he'd heard the chiming of bells and the strumming of harps.

There'd been other sounds in that dream, unheard above the music. Julia's troubled words. But now, as if some divine conductor commanded the bells and harps to hush ever so slightly their exuberant refrain—pianissimo, please—the lost words were lost no more.

*We won't marry, Jace. It's not necessary. I'll move to Chicago, Josie and I will move, and when you do marry, the woman you choose, the woman you love, will be a loving mother, too, for our Josie. I know she will be.*

"I love you, Julia."

"Jace, you don't have to . . ."

"Oh, but I do. *And I do.* I've loved you since London. Yes, since then. I was going to tell you on our last night together, and then I was going to convince you that it was best for you to forget all about me."

"Best? How could it be *best?*"

Jace smiled, and kissed her tears. The watery spill that had begun with sadness, with despair, was spilling still. But the tears tasted sweeter, ever more nourishing, as her glistening eyes glistened with joy.

"That, you see, is what prevented me from telling you the truth. *That,* Julia. Your fearlessness. I knew you'd go one-on-one with my demons no matter the risk. But what I didn't know was that you'd already driven them away. I changed in London, *was* changed, in London, by you. I became someone different because of you. Someone better, someone new."

"No," Julia whispered that single syllable yet again. And forcefully, too. But this *no* did not have him dying again. This *no* came with love. "You were you in London. You, Jace. *You.* The man who, once, had been an unwanted little boy, but who against all odds believed in love, and found it and gave it, and who dared, as you dared, to dream in that dream."

"I have been dreaming," Jace said. Very softly. And with reverence. "All these months. I've been dreaming all these months, Julia, of you."

Julia's lavender eyes shone, as softly, and so reverently too, she told him of her dreams. "You named her, Jace. You named our Josie. In April. In a forest of pines. In my dreams. Our dreams."

Neither spoke. Neither could. But both believed.

And why not, this woman and this man who'd soared where angels sang and reindeer flew and snowflakes forever danced?

They were soaring still, would soar always, in this magical stratosphere called love.

Julia took his beloved mangled hands, and tugged ever so gently, as a starving teen shepherd had been tugged toward love decades before. "Come meet your daughter, Jace. Come meet your precious Josie."

# CHAPTER
# TWENTY-THREE

*S*he curled her tiny perfect fingers around his crooked ones, and it was, Jace believed, all the healing his shattered bones would ever need.

And she tasted her mother's milk.

And Josie Anne Colton got better, grew ever stronger, throughout the summer day.

Her parents, both of them, became stronger, better, too. Love helped. Love cured.

And hot chocolate steamed a little healing magic, as did their decision to make Seattle their home.

"What is it, Julia?" Jace asked, in the early afternoon as they sat in the room where their Josie slept, smiling, and dreamed.

Josie's room in the Neonatal ICU could house as many as five desperate newborns. But this was a good time for babies in the Emerald City. Josie's crystal cocoon was the only one in use.

"What is what?" Julia replied.

"What is it that you're not telling me? Something, I know."

"Yes. Something. But for another day."

"Are you healthy?" Jace asked with such worry, the skeleton whose lab values would have landed him not as a visiting father but as a closely monitored guest in any hospital in the world.

"I'm *very* healthy, Jace."

"Is there someone else?"

"Who I love?" Julia's fingers, warm from hot chocolate, touched the greater warmth that was him. "Besides you and Josie? No. Never."

"Then whatever the something is, it's trivial."

"But it's not."

"Then tell me, Julia. Please."

She told him about Loganville. Everything there was to tell. He listened in silence, his broken hands clenched, and perhaps breaking anew, his eyes at once ablaze and cold.

Jace was silent, still, when she was through. And when he spoke at last it was to both of them, the woman he loved and the daughter who slept, smiling, in the nearby cocoon.

"I'm not going to do anything, Julia. I'm going to let it go."

"Because of us."

Jace Colton's dark green eyes looked at the *us,* his Josie, his Julia.

His family.

"Because it's what I want, Julia. You're my life now. You and Josie."

Silence fell again, so dark, so brooding, for him. Julia saw his search for answers in the brooding darkness— who the monster was, why he had done such a thing— and she watched but did not follow as Jace crossed to a distant window and stared in silence at the mountain. The lake.

He stood, staring, for a very long time. As if in a trance. Then suddenly, urgently, he turned toward her. But he looked instead, *glared* instead, at the distance between them.

And Jace Colton waited, with such fear, to see in that space, *the abyss he'd created,* the lash of fire and the fury of flames.

But no inferno blazed between them.

And the abyss? So vast, so deep? It was filled only with love.

"Grace would have loved your reindeer," he said to the woman whose golden glow filled the abyss, his heart, his world. "Winnie's reindeer. She would have loved the entire rainbowed herd. She spent that last day, that Christmas Eve, washing carrots for them. They needed carrots, she said, to see in the dark. Rudolph, she told me, always got three. Since he was in front. And she washed two each for the other eight."

Julia rose and walked to him, and touched his beloved face.

"Please don't decide yet what to do about Loganville. There's no need, yet, to decide. And Josie and I will be with you no matter what, loving you, *loving you,* forever and always."

Forever and always, even though it would be a while, weeks, before their precious little hummingbird could flutter home. She was still six weeks premature. But the time would come. Josie's parents whispered that promise to her amid so many promises of love on this Emerald City day.

And *sleep well, little love,* Josie's parents whispered before leaving their baby for the night.

It wasn't Josie's doctors who insisted that it was time for Jace and Julia to go. Or the NICU nurses, either. Jace and Julia made the suggestion, so gently, to each other. He saw the ever-darkening shadows beneath Julia's shining bright eyes, and she saw the exhaustion, too, of Josie's daddy.

Jace walked with Julia to the front porch of her Hawthorne Hills home. But once she'd opened the door, he told her that he was going to the motel.

"The motel, Jace?"

"To get my things and check out."

"We should have done that on our way home."

"I wanted to get you home."

Julia smiled. "And I wanted to get *you* home."

"I'm almost here, Julia, almost home. And I will be very soon. It's just that, well, I want to get the Canterfields angel you gave me. She's my symbol of Josie. And since our Josie can't be with us tonight . . ."

"*You are so beautiful,* Jace Colton."

"You make me that way." He kissed her sky pink

cheeks. And her mouth. "I won't be long, Julia. I promise."

She gave him her house key and watched from the open door as he drove away. Then she showered, she was a little cold without him, and dressed in her ruffled blue nightgown, the London one, and in the plush mauve bathrobe, several sizes too large, that she'd ordered from a catalogue but had yet to wear.

Then, because it was still a little too soon for Jace to return, Julia checked her phone messages.

There was one.

From Dolores Wilson.

"Oh, hello, Julia. This is the first time I've gotten your—well, I suppose, *our*—machine. But of course you're not there, not on a perfect summer evening in Seattle. It's SeaFair week, isn't it? Always a gala time. Anyway, here's the situation. Charles and I have decided to stay here, *move* here. The children are diehard East Coasters now. I haven't the foggiest how that happened, but it did! And the Virginia countryside is really very lovely, lush and green. So we have a favor to ask, Julia, and maybe I shouldn't do it on the machine. On the other hand, this will give you a chance to think it over, and we want you to be honest, which you *always* are, but also very polite. Anyway, here goes. We're going to have to sell the house. And according to real-estate agents we've talked to, we should get it on the market soon. Summer's apparently the best time to sell. Which will be, I'm afraid, a *terrible* intrusion on your privacy. We'd like you to stay, Julia, and you wouldn't need to put away your paintings every time the house was shown, unless you *wanted* to for privacy's sake, and we know we all agreed to an entire year, so if this is simply too much and you want to move out, we'll pay for your rent wherever you like, and . . . well, I think you get the idea, as random as this message seems. Please think about what you'd like to do, dear. And give us a call. Thanks! Is there anything else, Charles? He says no, that's *enough*. I guess I'm signing off. And don't worry, Julia. Whatever you decide is *fine*."

Julia almost returned the Wilsons' call, despite the lateness of the East Coast hour, to tell them she already knew who would buy their lovely home. Josie and Jace and Julia. The hummingbird family of three.

Julia's smile, for she was smiling, wobbled slightly when the doorbell chimed. Then curved anew. Yes, Jace had the key. But his hands would be full, and aching.

She flew to the chimes. To him.

Soon, and so gently, they would take each other to bed, to sleep, to dreams, as one. As three.

"Mr. Logan!"

"Please call me Troy."

"Troy. What are you . . . ?"

"Is Jace here?"

"Jace?"

Troy Logan's smile was forgiving. Kind. "I know who he is, Julia—may I call you Julia?—and that he's in Seattle."

"He's innocent."

Troy's smile vanished. But his solemn expression and

somber words gloriously reassured. "I know that, too. I've known it for twenty-two years. But the only way I can prove it and put the real killer behind bars is with Jace's help."

"You know who the real killer is?"

"Yes. I do. I've known from the start. But as long as an impostor named Sam was a fugitive from justice, Rawley could always say, *would* always say, that the killer was Jace."

"But it was Rawley?"

"Yes. It was. And I'm afraid that fateful Christmas Eve wasn't even the first time Rawley Ramsey's violent temper had resulted in death. In *murder.* May I come in, Julia? And tell you and Jace everything I know?"

*I*t took Jace almost no time to gather his things at the Silver Cloud Inn. He'd scarcely unpacked. He was ready to leave, was just lifting his duffel bag, when a single knock rapped on the door.

Jace abandoned his luggage and opened that door.

"Rawley."

"Sam."

"Jace."

"A killer by any other name."

"I didn't kill them, Rawley."

"No?"

"No."

"Any idea who did?"

Jace looked at the man who had tackled him that night

in the snow, had overpowered him with sheer might, and who, twenty-two years later, was stronger still. Who *wouldn't* be stronger than a skeleton with broken bones and with muscles that were cannibalized to mush? And, Jace imagined, as if Rawley's raw power wasn't weapon enough, a shoulder holster with a loaded gun undoubtedly lurked beneath the navy blue blazer that Rawley wore.

"Yes. I do have an idea. Would you like to come in?"

"Why not?"

"*J*ace isn't here."

"But he'll be returning soon?" Troy asked politely, and logically, since Julia had already opened wide the door to let him in.

"Yes. Very soon."

"Well, I could fill you in on past history, if you like, on various details that Jace probably knows, but you may not. Or," Troy raved quietly as he crossed the living room to the windowed wall, "we could just talk about this spectacular view. That, I take it, is Mount Rainier?"

"*I* was at the lake that night. When I heard the explosion I ran to the house."

"And then left."

"You told me they were dead, Rawley. And, if you recall, you refused to let me die with them."

"My apologies, Sam. Jace. On the positive side, you wouldn't have met Julia had you died."

"Which is how you found me."

"It didn't take much investigating to put her in London—with you."

"But you didn't mention to the State Department who I was."

"No. Or to the media. I wanted you home, safe, alive." Loganville's robust and powerful chief of police stared assessingly at the ravaged shell that was Jace. "*Are* you?"

"What, safe? Alive? Yes. I am. And will continue to be. Assuming, that is, you're not planning to kill me."

"*Y*es. That's Mount Rainier. And Lake Washington. And there, just beyond the first floating bridge, is Bill Gates's lakefront home. And, oh!" Julia exclaimed as a powerful arm imprisoned her, and a gun muzzle, that cold hard steel, pressed into the delicate flesh below her jaw. "*You.*"

"Me."

"Why?"

"I'll tell you, Julia. I will. As much as I can tell before Jace returns. Why not? But let's get you settled first, shall we? This chair—where *did* you find this hideous upholstery?—will do quite nicely."

The chair wasn't hideous, merely beloved. What was hideous was the ease with which he imprisoned her, the gun at her head, her wrists cuffed, both of them and easily, by merely one of his hands.

Then, together, they wandered; a scavenger hunt that took almost no time. The two items Troy Logan needed were in the garage. The silvery duct tape . . . and the paint thinner, purchased by the Wilsons long ago, but potent still.

Troy bound her tightly, with silver tape and plush mauve sash, in Gran's chair, then doused in the noxious solvent her hair, her robe, the ruffling blue.

Gran's chair. Where so peacefully Edwina Anne Hayley had fluttered away.

No such gentle departure awaited Winnie's sister. Julia would not even, as she died, be able to float to the cotton-candy clouds above the azure lake.

Troy had turned Gran's chair from view to door. Jace would see her that way, and understand the horror, the moment he walked in.

Julia would perish in flames, and Jace would be shot by Troy, and the true killer would explain to the local police, and with such heartfelt remorse, that although he'd ended the life, the terror, of the Loganville monster, he'd arrived too late to save Jace Colton's final victim. Julia.

The living-room inferno, and his own belated heroism, had not, Troy confessed, been his original plan. He'd envisioned a murder-suicide, a blood-and-brains scenario in which Jace, upon learning that his beloved Julia had learned the horrific truth of Loganville, shot her. Then turned his weapon on himself.

"This poor gun," Troy moaned with false sorrow. "It's been waiting so patiently, for over two decades, as have I, for the chance to execute, as it were, the perfect murder-suicide. It's not registered by the way, and as you can see—take a look, Julia—has a very nice silencer as well. And, just in case you'd like to know, it flew undetected from Colorado. With me. In my private jet."

Troy paused, as if it were her turn to speak, and Julia drew a breath, an instinctive gasp for air, even though breathing made the blurriness ever worse. It was an intoxication of sorts, this effect of noxious fumes on her exhausted brain. But there was no bubbly euphoria, as once there'd been with champagne, no buoyant voice that insisted despite appearances everything was going to be *just fine*.

If there was even a possibility of escape from Troy's lethal plan, it was eluding her, as it had been even before the fumes and the blurriness began. But it wouldn't elude Jace, whatever it was and if it existed at all. She needed to be awake, and as alert as she could be, when he arrived. To help him.

"You were going to stage a murder-suicide on that Christmas Eve?" she asked amid the fumes.

"I was. Starring Jace and Mary Beth. But Jace was a no-show then just as he's a no-show now. So I had to improvise. As now. Of course, even then I already had a little experience with death by fire."

"Mary Beth's mother."

"Very *good*, Julia. Yes. Louise. Who was a *bitch*. Speaking of which"—Troy withdrew from his jacket a pack of cigarettes——"these were hers. The bitch's. Her *final* pack. We shared a smoke, her treat, during which and without success I tried to convince her to stop meddling in Mary Beth's life."

"And yours."

"And mine." Troy lit a cigarette, which waggled in his lips as he said, "I'd offer you one, Julia. But you're just a wee bit too flammable."

"Did you kill Sam, too?"

"Mary Beth's beloved husband? Nope. Can't take credit for that one. Nor can Rawley, as it turns out. Not that I believe he'd have the guts. No, the good doctor's death was an accident, pure and simple. A gift of fate."

"But Mary Beth still didn't want you."

Troy Logan inhaled smoke, held it, and narrowed his eyes—at her—when he finally exhaled. "That's a brutal thing to say, Julia."

"But a true thing."

Troy shrugged. "Alas. I gave her one last chance, that Christmas Eve. I happened to have a wedding ceremony all lined up and ready to go in just three days. Do you know this, Julia? You're looking a little bored."

"I'm not bored." *Just so terribly blurred.* "I do know, however, that you were going to marry Carolyn."

"I was. And did. But it would have been *so easy,* the entire town would have understood, to have married Mary Beth instead."

"But Mary Beth said no."

"Mary Beth laughed."

"So you killed her."

"*Torched* her. Can you blame me?" Troy waited for a reply, saw it, and smiled. "Okay. So you can. You're probably not going to give me a ringing endorsement, either, for the next murder-suicide I have in mind. The one *after* this. But guess what? *I don't care.* It's going to be a murder*ess*-suicide, for the record, because it only makes sense—and *sense* matters in perfect crimes—for Belinda to shoot Rawley. Ah-ha! Puzzlement at last. Never heard of Belinda? Mrs. Bearce's only child? She's a *mouse,* she really is, and she's been pining for Rawley since junior high."

"Is Belinda's son Rawley's?" *The grandson who keeps the lovely Mrs. Bearce so lively and so young?*

"You really *are* a fount of Loganville lore. No. Robbie, the little computer nerd, isn't Rawley's. Seven years after Mary Beth's death, when it was obvious Rawley was in love with Mary Beth still, Belinda actually managed to find someone *else* to marry her. The conjugal bliss lasted just long enough for Belinda to have Robbie, who, by the way, adores Rawley as much as Belinda does."

"And who Rawley adores, too?"

"Yeah, unbelievably. He does. It's quite a sight, the jock playing catch with the wimp, and even more ludicrous—or heartwarming if that's your view—watching the kid show Rawley how to navigate the Net. Rumor has it that Rawley's actually asked Belinda to marry him. Which must make you wonder why, given the Norman Rockwell moments with Robbie's and Belinda's lifelong love, she'd shoot the man she's always wanted, then turn the gun on herself. *Aren't* you wondering that, Julia? No? I'll tell you anyway. Because even though it will be finally over, and Jace—and you, I'm afraid—will be *dead,*

Rawley won't be able to let Mary Beth go. It's been great fun, Rawley's relentless obsession with Mary Beth's un-avenged death. But now, well, I'm really in the mood to have Rawley Ramsey die. Of course if Rawley knew the truth, he'd swallow a gun himself. Would gobble it right up."

"The truth?"

"The *shocking* truth, Julia. About Grace."

"*I*'m not going to kill you," Rawley told Jace.

"Because?"

"I believe you're innocent. I didn't at first. I thought in fact that you were guilty as sin. But the more I thought about it, the more I became convinced that you couldn't have killed them any more than I could have. Or do you think I did?"

"I did," Jace said. "At first. I've only known the truth since earlier today. You seemed the obvious choice."

"And now?"

"And now." Jace's voice was soft. Low. "Troy."

As was Rawley's voice soft and low as he concurred. "Troy."

Soft and low. Like a distant thud on a midnight clear. The soft, low signal of destruction, and of death.

There was no other sound now, beyond the soft low tone in which each man pronounced the murderer's name.

But Jace heard that long-ago sound nonetheless. And

Rawley? He merely saw, and it was more than enough, the expression on Jace's face.

And even though Rawley knew that Troy had been in Loganville as recently as four hours before, and was to be notified *immediately* if Troy Logan left, he did not hesitate for an instant to follow Jace out the door.

"$\mathcal{T}$he truth about Grace?"

"The *shocking* truth, Julia. I think, I really do, that this revelation will wake you up. You're drifting a bit. The fumes, I know. But it will be more fun if you're awake when Jace arrives, and I definitely believe this little bombshell will do the trick. Ready? Here goes, and to borrow from Mark Twain, the rumors of Grace Alysia Quinn's death have been greatly exaggerated."

"She's *alive*?"

"I do have your attention, don't I? Yes. She's alive. At least she was when I saw her last, *when I got rid of her,* three weeks after Mary Beth's death."

"But . . ."

"How? She jumped from her second-story bedroom. Mommy's little angel believing she could fly. You can imagine my surprise, *and my chagrin,* when I discovered her. As, fortunately, I did. It was almost dawn, and the house had finally cooled down enough to remove Mary Beth's badly charred corpse, which Rawley did. By himself. He scooped her up and carried her out. She was not, I can tell you, a pretty sight. But Rawley cradled her, caressed her, and happened upon her shattered skull. And while he was orchestrating the immediate search for the most likely murderer, I wandered around to the back of the house. I still don't know why. True, what was left of Grace was going to have to be removed through her bedroom window, since the stairs were ash, and there were ladders lying around that I might have grabbed. I had no intention, naturally, of doing the grisly deed myself. But there I was, and there she was, covered in soot and snow, completely buried save for a telltale strand of golden hair. I assumed she'd be dead, frozen to death if nothing else. But she'd fallen into a snowdrift close to the house, where flames had blazed throughout much of the night. And where the soot that blanketed her was still quite warm. She was unconscious. But alive. And a potential eyewitness to my crime."

"But you didn't kill her."

"I *would* have. But you remember Carolyn? My bride-to-be? She'd *followed* me, to *comfort* me. I had to think fast. But you know, Julia, it's the surprises, and the challenges they present, that I enjoy the most. My life's been too easy, I guess. In any event, I told Carolyn that I wasn't quite as certain as everyone else seemed to be that it was Sam who'd murdered Mary Beth. That it might have been Rawley instead. Carolyn had witnessed Rawley's jealous rage on a prom night years before, so it wasn't a stretch for her to imagine him as a killer. And it was no stretch at all for me to convince her to help me keep secret the fact that Grace had survived. We wrapped Grace in my parka, and—how's this for taking risks?—I carried her right over to Rawley and held her as we spoke. She was *very* dead, I told him, burned as badly as Mary Beth. And when Rawley wanted to see her, I said no, as if I was his best friend and truly cared. I wasn't going to let him do that to himself, I told him. He'd seen Mary Beth, *held* her, and that was enough. Besides, I said, he needed to focus on finding Sam. I also suggested, and he agreed, that Mary Beth's autopsy would be intrusive enough, *agonizing* enough, and that Mary Beth herself would want us to spare such an invasion of Grace. Carolyn and I would take her, I told him, to the funeral home."

"But you didn't."

"Wouldn't have been much point, would there? The fumes are really getting to you, Julia. If Jace doesn't arrive soon, so we can get this show on the road, you'll end up about as spaced-out as Grace was when she awakened in my home later that day. Spaced out, bewildered, and blessedly *silent,* which was gratifying for a number of reasons, not the least of which was that her incessant chattering had always been annoying in the extreme. She didn't have a *clue* what had happened, that was apparent despite her muteness, but she was otherwise intact. She was able to walk when so instructed, and to follow even more complex demands. I won't bore you with how I secured the silence of the funeral-home owner. Or, for that matter, of the neurologist I imported from Denver just for Grace. *Julia.* You're looking like you believed I killed them. I didn't. Nor did I pay them off. Okay, I will bore you. They *cared* about Grace, what was best and safest for her, so they were as mute, as mum, as she. Carolyn also cared about what was best for Grace, although she and I'd decided *no* children and the idea of raising Mary Beth's beloved daughter . . . well, suffice to say Carolyn went along with what I presented to her as the suggestion of the most revered child psychiatrist money could buy, an expert who recommended that Grace be cared for in a psychiatric facility, the best of the best, until she was emotionally well enough to talk, or communicate in *any* way, at which point she'd be placed in a loving home *not* in Loganville."

"Where was the psychiatric facility?"

"Julia, Julia. Those pesky fumes. *What* psychiatric facility? If you were thinking more clearly you'd realize that the last thing I'd do was get her the kind of care that might help her remember the events of that night. Not that, the neurologist believed, she ever would. In fact, he believed, she might never remember *any* aspect of her previous life. Her concussion was that severe, and there was the emotional trauma, witness her muteness, as well."

"You could have given her that help. Safely. You just didn't want to. You wanted to *punish* her because she was Mary Beth's child with another man."

"The little zombie was all that was left *to* punish, wasn't she? Actually, I was rather fair with her. I didn't kill her. I gave her a chance. For all I know she's been spectacularly happy ever since." Troy cast a knowing, and disapproving, look at his raven-haired Joan of Arc. "You want details, don't you? How I cleverly got rid of little Grace so that neither she, nor the person *or persons* to whom I gave her, would have the slightest idea who she really was? So you can tell Jace? I admire your optimism, Julia. But you forget. You and Jace are already dead. And besides, just so you won't spend all of eternity obsessing about it, my eternal gift *to you,* even if I shared every detail there'd be no way of finding her. No way *at all.*"

Troy looked, suddenly, toward the door. And only then did Julia hear the sound of the key in the lock. Only then, and she'd been listening, trying so *hard* to. But she hadn't. Had not even heard the closing of the car door. And now . . .

"Hark," Troy whispered. And smiled. Even as Julia inhaled a lungful of fumes and cried, "Jace, *no!* Don't come in!"

"Scream all you like, Julia. The damsel-in-distress routine will only make our hero more eager to rush in. Is it a tricky lock? He seems to be having some trouble opening it. Oh," Troy clarified as the door swung wide and Jace entered the room, "I see. The trouble is with his hands. Greetings, Jace. We've been expecting you. You look *terrible,* and that's not even counting the expression on your face. Speechless, Jace? Really, I figured you for some macho command like 'This isn't going to work, Troy. Let her go.' Of course, I don't *have* her. That ghastly chair does. Smell the fumes, Jace? See this cigarette? Can you say *poof*? Can you say *anything*? Oh, I see, you think just looking at you will scare me to death. Or that if you get close enough—I see you walking toward me, Jace— you'll be able to grab the gun. That's not going to happen. Although, just to increase the suspense and because of your hands, which are a handicap to say the least, I'll let you get closer than I'd originally planned before I shoot. I'd been thinking a single bullet to the heart. But, you know, I really do want you to watch her die. So I think I'll go for the legs first. I'm a better shot, by the way, than those snipers in wherever the hell it was. You'll go down, Jace, on your knees, and I'll toss this cigarette, and it's entirely up to you just how quickly this little scenario unfolds. There's an imaginary line somewhere between you and me, and the second you cross it . . . that stopped you, didn't it? Wanna talk? No? You know what? Why don't I toss the cigarette first, and *then* shoot you to your knees?"

Troy Logan did just that, the tossing part. He flicked his burning cigarette, Louise's burning cigarette, toward Julia and her cocoon of fumes even as the bullet, from the kitchen, sped straight and true for his head.

Once upon a time Rawley Ramsey, volunteer football coach for the Loganville Wildcats, had tried to convince a teenage shepherd named Sam to join the team. Sam was a natural athlete. Rawley spotted that gift right away. And, he'd told the reluctant recruit, he knew he'd have good hands, terrific hands, the kind that could catch a football no matter how wild the toss.

And they were terrific. Those hands. Broken as they were. And the skeleton was an athlete still. And a shepherd always.

Jace caught the cigarette in midair, at the very edge of the fumes. There was a spark of light, the faintest flash. But it floated heavenward. And the demons below, in the invisible abyss, did not, would never again, sear and flame.

Jace extinguished the cigarette, crushed it in his broken hands, even as he fell to his knees before Julia—and not shot, merely grateful.

Jace freed her from her bonds, and from the fumes. Then he held her, cradled her, away from her drenched robe—he took it off her—and from the beloved chair.

"It'll be fine," Jace whispered as he held her. "I promise it will."

*It* was Gran's chair. In her confusion, Julia was so worried about its fate. Did the splattered solvent doom the chair to be destroyed?

No, Jace promised.

And Jace Colton kept his promises.

He'd come home, to her, just as he'd vowed.

Julia's confusion cleared, began to, as she inhaled safe air and the greater safety of him.

"Are you all right?" she asked suddenly, urgently.

"Me?" Jace smiled. "Never better. How about you, Rawley?"

"I'm good, Jace," Rawley answered from a few feet away. "I really like a house where all the outside doors open with the same key . . . and where you can't unlock a front door with a car key no matter how much noise you make."

Julia turned in Jace's arms to Loganville's chief of police. "You didn't believe the story I told you at the library, either."

"I would have, Julia, if I'd known you then. Or if I'd

spoken to the answering-service manager in Kansas before my investigators placed you on a flight to London seated beside Jace. It was entirely plausible, the manager told me, that you'd have made the trip to Loganville for a troubled stranger."

"And even more plausible," Jace said softly, "that she'd make it for someone she loved."

"Yes," Rawley agreed. "But I'm glad I didn't know about you, Julia. Because if I'd believed you and not followed through . . . I've wanted *this*"—he touched his foot to the dead monster on the floor—"so much, and for so very long. Don't look at him, Julia."

"No. It's okay. It doesn't bother me."

"But you're frowning," Jace said. "What is it, Julia?"

"Troy said some things."

"Such as?"

"That he murdered Louise. But not Samuel Quinn."

"And?"

*And besides,* Troy Logan had said, just so you won't spend all of eternity obsessing about it, my eternal gift *to you,* even if I shared every detail there'd be no way of finding her. No way *at all*.

"Julia?"

*All of eternity obsessing.* That torment. Not to mention, Julia thought, the rest of life on earth obsessing and tormented as well.

Which they would do. Both of them. Rawley and Jace.

She looked from Jace, who was waiting so patiently for her reply, to Rawley, the man who'd made a young boy feel so very special, as if he, the awkward Robbie, was a gifted athlete, too, and who was finally going to marry the woman who'd loved him, and would love him, forever.

There would be happiness, not torment, for Rawley Ramsey. At last.

As, at last, there would be for Jace.

But as Julia Anne Hayley looked again at the man she loved, would love forever, she knew that the choice, and the truth, was not hers.

It belonged to them, these strong and honorable men.

So she said, to both of them, "And he told me, Troy told me, that Grace didn't die."

# CHAPTER
# TWENTY-FOUR

"$\mathscr{I}$ have something to say."
The quiet but decisive words came a month later from
Mrs. Bearce.

It was September 12, Julia's birthday, and they, this
gathering of loved ones, were in a private dining room at
the Silver Cloud Inn. It was Julia who'd suggested the
Emerald City reunion. For Jace. The man she'd married.
The man she loved.

They'd flown their birthday guests to Seattle first class.
In seats 2A and 2B. And 2C and 2D. Mrs. Bearce and
Robbie. And Belinda and Rawley.

And Garek had come as well, from Chicago.

Garek McIntyre, the attorney—and the man—Jace
trusted absolutely, and whom Julia had trusted, too,
and needed so much, all those months, when Jace was
away.

Garek was strong. And handsome.

And blind.

The darkness had befallen Garek during a rescue mission, the kind dared by only the elite of the elite, the men who were trained, and did so willingly, to take every risk.

Garek had been one of them. The best of them. He'd been leading the mission, in fact, in which his eyesight had been lost. And it had been, for all save Garek, a dazzling success.

Now Garek was here, and Jace's Loganville family, and silent wishes had been made all around before Julia blew out the candles on her cake.

And now Mrs. Bearce had something to say.

Mrs. Bearce. Who, like Gran, was positively ferocious when it came to the ones she loved.

"We're going to try to find Grace. We all know that. The best investigators are already involved. And everyone who knew her in Loganville, Carolyn included, is finding photos, searching memories, helping in every way they can. And if our private investigating yields no results, we will, as we've all agreed, approach the media. We'll *just say no,* however, to anything Alexis Allen might want to do. And maybe we'll find our Gracie. And maybe we won't. But in the meantime *and always* we have to live our lives. That means you, Jace Colton."

Mrs. Bearce smiled fondly at the shepherd she had known as Sam. He wasn't a skeleton any longer. It was truly remarkable what hot chocolate and macadamia nuts—and love—could do. He was holding his sleeping daughter, and his shining gold wedding band glowed like the luminous light that shimmered within, and it encircled a finger which, like all his fingers, was becoming ever straighter—with love—with each passing day.

"Actually," Mrs. Bearce said, "I do believe, Jace, that you're doing *very* well. So . . . that means you, Rawley Ramsey. You're going to marry my daughter in March, as planned, come hell or high water."

"Mother?" Belinda interjected. "Rawley and I were actually thinking of moving our wedding date up. Like to a week from today?"

"That will do very nicely," Mrs. Bearce affirmed, and "*Yes*" Robbie enthused as he gave his father-to-be, who'd been his father for a very long time, a discreet high five.

"And that means you, Garek McIntyre."

"Me?" The eyes that were blind, and very blue, looked directly at Mrs. Bearce, a precise tracking that was a vestige from his many years of perfect sight. They appeared quite normal, Garek McIntyre's very blue eyes. The blindness had come from a traumatic injury deep within.

"A few years ago," Mrs. Bearce began, "I started having these bright, bright lights darting around in my eyes. It was reflected light, I eventually discovered, a scattering off the cataracts I didn't even know that I had. It was quite uncomfortable. The brightness, through the cataracts, caused a most intense glare. And it was dangerous, too. Especially when I drove after dark. My eyes are fine now. *Better* than fine. The cataracts are gone, and my world is clear and new. I know you don't have cataracts, Garek. But there are times aren't there, when sudden too-bright lights find their way in?"

"Garek?" Jace asked. "Are you seeing lights?"

"Yes. Sometimes. I am."

"For how long?"

"A while."

A while, Jace mused. While he'd been held prisoner and Julia had needed Garek so? And during the past month when Garek had worked tirelessly to orchestrate the search for Grace?

"We'll get that worked up." Jace's solemn promise was addressed to Mrs. Bearce. But it was made to Garek. "I'll arrange for Garek to see an ophthalmologist at the U. And, I think, I'll tag along."

"Good," Mrs. Bearce replied. "Now, I just have one more thing to say. But listen to me. Please. Grace was *so very loved*. By Mary Beth. And by you, Rawley. And you, Jace."

"And you, Mrs. Bearce."

"Yes, and me. And so many others. For every minute of her first five years of life. I've done some reading on this. But even if I hadn't, I'd know it was true. Her brain may have lost the memories, but her heart won't have forgotten. And it's that foundation of love, that *fountain* of love, that will see her, our Grace, through. She's all right, and she *will be* all right, whether we find her or not. We gave her the best we had to give when she was with us, and now, even as we're searching for her, we need to give the best, always, to the ones we love . . ."

The scene, in watercolor, had come to Julia at the moment when, amid fumes, Troy Logan had told her that Grace was alive. And the vision had remained, to be painted if she possibly could, sometime before Christmas. To give to Jace on Christmas Eve.

But Julia painted her watercolor scene that very night, just hours after Mrs. Bearce's wise and loving words, and while Jace and Josie slept.

And by dawn it was done, and she would give it to him today, because the extraordinary vision had been met, exactly as she'd imagined, as she'd hoped—because Julia had *three* muses now.

Winnie and Josie and Grace. This painting was theirs. They'd been with her, all three *and such good friends,* throughout the night.

The Christmas tree in the girls' painting was teal blue, as had been the tree in the London suite. And, like that tree, it had silvery bows and tiny white lights. There was a snowflake, too, at the very top. Just one snowflake. *The* one. Scattering rainbows from on high.

The girls' blue spruce had fuchsia needles as well. *Fuchsia.* A reflection, perhaps, from the billowy drifts of mauve-colored snow. Yes, snow. For this teal-and-fuchsia tree lived outside, flourished there, in Loganville beside the lake.

Moonlight caressed the lakeside tree, in glowing beams of aqua and gold. And stars twinkled in the Christmas Eve sky. Silver stars, and purple ones, too.

An angel shimmered on the mauve snow in the aquamarine light as she played her harp—of gold—beside the lake. The angel chose to be near the frozen water, the mirror so shining and so pure, so that her celestial music might be heard, would be heard, by the dancing girl who twirled on the ice.

She was blond, the spinning ballerina, and she reached with joy to a sapphire sky, and she smiled at what she saw, the sleigh that flew, and what she heard, the strumming harp, the chiming bells, and the fluttering, such fluttering, overhead.

And she sang, how she sang, as reindeer and angels, and harps and bells, promised for her—forever—a perfect midnight clear.

Warner Books is delighted to invite
you to enjoy more enchantment from
Katherine Stone!

Please turn this page
for a bonus excerpt
from her magnificent novel

*THIEF OF HEARTS*

available wherever
books are sold.

# CHAPTER THIRTEEN

*MAUI*
*WEDNESDAY, APRIL TWENTY-FOURTH*

Caitlin did not stop reading, could not—not for food, not for sleep, not even when the flight became so bumpy that most passengers abandoned their books, clutched their armrests, and gritted their teeth.

*Blue Moon* was dark. Sensual. Erotic. Dangerous.

And written by a man who could not possibly compete with his dazzling twin? An awkward and perhaps physically unattractive man *with an extraordinary imagination*?

Was it truly possible to *imagine* such passion? Before reading the lyrical prose Caitlin's reply would have been an emphatic *no*.

But now she felt the passion, its longing, its hunger, its need. Jesse Falconer made her feel it, made her *want* it.

Jesse Falconer? No. The moon twin was not the sorcerer of ecstasy. Graydon Slake was.

Graydon Slake, the alter ego of the shadow twin, the illusory author who created the most spectacular fiction of all: the fantasy of love.

Graydon Slake might beg to differ with her romantic assessment of his work. His thrillers were breathless journeys into the intimate recesses of murderous minds—and breathtaking journeys, as well, into the intimacies of sex.

Sex, not love.

Never once, not in the 600 pages of *Blue Moon*, did *love* appear. Not in the lyrical prose and most assuredly neither in the stylish repartée between hero and heroine whilst in pursuit of the killer, not in the provocative words they whispered in bed.

There was a definite edge to Graydon Slake's "hero," the ex-cop who understood so well—*too* well?—the desires of murderers. He was dangerous, and he could be cruel. In fact, the line between the hero of *Blue Moon* and its diabolical villain was fine indeed.

That gossamer thread *was* there, however. Without the slightest hesitation the hero had been willing to forfeit his own life to save the woman he "loved."

As Caitlin read the words of Graydon Slake—every word, more than once, during the tumultuous flight to Honolulu—she thought about the Falconer twin she did not know.

Long ago she had decided that Jesse was moon to Patrick's sun. He possessed not a kilowatt of his own dazzle and was both physically uninspired and socially inept. Passion smoldered within the moon twin, of course, passion for his writing . . . and for the snow lions of the world.

Jesse Falconer's passion was quiet yet fierce, serious and intense; identical, in fact, to Caitlin's own passion for saving endangered hearts. Indeed the *undazzling* twin was far more like her than Patrick ever would be.

But now Caitlin had read *Blue Moon*. Maybe, *maybe,* the novel afforded further proof of how similar she and Jesse were: irrevocably solitary creatures who were nonetheless achingly capable of imagining the wonders of love.

*But it was also possible that her assessment of the dark twin was all wrong.*

Well, she would find out. Tonight.

Caitlin's storm-delayed Aloha Airlines flight from Honolulu finally reached Maui in the late afternoon. Already the tropical tempest had imposed an early twilight on the Valley Isle. Already the Honoapiilani Highway had become a treacherous ribbon of black satin.

I *will* be careful, Caitlin had vowed to Timothy Asquith. It was a promise which implicitly precluded the notion of making the drive after dark. Arguably, for Caitlin, the cliffside trek would always be fraught with risk. She rarely drove. Her apartment on Barrington was directly across from the hospital, and Ariel's was just three blocks away. A bone-dry street at high noon felt somewhat foreign to her, and if one factored into the equation for disaster her recent lack of sleep . . .

Her mission *could* be put off until morning. Realistically, she and Jesse Falconer's blood would not be boarding a plane for the mainland until tomorrow. But she had come this far, and it seemed important that she complete her journey tonight—while it was still her birthday, and when the heavens had become the sea, pouring sheets of liquid magic onto earth.

She would arrive at the mountain-top hideaway a little frazzled perhaps. More than a little. Weary and raw. But she would arrive.

Even though her hands were threatening to spasm from their death grip on the steering wheel and her eyes stung from peering through walls of rain—*already* and she had yet to reach Kaanapali. Twilight lay far behind and her destination lay far ahead. Beyond Kaanapali. Beyond Kapalua. Beyond Pineapple Hill.

She was virtually alone on the rain-slick roadways, making it safer for all concerned, and streetlights glowed overhead, illuminating her journey into liquid blackness . . . until, that is, she made the turn-off onto the private road to Jesse Falconer's home.

Apparently the reclusive author chose not to provide his nighttime visitors with any insight into the perilousness of their winding ascent—or the precariousness with which they teetered on the edge of eternity.

Visitors? One did not live in a place like this if one wanted visitors.

Well, Jesse Falconer, I am coming to visit, and I'm almost there. At any moment this tortuous road will become a driveway, and there will be lights. Won't there be?

Yes. Surely. Unless . . .

The mind that had been deprived of sleep by the haunting rampages of ghosts and ghouls began to conjure disturbing images of Jesse Falconer's "home." A medieval castle, perhaps, complete with chilling drafts and dank dungeons. Or, for the man with a passion for murder, something quite Frankensteinesque, a turreted monstrosity more suited to the Bavarian Alps. It was even possible the murder maven's tastes ran to the truly macabre, a home for Count Dracula himself, a Transylvanian bungalow with coffins in every room.

Surely Timothy Asquith would have alerted her to such architectural eccentricities. But Gemstone Pictures' CEO had arrived here during the brightness of a Hawaiian day. Even the most gothic of castles would seem enchanting in such a benevolent light. Timothy Asquith would have no way of knowing the dramatic transformation induced by nightfall, not to mention a ferocious storm; a transformation as profound, perhaps, as the one Jesse Falconer underwent every time he became Graydon Slake.

Was the famous author writing now? Was he crafting the most black of terror—and the most stormy of passion—in this fierce and unrelenting darkness?

Darkness? *What* darkness?

Suddenly, stunningly, the world changed. Brightened. Glowed.

*Glared.* It was daylight now, the full luminescense of a tropical sun, a blinding brilliance made all the more intense by the prism effect of the falling rain. The golden floodlights illuminated the rain-kissed stone on which she drove. It was slate, an entire teal-green driveway of it, and spiked green steel fenced the perimeter of the drive—a lofty barrier, unmistakably forbidding.

The spear-sharp barricade lay before her as well, a massive gate suspended from pillars of slate. An intercom adorned the driver's-side pillar, modern technology embedded in stone. Was there a camera lens, too, zooming in on her face? Was Jesse Falconer studying her image, faultlessly clear despite the rain, thanks to the powerful wattage of the penetrating lights?

Yes, Caitlin thought. He is staring at me.

She *felt* the invisible appraisal, intense—and disapproving. The dark twin was noticing the dark circles beneath her eyes, and the harrowed tautness of her skin, and the bloodless hands that clutched the steering wheel.

Would he take pity on the orphan of the storm, permitting her to venture farther with no questions asked? Or would she need to compel her fingers to uncurl, if such motion were possible, then lower the window and plead her case to the intercom framed in stone?

The answer came quickly. Apparently Jesse's interest was piqued. Or maybe a face-to-face inquisition appealed to him more. In the dungeon. Where intruders were tortured until they confessed all.

Whatever the reason the spiked iron opened, a somber parting, and a silent one; and yet as she saw the gate close behind her, Caitlin sensed an ominous clang, like the barred doors of a jail cell slamming shut.

Her heart began to pound, a primal reflex of pure fear, even though there was nothing fearsome in what she saw. The world had changed again, gentled. The glaring floodlights had been dimmed, replaced by a golden mist that drifted from lampposts amidst an ocean of fluttering palms. The slate gentled, too, becoming a river of teal that meandered through gardens abloom with every hue and blossom of the tropics.

And Jesse Falconer's house? Caitlin saw it at last, as she rounded the final bend of the river of slate. It was not a medieval castle. Neither was it the secluded citadel of a scientific madman nor the night-black dwelling of a vampire prince.

The sprawling white structure most resembled a lustrous strand of pearls nestled amid a rainbow of flowers.

Caitlin stopped the car at the foot of a flight of teal-green stairs, the final ascent to the pearly home. She compelled her fingers to uncurl, an unfurling that precipitated a burst of tingling pain—and a clumsiness the surgeon had rarely experienced. Sheer will enabled her to turn off the ignition, set the brake, douse the headlights, unfasten her seat belt, and open the door.

Then she was outside, standing in the rain, her every muscle trembling in relief and release from its isometric clench. Trembling, yet paralyzed.

Or was it *mesmerized,* transfixed by the apparition at the top of the stairs? It was as if the rain had parted, *as if he had made it part,* for Caitlin saw him quite clearly— as clearly, that is, as a shadow could be seen.

He was a faceless silhouette. But his shape spoke volumes. Jesse Falconer was physically quite whole, distinctly unmaimed. Lean, elegant, powerful, commanding.

But perhaps there were scars on his shadowed face—

the ravaged face of the moon—disfigurements so grotesque that no woman would want him even in the black veil of night. Caitlin would know. Soon. For he was emerging from the darkness.

The lamplight fell first on his hair. Like hers, it was the color of midnight. Thick, lustrous, shining. Then the golden beams illuminated his face, revealing it, exposing it.

There were no scars. There were only hard planes and harsh angles, classic features carved in stone. Quite flawless, quite breathtaking, quite—

All of a sudden, through the parted curtain of rain, Caitlin wondered if she saw scars after all, deep slashes carved in the heart with knives of pure pain. The moment passed swiftly, the vicious wounds merely a mirage, false shadows on this night of authentic ones, and Caitlin saw the real Jesse Falconer once again.

Meek. Socially inept. Physically unattractive. Those were the words by which she had decided the moon twin would best be described. Such safe words, such comforting images. They were shattered now, splintered like fine crystal on a river of slate.

And the words that took their place? They came on a gust of wind, a force of nature that seemed—like the rain—completely in his command.

Dark, the wind hissed. Sensual, it howled. Erotic, it mocked. Dangerous, it warned.

The gusting wind swirled with the same adjectives that Caitlin had assigned to Graydon Slake's thrillers of passion and murder. And as for the extraordinary imagination she had given him? Quite possibly Jesse had no imagination at all. The lyrical passages of intimacy had merely to be recalled from his own vast array of erotic interludes.

Lyrical passages of intimacy? You mean *sex*. Pure and simple. At least *simple* for Jesse Falconer, for whom such uninhibited sensuality was surely as instinctive and *as necessary* as breathing.

The man who stood before her wrote bestselling novels; and he had at his command the wind and the rain; and for light entertainment he enjoyed watching unwelcome visitors attempt to reach his home in the pitch-blackness of night.

But all these enterprises were trivial diversions, amusing ways to pass the time when Jesse Falconer wasn't where he belonged—in bed, making love.

Caitlin was in the presence of an alarmingly sexual creature. He was moving toward her now, a powerful gait of predatory grace, and at last she saw his eyes. They blazed with a dark green fire, a glittering inferno that sent both warning and promise. Like a Graydon Slake hero, this man was dangerous, and he could be cruel. He was separated from sheer villainy by the most slender of threads.

The stealthy prowl halted a short yet generous distance from her, not crowding her, not invading her space—at least not physically.

Jesse Falconer did not smile. But he did speak. And his words, low and deep, felt oddly protective.

"Let's get you out of the rain."

He was as drenched as she. But he supplied her with all the towels she needed before attending to the dampness of his own hair and face.

"So," he began at last. "Who are you?"

"Don't you know?"

"Should I?"

He had seemed so unsurprised to see her that Caitlin had assumed he had been forewarned after all, that Timothy Asquith hadn't kept his promise of silence any more than she had kept her promise to be careful.

"Didn't Timothy Asquith tell you I was coming?"

"Not a word. And the last time we talked was about two hours ago."

"Well, I asked him not to tell you."

"And he agreed? That doesn't sound like Timothy. The two of you must be very close."

"What? Oh, no. Not really. I know his wife fairly well, and his son and—"

"Okay. Somehow you managed to convince him to conceal from me the fact that you were coming. The question is, Why?"

*Because I wanted to catch you by surprise. I wanted to be certain that, once warned, you didn't flee rather than confront the bitter memories of your past.*

What a foolish notion—one that rivalled the image of him as unattractive and meek. This man, this predator, would never be caught by surprise. Nor would he flee. Not ever. Not from anything.

*Because I wanted to offer you the chance to become*

*the sun, to be as dazzling as your twin, to save an endangered heart.*

But Jesse was not the moon. He had his own light, his own heat. True, the fires within were quite different from Patrick's glittering gold. Dark. Fierce. Dangerous. Yet dazzling nonetheless.

And as for *neediness*? That was the most fanciful notion of all. Jesse Falconer had not been waiting for Caitlin to offer him the chance to help his twin.

Jesse needed nothing from Caitlin. *Nothing.* What needs he had—well, he could have whomever he wanted whenever he wanted her. Perhaps there was someone here now, a woman with whom Jesse shared sophisticated passion and stylish repartée. Perhaps she was in his bed, impatient and restless.

*As was he.* Caitlin saw his restlessness, and the immense power of his control. The restlessness was coiled tight. But like his sexuality, it smoldered.

"Why?" he repeated, his voice dangerously soft.

This was a man to whom one could not lie. At least Caitlin couldn't. Jesse would see the lie, and the blazing green fires would sear her soul.

*Because I need your blood.* The prospect of getting Jesse Falconer's blood suddenly seemed beyond daunting. It seemed impossible.

The magical confidence of the sea was gone, drowned by the storm that was part of him. Caitlin needed time to recover *and* to prepare an entirely new script, an alternative approach to this man who was so very far from the kindred spirit she had envisioned.

She temporized. But she did not lie. "Timothy asked me to read your screenplay." *And I will, when I return to LA, as soon as I've finished giving Stephen Sheridan samples of your blood.*

"And you came here to discuss it with me? In the middle of the night? Despite a raging storm? This sounds serious."

His green eyes glittered, amused—and not the least bit troubled by her apparently major concerns with the script he'd written for *Thief of Hearts*.

Jesse Falconer was amused. But he was not fooled. And now there was a slight but ominous change, and Caitlin saw his amusement for what it truly was: contempt.

"Yes," she asserted. "It is serious." *Your twin is dying and I am going to convince you to save him.*

The magic of the sea was returning, or perhaps it was the power of her own passion for endangered hearts. *Saving hearts is what I do, who I am, all that I am.*

Caitlin's surging wave of confidence was preempted by a sudden chill. The raindrops that had evaded her hurried toweling had apparently made a bee-line for her bones, where they had promptly turned to ice.

"You need to shower and change before we talk."

Caitlin answered through teeth that threatened to chatter. "Yes."

"And sleep? Can our discussion wait until morning?"

It was a gift from him to her, an overnight reprieve during which she could regroup. "That would be fine. What time?"

"Whenever you wake up."

"Should I call you then? Before I leave?"

"Leave where?"

"Kapalua. I'll get a room at the hotel there."

It was faint, just the trace of a flicker, but Caitlin convinced herself it was real. *Surprise,* in the man who could not be surprised. And now his gaze seemed even more intense, as if appraising her anew—as if her willingness to descend the treacherous road despite her quivering fatigue made him question some judgment he had made about her.

"Not a chance," he told her. "You'll spend the night here, in the guest wing where Timothy and Lillian stayed."

Lill*ith,* Caitlin amended silently. "Thank you."

Her faintly blue-tinged lips offered a smile, which was not returned. The flicker of surprise and the possibility of a more positive reassessment of her were long gone.

"I have one final question," he said to his shivering guest.

"Yes?"

"Do you have a name?"

*Look for the rest of Katherine Stone's*
***THIEF OF HEARTS,***
*available wherever*
*books are sold.*